ECHO'S LIGHT

BRYAN JORGENSEN

FriesenPress
One Printers Way
Altona, MB R0G 0B0
Canada

www.friesenpress.com

First Edition — 2024

ISBN
978-1-03-831641-7 (Hardcover)
978-1-03-831640-0 (Paperback)
978-1-03-831642-4 (eBook)

Fiction, Science Fiction, Alien Contact

Distributed to the trade by The Ingram Book Company

This is a work of fiction written before the events in Israel on October 7, 2023. Any similarities are purely coincidental.

PROLOGUE

"Do you sense it? The future doom of another civilization. The end of life. The end of their existence," one sheath conveyed to another.

These three entities were inside their energy spheres, floating in an orbit above a planet they were studying, when that sense reached them. Sensors that were never turned off as they were continuously sniffing space like cadaver dogs, trying to pick up the scent of peril.

"It's different than the others we've detected." The sheath sniffed again. "It's coming from very far way. From an area we have yet to explore."

It wasn't just a different scent it was…unique, unique to the universe.

"Is it the perception of a natural catastrophe?"

"I'm not sure."

"Let's go…"

They sped off in their own distinctive way, towards that signal of a future event that was so destructive and so powerful that it ripped back through time. No detours. A straight line on a mission to try and save another world from imminent annihilation and perhaps, for the first time ever, on a mission that could free their own species from the grips of slavery.

CHAPTER 1

Sunday October 19
10:30am local time

Joel was a mess. Mentally and physically.

He laid out like an ironing board on his dirty bed, wearing only a pair of foul boxers, which, along with his sheets, had not seen a washing machine in weeks. It was the only bedroom in his small, rented Pueblo-style home on the outskirts of Tombstone Arizona and was also the only Pueblo-style home in the area. His nearest neighbor was a football field away, or ten seconds by tumbleweed.

It was early Sunday morning when Joel slowly opened only his right eye, as his left eye was just too damn swollen to be of much use and, for the life of him, he could not remember how it got that way. With his working eyeball, he followed a fly that was gleefully darting about, feeling just at home in this dump as Joel was. *Mi tugurio es su tugurio,* he mused to himself.

He did find one of his senses working, took in a breath, and was met with the familiar stench of body odor. A sad groan was the result. Next, he decided to ascertain the time. There was one large window opposite his bed, and the light filtering through it did not indicate the afternoon. His best guess was a quarter past ten. He was fifteen minutes off.

Joel slowly regained his faculties, and it wasn't long before last night's escapade revealed itself. *My god!* He groaned again and used both hands to massage the stubble on his face then moved up to his forehead, careful to bypass his peepers. He felt a slight oily residue between his fingertips from his scalp, but he didn't really care as the altercation in the bar last night was clear now.

Embarrassment... shame... patheticism... but most of all, pity filled his soul.

What the hell am I doing!

It was a phrase that had come up plenty of late. And a phrase that summed up his life for the last six months. As for last night, once again he drank too much. Before he moved to Arizona, he rarely drank at all. Well, that was not entirely the truth. From his early teens to the age of twenty-seven, he got lit up on a regular basis. Then he met the most amazing person to ever enter his life and for fear of losing her, he all but stopped drinking as his love of her overpowered his love of alcohol. Recently, however, sobriety is his mortal enemy.

Joel struggled to pull his depressed body out of bed. He was awash with fatigue and light-headedness as his feet dangled over the cold tile floor.

Joel shook his head and scolded himself. *What was I thinking? Stupid! Stupid!*

The reason for that was his foolishness in stirring up trouble in the bar. Joel was not a young man at fifty-five years of age, or an overly tall of beefy man either at just a hundred and seventy pounds and five feet ten. Unfortunately, every patron in that bar was beefy, half his age and twice his strength; he was a shrimp compared to the behemoths that pounded on him last night.

Oh well, what's done is done.

There was a cracked dresser mirror, slightly askew, about ten feet away and his image was appalling to him.

"Jesus Christ," he mumbled.

He wished he could step though the mirror and see himself on the other side and the life he had just six months ago. Perfect, it was, save for that one horrific decision he made that ruined everything.

His swollen lower lip was easily visible. There were two fist sized welts on his lower left rib cage, courtesy of a couple of rabbit punches from two large bunnies. Just off to the right of those bruises was the partial imprint of a boot, residual evidence of a crime against him that he would not report. Nothing broken, he believed, and if something was, he didn't care.

The top of his head was shaved three weeks ago, a fresh look that he hoped would lead to better decisions. All it did was make it easier to see a three-inch cut, and a raised bump, no doubt from a beer bottle tossed at him for something obnoxious Joel did or said.

He decided to shower later, if at all. Instead, he was thirsty but needed some fresh air first; anything must be better than what reeked inside. He took a slow walk through his barren living room and realized he didn't even lock the front door. Whoever he pissed off last night could have easily followed him home to finish the job.

My bad, he mouthed, but was thankful to still be alive.

He opened the door and was greeted by warm sunshine a refreshing breeze and a sky that was a brilliant blue save for an odd large area of black that came and went. At least the weather was not against him. He looked to his right and there was nothing but dried scrub brush and a long dirt road. To the left, he heard a squeaking noise and saw an odd figure on a red bicycle. He blinked as best he could to clear the haze and saw a man with a long, black, flowing mullet peddling this red bicycle. This stranger took one creepy glance at Joel, then continued on his way.

Joel was overcome with worry as he imagined this stranger as a scout for a jealous husband or boyfriend. This brought on more memories of last night. Having not been intimate with a woman since that tragedy six months ago, his obnoxious, incomprehensible, and anxious behavior had creeped out a lot of women in that saloon, thus annoying many of their dates. Being jammed up was affecting his judgement.

Being out in the open didn't seem like a good idea either, so he turned to go inside but heard the bell on that bicycle ring three times. Joel nervously looked back, and the stranger was gone. Completely out of sight, which was impossible.

What the hell! He wanted to shout, but he could not get his parched throat to make any sounds.

He scratched his chin and did some rough mental calculations. It was at least a thirty-minute bike ride from the nearest town using a good bicycle, not that rickety one he saw the stranger on. When he was young, he remembered using a bike just like that to pull a wagon while delivering thick catalogues door to door, oddly on that exact kind of bicycle he noted again. But that was forty-five years ago, as a ten-year-old. That childhood memory made him chuckle, then made him wince as he caressed his tender ribs.

Once in the kitchen, Joel poured himself a glass of orange juice and continued his memory as a kid, bicycling down to the local library to fetch the college football scores from the Sunday New York Times. The wooden stick it was attached to could barely hold the weight of the thick paper.

Joel had been a stats and sports nut since the age of eight. Back then it was all about pen and paper. He would write down all the scores and standings of hockey, football, and baseball, every day. Why? It was his idea that in thirty or forty years, he would have the answer at his fingertips to any sports question asked.

If someone in the year 2018 wanted to know how the Dallas Cowboys did in 1979? Ask Joel. If someone needed to know which hockey team scored the most goals in the 1980/81 NHL season, ask Joel. What a waste of time, he thought, because who needs to ask Joel when all they have to do is ask Google.

And now all those boxes of stats, piles and piles of papers, lay in boxes in his only closet. Useless to anyone, but a memory of his early days as a youth that he could not throw away.

Joel was currently living the life of a minimalist. He had no cable and limited internet by choice and if he was lucky, he could get one bar of service on a clear day. Joel figured he was already depressed and lonely, so why not go all in. Of course, he had plenty of money in the bank to afford to go back on the grid. A quarter million dollars from a spousal death benefit that he could not bring himself to spend. So, until that guilt went away, that money would remain untouched.

Joel drank the entire glass in one try, then was startled by a noise coming from the living room. He got up slowly and peaked around the corner and saw the man from the bicycle standing in front of his television. He squeezed the empty glass until it almost broke then softened his grip and now he had a weapon to use. Joel did have an ancient landline to dial 911. However, that landline was attached to a phone jack and the phone was on a table near the intruder. He decided to size up his opponent in case it came down to hand to hand combat. The man was thin, and an inch shorter and frail looking, perhaps a homeless man in need of shelter. However, in Joel's depleted condition, could he be in for another beating?

"Can I help you?" Joel asked carefully.

"It's how I can help you. Here, take this." He handed Joel the remote control for his television. "I'm all finished here."

"Finished with what?"

"Here, take this please." Joel took the remote then backed away slowly. "Turn on that device," the vagabond advised.

Joel followed the instructions and the small flat screen attached to the wall came to life. The picture was crystal clear, and he recognized the familiar show right off. It was Sportscenter doing its usual thirty-minute loop of last night's highlights. He now had cable, which he didn't ask for nor made an appointment for one to be installed.

"Why?" Joel asked.

His mind tried to desperately link this to last night. Was it a husband thanking him for making a fool of his ex-wife? That was a ridiculous conclusion.

"I'll be in touch," the stranger said, then left through the front door.

"Don't forget your..." Joel was going to say tools, but there were none around, and the man had none with him. He went as quickly as he could to the window and looked out. No cable truck and no one in sight, just an odd vibration like being touched by a tuning fork.

Whatever! was all he could think.

He needed to sit down. His couch was quite comfortable and fitted well to his form as he decided to just relax and watch his new gift. First was a headline that was in bold, black large type: CARDINALS EMBARASSED BY LOWLY LIONS. Then he listened to the announcers as they explained how Arizona lost 31-17 to the winless Lions for their first loss of the season. Odd that he didn't bet on that game as one of the few joys left in his empty life was placing small wagers on sporting events, mainly the NFL. Odd that he didn't even remember watching the game.

Joel grew up and lived his entire life in Calgary, Alberta. As a child, he went to every Stampeders game with his dad and continued that tradition with his wife and two daughters. They would often embark on road trips to Edmonton and to see the Roughriders in Regina. One especially memorable trip was to see the Seahawks in Seattle. His girls were thirteen and fifteen at the time and the fond memories of their drive through the beautiful Rocky Mountains returned at this most inopportune time.

He tossed the remote down and leaned back. His eyes welled up for, well, he lost count as to how many times. His two girls were in their late twenties now, living out their own lives. He looked at the phone beside him, wanting so badly to reach out to them. Joel had not seen them since their mother's funeral. Between their anger and his guilt, not much was said during the service, and nothing had been said since that day.

They hated him and he knew it. They so much as said so when they returned home from the cemetery. There Joel was, a tough, rugged man cowering in his living room chair, gripping the armrest tightly while taking their verbal barrage. Each angry word from his girls ripped a piece of his heart away until his chest was a mere cavity.

How could he fight back when he knew they were right. He was responsible for their mother's death, and he felt no explanation or plea for forgiveness could change that perspective or their feelings. He should have stood up and apologized but decided to let them vent. He was feeling equally angry, completely at himself. The light of Joel's life had been snuffed out by him and his selfish actions and his emotions took a final fatal blow from his daughters' last words, which were imprinted on his mind like a hot branding iron.

We never want to see you again!

He tried, with all the courage he could muster, to text his girls… to call them, but they were ghosts. How many times could he say sorry? Would time heal all wounds? Well, almost six months had gone by and here he was, a coward, fleeing from the people who meant the most to him.

He had decided to sell his house shortly after the tragedy and move here to live with a friend. That only lasted one month as he was kicked out, more accurately, physically removed, after returning one night in a drunken stupor. Now he lived alone, estranged from his family and friends with only scant Facebook posts to remind him of what he was missing.

He rubbed his eyes dry then continued to watch the highlights, only half-heartedly caring what the sportscasters were saying. Joel's soul was in such an abyss that he wasn't even startled by the ringing of his phone. Not his cell phone, which was more of a paperweight, but his old-fashioned land line. It was an annoying ring that would go on and on if he didn't pick up. After the eighth ring he knew who it was. On the tenth ring he answered it.

"That you, Billy?" Joel asked.

"Who else would it be? I must be your only friend down here."

"I thought it might be the cops."

"Only if you called them. You're lucky I was there. You're lucky most of those mastodons know me, or you would have been a lot worse off. I had to do a lot of fast talking to get you out of there."

"Come on, Billy. It wasn't that bad."

"Have you looked in the mirror. You did a lot of swinging and a lot of missing. Can't say the same for them."

There was no response for 5 seconds.

"Come on Joel! If this doesn't knock some sense into you, I don't know what will."

"Let it go, Billy."

Billy then touched on a sore subject. "Joel, call your girls."

"Let it go!" he said again.

"Reach out to them. I am sure they want to hear from you."

"They don't need me," Joel said in an emotionless tone.

"You've said that so many times in your own mind that you've convinced yourself it's true."

"Can we change the subject?"

"Fine," Billy relented. "Did you want to come with me to the game?"

"What are you talking about?" Joel was speaking with the phone up to his left ear while watching the television with his good eye.

"I told you Thursday I had two tickets to the Cardinals game today. Should be a slaughter. The Lions stink."

"Well, this time it was the Cardinals who stunk. They turned the ball over five times." There was no response on the other end of the blower. "They lost by fourteen points, Billy."

"Now what are you talking about?"

They were both confused, and both were waiting for the other to speak.

Finally, Billy said, "I think you're still a little woozy from the shit kicking. Arizona is twelve-point favorites, six and zero, and the Lions have not won a game this year. You know that. And Detroit is down to their third string quarterback."

"It wasn't just me who got the shit kicked out of them, Billy."

"You're crazy, Joel. At least I'm putting my money where my mouth is; I put five c-notes on them to cover."

"Looks like you should have put a thou on Detroit to win by fourteen. You would have won a bundle."

"What! Wait, I'm confused. Why does it seem like I am talking in the present and you are talking in the past?" All Billy heard was heavy breathing from the other end of the line. "Listen Joel, why don't you rest, kick back and heal up? I'll drop by after the game."

Joel was beginning to wonder if he was in his right mind. He flipped through the channels and all of them were blank. He returned to Sportscenter and took another look at the top of the screen to confirm his sanity. "Billy, I'm watching the highlights now. They always show the highlights Monday morning."

"Joel, today is Sunday. You should see a doctor."

"I would if I had the money."

"Listen, I gotta go. Now that I have an extra ticket, maybe I'll take Jennifer. She knows nothing about football, but she looks great in a pair of shorts."

"Good luck with that."

With that, their conversation ended. Joel continued to gloss over a few more stories noting one that informed him of the death of a Nascar driver during Sunday's Bank of America 400 race at the Charlotte motor speedway. He turned off the tube and then looked around at his empty flat. So quiet. Not what he was used to back home. Then that fly came back, buzzing loudly, hovering, then landing on the rim of an open garbage can. No doubt in a few days, maggots would be crawling all over his floor.

He didn't know what to do with the rest of the day. Just waste it like the others, was his decision. However, if he had been more observant, more on the ball, he could have placed a bet that would have made him a very rich man.

CHAPTER 2

Three hours earlier
Interstellar space

"Beautiful. Absolutely beautiful."

"One of the best views I've ever seen," said one sheath to the other.

To use the word *said* implies speaking, which produces a sound that travels through a medium like air. At the moment, these two sheaths were in space, in a region outside of the spiral galaxy best known as the Milky Way. Surrounding each sheath's sphere of energy was a protective barrier that kept the cold, dark vacuum of space on the outside, where it belonged.

These sheaths had no physical bodies. Inside each individual sphere was a small bundle of their individual cohesive energies, bundles of electrical impulses that were made up of their own thoughts and memories. The barrier keeping them safe was strong, which meant they felt no cold, heat, or radiation. These two ancient beings were in a state of eternal comfort.

Their consciousness and their will to survive kept their beach ball sized spheres of energy from breaking apart. To an outsider, say like an astronomer from Earth, they would be perceived, through instruments, as normal background electrical radiation, or a simple miniscule speck that made up the many properties of space, nothing that would attract attention, and completely invisible to the naked eye.

These two specks had just travelled from a place classified as Earendel, billions of light years away from earth. They were there studying a planet.

These sheaths arrived so quickly at their current location from the Earendel system simply because they wanted to be here. Freedom to travel anywhere in the universe just by thought was one of their abilities. An ability they could give others if they found the right dire conditions. Does their rapid form of movement make them time travelers? Perhaps, but a better term for their abilities could be described as... necessary.

To be precise, there were three sheaths. However, the third had gone ahead to try to pinpoint the origin of those future waves of peril they had felt not long ago.

An exceptionally long time ago, these three all had physical bodies, but for the most part they now spend their lives travelling the universe in electrical form. As for the rest of their species on their home world, they are also beings of electrical energy, but have kept themselves in physical bodies which they use as mere containers or sheaths of convenience and necessity. A container with arms and legs to house their electrical energy. These physical bodies are needed to move about their planet and to build structures. However, it was only these three emissaries that have been given the task to leave their own star system and explore the universe. These three could move among the galaxies at a snail's pace to enjoy the sights, pausing at any point like a bus making stops, or with just a thought, be anywhere in the universe they desired.

For this mission, these three were moving nonstop from Earendel until they reached the outer boundaries of the Milky Way. They proceeded to travel inward toward the thoughts of that third sheath, using their imagination and their desires to go where they wished. Occasionally, they would stop and sniff the air like blood hounds, searching for more thoughts of doom, or at times to briefly pause and absorb an awe-inspiring sight. Here, they found both.

These two sheaths, and the third currently investigating the source of the disturbance, were the only three of their kind that had their special abilities which they used to fulfill their main purpose, to search out and give sentient civilizations the freedom to explore the universe in the same manner they can. Yet before that could happen, these civilizations had to meet a strict set of criteria. However, there was a dark side to this process that these sheaths have kept secret for eons.

So, how many of these civilizations have they given universal exploration to? So many that the chance of encountering someone from past missions was not uncommon. Even despite the enormity of the universe, every now and then, they would come across some of the species they gave the gift of eternal life and freedom to.

Two individuals that they had freed long ago were nearby and those energies touched the thoughts of both sheaths.

"Are you sensing them?" the one sheath thought to the other.

"Yes. They are approaching our position."

They slowed their velocity and now there were four spheres of mental energy floating in space. They hovered in proximity, not affected by the push and pull of nearby bodies, but were wafting in the interstellar winds, like four divers being moved by gentle ocean currents.

"How are your travels?" sheath one asked.

This sheath could sense the arrival of one female and one male thought pattern. It was the male who responded.

"Amazing… and agonizing at the same time," he conveyed in his own language which was unique to their species.

"I'm sorry to hear that you have had such sad experiences."

"Thank you. Let me introduce ourselves. We came from the Jennai spiral galaxy. You visited us five thousand years ago and gave our people your gift. Unfortunately, a hundred years after you left, we both perished in a transport accident, and have been travelling the cosmos ever since."

That was one of the caveats. Eternal existence and the ability to travel the universe was only given after death.

"Have you been back to your planet since?"

The female said, "Many times. We would occasionally connect in space with family members who had passed on and they would regale us with new stories of great accomplishments of our people. Even though we can never return to the surface as in our original physical bodies, we are at least able to drop in now and then and enjoy, from within our sphere, the progression of our species over thousands of years. An amazing chance to witness our civilization's development over such a vast amount of time."

The male added, "We have witnessed our race put colonies on our three moons, and we even have floating cities in space. I learned my grandson six generations removed and his wife was living on one of the moon bases. It was all amazing."

Both sheaths could sense a drop in energy of both travelers.

"Then..."

"Something happened?"

The male took over with the story. "We had met a lot of our people during our travels, but then one of the times we were returning for a visit, we were suddenly bombarded by more voices than usual. As we would find out, they would be the individual energies of our entire population. Our entire race is now spheres of energy. All a result of a catastrophe that befell our star system."

"We were advised to stay away," the female added.

"But you didn't," the first sheath said.

"That only fueled our desire to confirm what they described. That our star was... gone. As were the six closest planets, including the two we once lived on. Our sun had gone nova. Everything and everyone were lost."

"I am so sorry," the first sheath thought to the pair.

Not only were the thoughts heard from sphere to sphere, but also the emotional intent. These emotions were fused to the telepathic vocal waves. In this instance, the sheaths sent out waves of sympathy that the male and female new arrivals were receiving and were appreciated.

"Sometimes being immortal means having to experience death in all ways and at any time. It can become too much to bear for some. Remember, immortality does not have to be an infinite sentence. There is no shame, or offense to us, when some want to discontinue their existence. Many have before."

"Thank you for your kind and reassuring words," the female said. "We never felt this way until the time we witnessed the destructive aftermath of our star system. We have thought about whether it was time to travel into a beautiful star and cease to exist. If we do decide, we will be at peace with the decision."

"Have you come to that decision?" asked the second sheath.

There was no response to that question, yet. Each lifeform inside each sphere had the individual ability to put up a barrier to block others from sensing their emotions. Both these newcomers had done so, and the sheaths waited patiently for them to continue. After about a minute, the barriers went down, and one of the sheaths continued with the discussion.

"We have also enjoyed being witness to natural events that not just took thousands, but millions of years to play out. We saw the formation of a red giant which turned white then its subsequent demise into a black dwarf three million years later. We witnessed the collision of two stunning spiral galaxies, returning every few thousand years to see the changes that resulted, like the birth of new planets. We have both been in awe of the explosive nature of the universe as well as the beauty in the creation of existence."

"It's staggering to think of how long you've been alive," the female noted. "It pales in comparison to our short lifespan. Perhaps when we are finished here with you, the decision to continue our lives or to end our lives will be made easier. We were hoping to run into you one more time, and finding you was not easy. But now that we have, we can at least cross that one desire off our list. We just wanted to say... thank you for everything."

"Well conveyed, my love." The male then focused his thoughts on the sheaths. "Can we ask you a question that has been on our minds since the death of our system?"

But before it could be answered, the female interrupted.

"I'm not so sure I want to know anymore," she admitted.

"I understand, but I would like to know. Perhaps I can find out, then fill you in at a time when you are ready. If you like, you can close your mind off to our discussion," suggested the male.

"That's a good compromise." She paused to consider, then decided, "No, no... I will keep my thoughts open. We have shared a lifetime together. Why stop now?"

"I can sense a natural loving bond between you, but I also sense you are troubled by something," one of the sheaths noted. "Please, ask your question. We can go from there."

There was a moment of silence as the male mustered up his courage. The four souls were separated by about thirty feet of darkness and cold, but inside their energy bubbles, it was warm, comfortable, and soothing.

"Did... did you give us... give our people your gift because you knew our world was coming to an end?"

Both sheaths were quiet. It was an often-asked question, and in all instances, they gave an answer that was the truth, save for one fact they have never revealed. Was that fact a lie by omission? It was a lie out of necessity.

"Yes, yes, we knew. We call these visions of future disasters *Spectacles*. We sensed your future doom, your future *Spectacle*, which is what drew us to help you. Some worlds are doomed through their own actions. If we sense that to be the case, we can give gifts to selected few to try to stop their own destruction, but there are instances, like yours, natural events like the death of your star which is too massive and irreversible for any one of you to prevent."

"This is who we are and what we do," the other sheath added. "To give immortality to those who are about to die. It's what we search for when we travel the universe. Sure, we can offer this gift to those not about to face extinction, but since there are only three of us, we must make those civilizations that are in peril a priority. Coincidentally, we were on our way to that next Spectacle when we met you."

"Then we are so sorry to have delayed you."

"Do not worry. Our third is already there, and we will join our friend shortly."

"Why did you decide to tell us of your purpose?" asked the female.

"Because we are sensing in the both of you an emerging desire to terminate your existences. Is that true?"

There was a moment of delay, which the sheaths interpreted as a calming symbiosis between the two visitors. The confirmation of this came shortly after.

"Yes, it is. It's time to end to our exploration," said the male. "However, there is one more thing."

"What is it?"

"Can we travel with you? Just for a bit? We would like to find a suitable place to... relinquish our lives, together. Perhaps a colorful nebula or the beautiful birth of a star."

"Of course. We passed a twin jet nebula not too long ago?" the one sheath suggested. "It was awash in amazing colors. Blues and aquas and fiery oranges. Swirling gasses mixing into a gorgeous palate."

"That is perfect," the male confirmed. "Orange was always your favorite color, dear. Could the two of you come with us? Show us the way?"

The female added, "We would like your guidance in how to become one. To join our spheres, not just in mind and spirit, but in energy. We want to touch each other like we did when we had physical bodies, but we don't know how."

The second sheath said, "We are sorry that we can't return you to your physical state. That is only possible for us, and even that comes at many risks and incredible cost to our energies. We would be honored to go with you and show you how to combine your separateness into oneness."

"It will be a truly wonderful experience," said the first sheath.

"We've already said our good-bye's to as many of our family as we could find, so can you guide us?"

The four spheres of energy left for the twin jet nebula, about fourteen thousand light years away, and reached it in no time at all. Once there, the two sheaths supervised the joining into one union of the two lovers. For thousands of years, they were separated from physical touch. Now their feelings, memories and emotions intertwined, feeling warmth comfort and joy. Arms, legs, and bodies together in a metaphysical embrace. Peaceful and harmonious it was. A perfect end.

They were now one sphere, having converged like two chromosomes into one cell. The sheaths guided them into the nebula and the two lovers' energies scattered like ashes. The sheaths remained in silence out of respect for lives just lost until one thought to the other.

"Do you think they knew? Knew our secret."

"We would have sensed it. If they knew, we would have heard the objections. No, I don't believe anyone has ever found out."

"It will come out, eventually, don't you think?"

"Perhaps."

"I have wanted for a long time to tell someone the truth behind our intentions."

Without responding, the second sheath sent a thought that was one of hesitant agreement. Was it time to confess? Perhaps they would reveal it all to the ones they would come to next.

They continued their journey to the third sheath, who was a free-thinker they didn't want to leave on its own for much longer. Therefore, with a simple thought, they arrived instantaneously at their destination.

They glided quickly past all the large planets and took some time to do some studies of only the largest asteroids and moons to see if they could sense any signs of existence. Eventually they did a quick survey of a large, cratered moon before coming to a stop halfway to their target planet.

Earth.

They sensed some sentient energies in the space around them, however, these energies were of those they helped long before. They were visitors from other parts of the universe that had come to enjoy the view of this giant blue orb, simple tourists who had left their physical bodies long, long ago. The sheaths found an area where they could be alone and began their analysis using their regular telepathic conversation.

"What's your opinion?" sheath one asked. "Conditions seem optimal to help them."

"I agree. But we must be sure this species does not already have an afterlife. You know the consequences of giving an afterlife to a species that already has one."

"I do… I do. Our third member has been down there for a bit. There is no telling how much trouble it is getting into."

"We haven't narrowed down the time frame of their annihilation, so it's difficult to know how urgently we must proceed."

"You never stop hoping that one day we can be precise, but as usual, we can only generalize. In this case I am sensing that it will happen to them soon."

Soon, to beings as long lived as them, could mean a lot of things.

"The event that caused their destruction will become clear at some point. It always does." "Then shall we begin?" asked the second.

"After you, my friend.'

CHAPTER 3

Sunday October 19
8pm local time

Joel was doing what he did every evening since his wife's death: nothing.

Well, nothing productive, that is.

He stretched himself out on his used, beer-stained sofa and aimed the remote at the television attached to the wall. It was slightly askew, which added to his discomfort as he tilted his head nine degrees to compensate. It wouldn't take much to straighten out the television, but that would necessitate need or a vitality. He had no need, and it was not vital to Joel.

Channel surfing was about the only exercise he would do today, and as far as he was concerned, that counted as a fitness workout. One could confirm that through his Fitbit, but it was lying behind the toilet in his bathroom. It had fallen off about a month ago and was now stuck to the floor.

"Sweet!" he said as he stopped when he saw the Nascar race.

Then he furrowed his brow because, while he liked to watch these cars race around the track and crash into each other, he never wanted anyone to get seriously hurt, let alone die. He recalled seeing that driver Anton Nash died in a horrific crash on lap seventy-one during this race.

Then he furrowed his other brow as he noticed on the upper right of the screen was the word *LIVE.* Something wasn't right. According to Billy, this was Sunday, and Joel was ambitious enough to confirm it was

Sunday. Also, Nascar races had been running Sunday prime time for the last few years. Even the announcers on occasion mentioned the live broadcast. Joel continued to watch, as the camera would pan across the large scoreboard and readjusted his head as he saw the time in big bold lights. It read 10:04. He looked at his wrist, but it was bare, and he had to find another source for the time and found it through the doorway on the kitchen stove.

It all seemed right, accounting for the time zone.

All this furrowing and head bopping was zapping his strength. He wasn't sure what to think. Could it all have been a hangover induced hallucination? He would find out in a few laps. Sixty-eight... sixty-nine... seventy. Joel swung his legs around and leaned in as the cars flew around the first corner on lap seventy-one.

Joel knew Anton Nash was in car fourteen, and never moved his eyes from the bright yellow auto as it skidded into the concrete outer wall, bounced violently off, then careened into the closely bunched hot rods that were in pursuit. This caused him to flip end over end. Most of the experienced drivers were able to avoid Nash, except for car number seven who struck Nash at a hundred and ten miles per hour.

What little skin was left on the car was torn away, leaving only the frame. Nash was exposed not only to the flying debris, but to all the television viewers, one of whom had his jaw down almost to the floor.

Car number fourteen finally rolled to a stop, and it wasn't long before the track lit up with emergency vehicles. Joel strained to see any detail as the cameras stayed a respectable distance away. Joel craned his neck and moved his body as if there were rows of spectators in front of him blocking his view. There was no doubt to Joel as to the gravity of the situation, because he knew Nash's fate. Fifteen minutes later, he was pried from the wreckage and an ambulance left the scene.

"What the fuck!" The fuck part was said under his breath.

Then he heard the phone ring but unknowingly not until the fifth ring, as he was so engrossed. More rings later, he knew who it was. He felt his way to the phone as he could not take his eyes off the screen.

"Hey, you won't believe this," Joel blurted out without even asking who it was on the other end of the blower.

"Never mind that. How, how could you know?" Billy asked.

Of course, Billy was referring to the football game, but Joel was still immersed in the crash of Anton Nash.

"I didn't know fully. I mean he hasn't died yet." "Died? What are you talking about?"

"Anton Nash."

"Who does he play for?" "What?"

"Hey dude, this is not working out." Billy said, then sighed.

"Okay, why did you call?"

"The Cardinals! They lost 31-17 and they turned the ball over 5 times!"

"I know that. Now let's get back to that Nascar race. I..."

"No, I've got a lot of anger that needs to be vented first, then we'll get to your problem."

"Fine," Joel said, and then Billy continued.

"Joel, I've only known you three months, and I know two things. You are a terrible drinker and an even worse gambler. Then you come up with this shit about the Lions winning so naturally I put five hundred bucks on the Cardinals. Not only did you predict the exact score that no sane, knowledgeable person would ever predict, but you also knew how many turnovers Arizona would make."

Nothing was said for a minute then Billy heard Joel's response.

"I did? Hmmm, come to think of it, I do remember telling you that. But how?"

Joel still wasn't putting the two events together. He was instead thinking why he didn't put a huge bet on the Lions.

"Billy, my head's still not feeling right. I need some time to figure out what's going on."

"Does that also include what you wanted to talk about?"

"Yea, it sure does. It sure the fuck does."

"Fine. Listen, I was able to finagle a second date out of that girl I went to the game with, you know, the one I lost all that money on," he repeated. "And I'm going over to her place tomorrow. She has a sister, an older sister. She's available and... well, she's just available. Why don't I come by and pick you up...?"

"Thanks, Billy. But…"

"I know. You're not interested. Man, you've got to snap out of it. Hey, I'll stop over anyway, and we can chat."

"Sure. Why not." Joel conceded.

"Oh, and get a cell phone, will ya?"

Joel heard the click of his land line followed by a dial tone. Without further ado, he went back to watching the events unfold. Sure enough, by the evening's sports report, he sat mired in confusion with a small invasion of butterflies in his stomach, which grew to a swarm when they announced the death of Nascar driver Anton Nash.

Joel tried to recall how hard his head was bashed in and how much alcohol he had consumed, which could explain his premonitions. He grabbed his head tightly as it felt like it was floating, unattached to his body.

"Whatever!" he called out and hoisted himself off the sofa. "Time for a drink."

Hell, why make this day any different from the others?

CHAPTER 4

Monday October 20
3:45pm local time

The sand was white, soft, and perfect. The gentle rippling water lapped at his bare feet. He walked slowly along the shoreline letting the warm breeze soothe his body. It was perfect. Yet why was Victor in a sullen mood? He really didn't want to be here. It was an odd feeling: who wouldn't want to be in this paradise.

This stunning private island, aptly named Island of Solitude, was a paradise thirty miles east of Fiji. This was Victor's private island, with seven tiki styled chalets scattered about that he would share with many of his common employees. Victor wanted for nothing. He was the founder and CEO of a global telecommunications conglomerate, and a noted philanthropist. He wasn't always that. At one time, he hoarded his cash like most other billionaires with a net worth that could rival anyone else.

So back to his sullen mood. How could that be with all he had? It had to do with an anniversary of sorts. Not a wedding anniversary. Not an anniversary of an invention or an acquisition. Certainly not retirement, as he was only fifty-three and still had no desire to retreat from work, especially since becoming a major player to garner contracts in the race to the moon.

This anniversary signaled exactly one year since the death of his one and only child, daddy's little girl.

This should have been Charlie's first year in college. The details of her death were still so fresh in his mind that it trumped the beauty of this place. The image of her contorted body in that cold casket was tormenting him even here. He should not have gone to view her body one last time. His wife even begged him not to, yet he wanted closure.

And closure is a risk. It works in some cases but failed for Victor. All his attempt at closure did was to continuously open bad memories and emotions that he could not get out of his mind.

And three of those emotions were anger, frustration, and at the top of his list, vengeance.

Sure, they caught the man responsible and while he was just four months into his seven-year sentence, he was still breathing and alive while Charlie was not, and Victor was dead inside.

His wife of twenty-seven years was back at their luxury beachside bure waiting for his return. She had wanted to come on the stroll with him, but Victor wanted to be alone. It was apparent that the tragic death of their child had not brought them closer together but had formed an invisible wedge that time had not been able to break down.

Each of their grief had manifested into different actions. She would celebrate their daughter's life by living and being happy, just what Charlie would have wanted, whereas Victor instead plotted how to exact revenge on the man who had killed his girl. Running for political office to bring about justice reform was on the front burner. However, his eye for an eye platform was way too radical to be taken seriously and would only being endorsed by the most fanatical of voters. Victor's public form of justice was seen as far too brutal for most citizens to stomach. The only thing keeping his cause going was that he had the funds and the pent-up vengeance to keep his agenda going. Of course, those close to Victor tried to convince him that his ideas were outlandish and barbaric.

His wife was waiting back for him shortly, so he decided to walk a little further. This stretch of beach was particularly private and only accessible for those staying at his bure. To his left was a long, lush stand of palm trees and tropical foliage. However, his eyes were focused on an object about fifty meters down the shoreline. It appeared to be the silhouette of a man. His guard went up, as he was sure that figure was not about to do the fandango.

Victor was closer to the stranger than he was to the resort and thought about a carefully performed retreat, followed by a complaint to the resort manager. He paid well for privacy and wasn't getting his money's worth. There was supposed to be a patrol boat employed by the island to keep any desperate pirates from kidnapping the wealthy for ransom, which was foremost in Victor's mind.

The good news was that there was only one figure, and the bad news, it was approaching, not retreating. Victor wasn't a big man at five foot eight, but he had some speed and agility still left in those old legs of his. Whether it would be useful here is still to be determined. Victor tested the sand with his bare feet. It was compact, which meant a good surface for sprinting.

They were now fifty feet apart, close enough for him to see it was a man of average height, but ill dressed for this humid afternoon. He wore long white pants and a white shirt but a long black overcoat that could easily hide a machete or a long gun being held together by duct tape. Victor was frozen in place by fear but also by a weird sense of… curiosity. Yes, curiosity.

The man in the trench coat kept approaching, then stopped twenty feet away. There was an awkward silence that lasted a solid thirty seconds before the stranger spoke.

"Your name is Victor," he said in perfect clear English.

His tone was soothing and nonthreatening, so Mr. Sierra responded in kind.

"Yes. Have we met?"

"Of course not."

"This is a restricted beach. Are you from the resort?"

The stranger looked around then held his arms out and said, "I am from a place not like this at all. I am here, in this place, to find some answers. I am here to help you."

Those open arms sent a tingle through Victor, as if his body was sitting in a massage chair set on gentle.

"Thanks, but I am doing fine. I really should be getting back." He backed away slowly. "Nice to meet you though."

He was truly back peddling slowly because that curiosity was overwhelming his desire to leave quickly. Then the stranger's next words froze him in place as if the sand were made of glue.

"You lost a loved one, not long ago."

"Who, who are you?" Victor replied, noticeably frustrated. How dare this stranger go and open wounds and get them bleeding.

"A friend."

"I don't know you."

"I can help you. We can help each other. Not tonight. Tomorrow. Just *want* to talk to me and I will return." Again, his soothing tone kept Victor's anger from elevating.

Victor didn't know how to react. He turned to look back at where the resort was, then when he looked back, the figure was gone.

What was that all about?

He began to question his state of mind and wonder if any of this had really happened. He also questioned this feeling that the stranger left something behind, inside Victor. It was hard to explain, so he didn't even try.

Then he saw two footprints cast into the sand exactly where the man was standing, which meant it did happen.

"Juliet, you will never believe this, so I won't even try explaining," he said aloud.

Victor began the long, lonely walk back. He pulled out of his back pocket a picture of his daughter. She was in a wheelchair, slumped to the side, in front of their dining room table. She was surrounded by eleven family members and behind the paralyzed Charlie was the banner, Happy 18th Birthday. She was smiling, crooked though, with a small amount of drool dribbling down her chin, and despite her condition, was aware of what was happening around her. Charlie was wearing a beautiful flower dress down to her knees that revealed her shriveled up legs. Tragically, she passed away three weeks later. Why he kept that photo with him could be for two reasons. One, as a last memento of a happy time in his daughter's short life. Another, to keep the embers of his anger from cooling off.

He carefully tucked the picture away and remembered that they still had six more days here, and he knew he would be back here tomorrow and stand on this very spot and *want* to speak to that strange man.

CHAPTER 5

Monday October 20, 11am local time

"For the last few weeks, we have been focusing on what is God, who is God, and what does he represent," Professor Matthew Danieli, of the Jerusalem School of Theology in Israel, began.

He then noticed the hands raised of about five of his female classmates. "Excuse me, or what does *she* represent."

He smiled as all the hands among the fifty-six students sitting in this modern lecture hall went down. "However, for the ease and familiarity of discussion, I will use the pronoun *he*."

There were a few more groans, but no more hands went up.

Professor Danieli left his lectern and strolled to the middle of the stage, in full view of his students. "On Friday, I asked you to submit a short essay on what each of you believe God is and what his purpose is. I read a few of them and we have some interesting viewpoints that we can discuss." He folded his hands and scanned the students' faces in the seventy-seat auditorium.

They were five weeks into the semester, and he had become familiar with all the faces. Except for one. He remembered her during his 9am class. She was new. Sitting up in the top row, with no books, no laptop, no paper or pencil. Just quietly listening. What really grabbed his attention was that she remained in her seat after the class was dismissed, just observing him. While he packed up his briefcase, he would look up at her, then down, then up and she was gone.

He wasn't sure if she was real to begin with, yet there she was again, same seat, top corner. To confirm her reality to him, she raised her hand and spoke.

"Professor?"

"Yes?" he responded hesitantly but not nervously, as her voice was soothing and comforting.

"Do humans continue to exist after the body has died? Does belief in a religion guarantee life to continue beyond death?"

"The answer, it seems, would be the same to both questions, don't you think?"

"Then there is life after death?"

"Most religions believe that to be the case."

"I see. Is there proof of this belief? Has anyone returned after death and described their experience?"

Professor Danieli moved closer to the left side of the stage to get a better look at the questioner. She appeared older than most of the students. He studied her a little more. She was in fact older than all his students by a good fifteen years. Long silky black hair, pale complexion. She was wearing a long black coat. Very out of place.

"Returned after death? Sure, there have been examples of people being clinically dead and revived to tell us of bright lights, but nothing that can be proven. I guess if there was proof, then that could make my studies and teachings irrelevant? Redundant?" Among his students there were whispers and all of them got a glimpse of the new girl.

"Can we ask if anyone in this room has lost someone that has come back to life to tell of their experience in detail? If so, I would like to meet them."

"I don't think that would be appropriate," the professor responded, and that sentiment was backed up by the mumblings of some of the students... but not all.

The stranger continued. "There is a girl sitting in the second row third from the right, my right, that lost someone close to her not long ago."

Suddenly all the attention was on that girl in the second row, third from the right. Her name was Naomi. She had shoulder length silky black hair with highlights of green. Greener than black, to be precise. She was just a shade over five foot five and though she slouched in her chair, even that wasn't enough to keep her hidden.

"Could I ask her a question?" the stranger asked.

Secretly, Naomi was the professor's favorite student. She always offered an opinion that was insightful, creative, and often worthy of debate. At times, her thirst to know the answers to everything would lead the students in a debate that would last past the end of class. He could tell this time, however, that she was uncomfortable with the attention.

"Naomi? Do you mind?" He decided to let her decide.

Naomi sat up straighter and glanced at the girl in the back. "How? I don't know you. We've never met. How could you know?"

"I know."

There were more whispers, but everyone had their phones and tablets down in anticipation of a good debate.

"What... what's your question?"

"If someone you loved who had passed away, could be brought back to life to only answer that one question about existence after death, would you want that? Would the answer be worth the pain of losing them once again?"

Every face in the room could see a small tear leaking out of Naomi's left eye.

"If the answer is that they experienced nothing, then it wouldn't be worth it," a student next to Naomi offered.

"But what if the answer is yes! Isn't that truly the answer to all religious beliefs?" That remark came from a student in the next section.

Another student chimed in. "That proof would need corroboration. If that were to happen, it would be one of the most uplifting, spiritual discoveries in all of history."

"Let Naomi answer," Professor Danieli insisted.

Naomi shook off her fixation on the stranger. "Isn't this whole debate moot, because it's simply not possible to reanimate the dead in order to answer that question. This is the stuff of science fiction, not reality."

"Hypothetically, then," the stranger said.

"Hypothetically?" The professor decided to weigh in to take the pressure off Naomi. "We study and learn and strive to find the answers to the tough questions. The Book of Revelation and the Book of Enoch say afterlife is a possibility. Neuroscientists have proposed that all our reports of life after death experiences are simply a chemical reaction in the brain to protect us from trauma. These same hallucinations can easily be recreated using simple drugs."

"It sounds like you don't have an opinion one way or the other," one student remarked. "And if we did have that answer, we wouldn't need to take this class anymore."

Some of the students laughed at the comment, but most agreed.

"First, to answer the lady in the back row, in this case, it would not be worth it. The world needs to *believe* there is an existence after death more than they need to *know* there isn't. And I guess that answers the other question as well."

Naomi cleared her throat. It would appear she had gained a lot of respect among her peers in just the short few weeks they were in class together, and the room fell silent.

"You're right, Professor: the wrong answer can destroy a civilization. It can destroy all the hope a religion is meant to bring out in people."

"From my experience, that is rare," the stranger said.

Naomi furrowed her brow in confusion, which was shared by most. "I don't understand what you mean, 'in your experience', but it's my opinion that it's not worth it. I want to continue to believe that my sister is happy and existing somewhere in some form or some plane of existence, which goes against most of my scientific beliefs and my need-to-know new things. But to know the opposite? It's just not worth the risk. And as I said before, this is all moot, as no one can reanimate the dead anyway."

"Now, ma'am..." Professor Danieli said, believing the debate had ended, but when he looked up at the back of the theater, the lady was gone. The room fell silent save for the rustling of fifty- five seats, all of whom were left wondering if she was really there or not, and Naomi? For the rest of the class, she could not get her mind off who that stranger was or even if she had been there at all.

CHAPTER 6

Monday October 20
2pm local time

Naomi was kicking at the small stones with her open-toed flip-flops, careful to leave the big rocks alone. This dusty, dry dirt road was the only way home from the university, which on most days would take her thirty-five minutes. Neither the hot sun nor the potential for danger could stop her mind from analyzing the events in class today.

She should have paid more attention to the potential for danger from the religious tensions that were on the rise in her country, as well as the ones that bordered on all sides. Nerves among the population were frayed as an all-out war could be months away which would devastate an already demoralized region.

Naomi was especially affected by the tensions, as eight months ago her parents were kidnapped and taken hostage. Their crime: escorting refugees that had escaped the war in Syria from Jordan into Israel. The Israeli government informed her just three days ago that they would continue to follow up on any intel, but for the most part, they considered her parents casualties of the insurgents and officially, their whereabouts were listed as unknown.

Unknown.

Unknown.

That word dug into her soul like an ice pick. And to thrust that pick even further in, her older sister, mentor, and best friend, who sacrificed everything to keep Naomi in school, was brutally gunned down, no doubt by the same insurgents, not long after her parents' kidnapping. This road was where the killers had come and she had no choice but to relive those events, in clarity, every day, as this was the only road home from school.

Then, that stranger had made her more emotional than she would ever admit. Naomi was halfway home when she tried everything to not look at the burnt-out metal shells of vehicles littering the road on both sides. A yellowhammer passed her, flying just high enough to see that there wasn't much to see but a junkyard. Most of the animals and birds lurking about were scavengers, which was not a healthy distraction either.

She kept walking and the scenery passed her like a cartoon background from the Flintstones. Concrete homes of similar construction were scattered here and there, some abandoned, some damaged by mortar shells, most pitted with large caliber bullet holes. She was walking at a good clip but slowed as she passed the remnants of a military Humvee, burned and scarred. The scorched bodies were long ago removed, long before the vultures and four legged scavengers could profit from man's hatred toward man.

Walking quicker, she passed on her right a Hatehof Wolf armored gunner. The body panels were in decent shape, but it was flipped over. The undercarriage was a spaghetti mess of blasted out machinery, making it only useful for parts. The insurgent driver and gunner had escaped only to be blown to bits by Israeli forces who had come too late to prevent the memories haunting Naomi.

It all began right at this spot, she was told, and at about this time of day four months ago. Naomi was carrying a small basket of groceries home from a market when she heard faraway sirens. These were warnings of a potential or impending attack. She had heard them about a dozen times in the last eighteen months, but most were either false alarms or from another region adjacent to her small village. This time she was deadly wrong!

She looked back over her shoulder and was horrified to see a cloud of dust trailing half a dozen vehicles. Naomi tried hard to hold onto her groceries as she sprinted home but let them go to pick up speed. Years and years of government drills and emergency preparedness were all she was drawing on as she knew what was coming her way. A body pumped up full of adrenaline was also keeping her focused, as her life would depend on both because she knew the Israeli defense forces were allocated elsewhere and any help could be hours away.

Her short, thin legs never quit until she was close enough to her home to see her sister at the front door, waving frantically until they were both inside. They briefly argued as to who would hide in the tiny crawl space dug only for one because the other had to remain up top to cover it up. It was never a question as to who would live and who might die, until now, but it was big sis with the final say as she forced Naomi into the cramped dirt hole.

There was barely enough room for Naomi to turn her head up, but she did just before her sister slid the floorboards in place. There was enough light for her to see her sister mouth the words, *I love you,* then there was darkness as the large living room rug was her last barrier to sight. If it could have barred the sound also, then the depth of Naomi's nightmares might not have been as deep as an ocean trench.

She cried and wept as silently as she could, wincing as each thunderous bullet felt like they were striking her. Naomi counted slowly to herself to keep her mind from totally disintegrating. She estimated, no she prayed, that help would arrive, yet all she could hear was the pounding of heavy boots on the floor above her. Friend or foe, she wondered but dared not ask. Please, she begged, let her sister live. Please, she begged, let her sister escape unseen. The gunfire was sporadic now. Above she heard muffled wails, men's voices, and the cries of her sister but not one word from anyone that she could make out clearly.

Any second they would discover her hiding place, or maybe they already had, and their guns were ready to riddle her body with lead. She felt ready to pass out, but hope came in the form of the sound of the rotors of a helicopter. Not just one, but many. Frantic yelling in a language she couldn't comprehend followed by one gunshot and then the heavy clod boot steps grew distant. The aggressors knew they would be made into mincemeat if they overstayed their welcome.

Now all the sounds of the war were outside so she tried to push up gently but couldn't budge the floorboards. She would later learn it was weighed down by her sister's beaten and bullet ridden corpse.

That was four months ago.

Today, she was nineteen, on her own, still with dreams, goals, and ambitions and she vowed, as her sister would hope, to excel and to learn to the best of her ability. Perhaps she was going overboard in following her sister's wants as she was studying and learning about everything and anything, wanting to know the answer to anything and everything, which helped in one especially important way: it kept her mind off the worst that humanity was bringing to bear.

Naomi wiped the tears away using a small cloth. She could see her house clearly now. She shrugged off her backpack and foraged around one of the pockets for her key. While she was searching, the events in class returned to her mind. She found it, then looked up to see a figure sitting in a chair on the front porch. A figure that was not there before. Her guard immediately went up. She thought of slowly making her way to the stone house on her left, one of the very few neighbors that remained in this sparse town.

Then the figure, dressed in black, showed her face fully to Naomi and she knew instantly who it was. It was the girl in the back of her classroom. The one they talked about long after her departure. As mysterious then as she was here. The figure stood, then smoothed the wrinkles in her coat. Naomi felt oddly relaxed and confident in approaching her.

"How dare you!" Naomi barked out. She readjusted the heavy backpack and came to within a few feet of the woman. "I spent an hour looking for you all over campus."

"I apologize."

Naomi was having nothing to do with the stranger's apology. "How dare you mention that in class! In front of my peers. You could have waited until now."

"Forgive us. Forgive me, but first contact can be... difficult on both of us." The stranger casually looked skyward to see the formation of small black spots forming high in the blue sky and frowned. "I meant no harm. In your class, I needed a..." she paused and stepped closer. Naomi stepped back just one pace. "I was hoping to get some answers to some questions, that is all. Again, I am sorry."

Naomi was still confused as to what the stranger was saying, yet still found it in herself to forgive her, so softened her tone.

"Who are you?" She moved under the protection of the porch. The shade felt good. "Aren't you hot? I know mystery seems to be part of your personality, but a long black coat is hardly practical." She put the key into the lock and turned it but did not go in. "Since you know of my loss, why bring it up? Why pick on me?"

"I can help you. Let me rephrase that. We can help each other."

"How?"

"It's complicated. Now's not the time. I can see by the expression on your face that you are disturbed by my appearance. I would like to return later when you are more comfortable." The stranger waited for a response, but none was coming. "You can trust me. I am here to help," she reemphasized.

Naomi opened the door fully and took one step inside. With her back still to the stranger, she said, "It's hard to trust someone who would choose to wear a long black coat on a hot sunny day, but yes, I would like to talk further."

Curiosity was a powerful desire. It overrode her suspicion of this stranger. Many a terrible thing can start with the phrase *you can trust me*. Naomi felt a strange energy coming from the stranger. A calming vibration that felt... good? Her intuition said she was in no danger. She turned around to say good-bye, but the woman was gone, leaving her to wonder if this had really happened at all.

CHAPTER 7

Monday, October 20.
3pm local time

"There's been some weird shit happening the last couple of days," Joel remarked.

He took a large gulp of his beer, which finished the can, then grabbed another from a cooler bag at his feet and continued where he'd left off. After a disgusting belch, he placed his hands behind his head.

Billy sat across from Joel with his feet up on the patio table and scanned the sky. It was clear of clouds and only the vapor trail of a high-flying jet broke up the canvas. He used his cell phone to call up a flight tracker website.

"Want to know where that plane is going?"

"Why would I care about that shit," Joel replied.

"It's..." Billy shook his phone as if the jostling would make Joel's internet connect faster. "An Aerolineas seven-thirty-seven flying from Buenos Aeries to New York."

"Like I said."

"Joel? Why don't you get rid of AOL and get with the times?"

"Never mind all that, Billy. I went into town this morning."

"You what!" Billy interrupted. "You do know that you are persona non grata there."

"I was out of liquid refreshments."

Billy shook his head. "Haven't you learned anything from Saturday night?"

Joel drank again from his can and then wiped away what missed going into his mouth.

"I guess not," Billy sighed.

"Just listen, please."

Billy gestured with his hands that he would.

"I ran into someone as I was coming out of the store. Someone must have followed me as I was walking to the taxi stand. He rode up behind me riding this bicycle."

"Ya, so?"

"It wasn't an adults' bike, but a kid's bike, kinda rusty, even like an antique. Funny thing was, I had a feeling I've seen him before. He was just sitting beside me on this bike while I was waiting for a cab and he said to me, *I'm here. You thought about me a few minutes ago and I came.* Then he says, *I'm here to help you.*"

"With what?"

"I don't know, he wouldn't say."

"What did he look like?" Billy asked. "I know most of the weirdos in town."

"Odd. Very odd. Maybe mid-thirties, with this ridiculous black mullet. Yet he didn't seem out of place on that bike."

"I've never seen anyone like that around town. Man, that's fucked up, just like your take on the football game."

"I told you I saw all the highlights?" Joel said as a question and not a statement. Joel raised his brow and sat up straight. "Now I know where I saw him before! Him and that bicycle!"

Joel sprang from his chair with the most energy he had mustered in months and dragged Billy by the shirt into the living room. Billy had to dodge some nachos that were strewn all over the floor while trying to release Joel's grip on his sleeve.

"Sorry, Billy." Then Joel turned on the only channel he could get. "Don't you see?" Joel asked while pointing at the screen.

"I see you finally got cable, that is all. What is going on."

"No, look at the date!"

Billy carefully stared at the television like an old man who forgot his bifocals. "Tuesday October twenty-first. Ya, so."

"That man I met this morning, he was in here monkeying with that. The program is a day ahead, don't you see?"

"Come on." Billy knew Joel and was sure he wasn't drunk nor high.

"I'm not high." Joel commented.

"Must be a typo. A data error."

"Then how do you explain how I knew the results of the football game in such detail?"

"Yes, come to think of it, you are the worst sports better of all time."

"Then there's that race car driver."

Suddenly all the excitement drained from Joel like the collapse of an above ground pool. Billy walked over to him and put a hand on his shoulder. He knew that, when sober, Joel was a kind and caring person.

Joel had often talked about how he and his wife Kelly were advocates for the poor. They organized rallies and on-line petitions, their goal to decrease the gap between the rich and the poor, which, if widened, they felt would lead to dire conditions if not corrected. Billy also knew the death of Joel's wife had set him on this downward spiral. Joel had revealed a good amount of detail as to why he moved here. If only there was something to renew his interest so that Joel could continue that cause in his wife's name and get out of the funk he was in.

Billy decided to be supportive and diplomatic to Joel's claims. "I must admit I am at a loss to explain it. What you need is another..."

"I'm way ahead of you. That man said all I have to do is want it. I think I'm ready for another meeting!"

"Just be careful, Joel. You know how weird people can be. That man might be up to something."

"I will, but I believe this is just what I need in my life right about now."

Billy could see determination in Joel's face, and it was good to see. "If you need me, I'm just a call away." He patted his friend on the back. "I'll see myself out."

Joel was left to himself and was about to drink the rest of his beer in one giant gulp but as the can reached his lips, he changed his mind. He ran and poured the alcohol down the sink, crushed the aluminum can and then tossed it onto the table.

Yes, this could be just what he needed.

CHAPTER 8

Monday October 20
8pm local time

Victor tried his best to unwind since that unusual meeting. Some wine and an hour soak in the hot tub were not the tryptophan he was expecting. Instead, the mystery man was a stimulant causing him to spin theories in his brain. To distract from his obsessive thoughts about the stranger, he spent some time with his wife, had a meal, and even managed a little zip-line adventure. Still, while high on that line, he wasn't focused on the fauna and foliage, but whether he could spot the man in the black coat. And all the while, he never discussed the stranger with his wife. Hell, he couldn't even explain it to himself.

Curiosity and superstition had him on this beach here, in the same place, even to the point that Victor was walking in his footprints from earlier that day and wearing the same clothes. Confident that he was alone, he scanned the environment. Isolation and privacy: his investment was paying off. The ocean was a little rougher this evening and the breeze was slightly cooler. There were no ships within eyesight, no dinghies or rowboats, nothing that the stranger could be using to come ashore.

Anger put a damper on his anticipation. Victor rubbed his chin. Was he being played? He could have easily brought a weapon with him but had decided against it. Now he was just alone with his simple faith as his only companion. *Just want to talk* was what the stranger said.

"All right here goes," Victor said aloud.

He closed his eyes for just an instant, then flung them open. His heart raced as the figure stood there before him. He blinked a few times as he could have sworn the stranger's shape was not quite solid when he first laid eyes on him. Like he had disassociated for a brief instant but was now a solid. Maybe it happened, maybe it didn't. That would have to be analyzed later. Right now, the stranger was standing thirty feet away, just as he had been earlier. Victor honestly believed he was experiencing something amazing, invigorating, and unexplainable.

"I wasn't sure you would return," Victor said without further ado.

"I was certain you would. They always do." The figure answered.

"Then let's get right to this. What do you want? What is it that you can help me with?"

"It's more what we can help each other with."

Victor shook his head. "There's always a catch. Just another slick salesman with a pitch." His thirty years of high stress business deals and meetings with hundreds of hucksters had hardened him to the point that he could ruin this before it ever began. He turned his back and took a step toward his villa, but the stranger said something that made him turn to stone.

"I can bring Charlie back. The daughter you lost not long ago."

"How dare you!" Victor snapped. He gritted his teeth.

"Would you like to speak to her?"

"She's gone. I already said good-bye to her. She isn't coming back."

He spun around, part of him expecting the stranger to be gone and all of this was just his imagination. Or a hidden desire that he would still be there, and there he was.

"Why would you offer such a thing? She's gone. She only remains here in my heart and in my thoughts."

The stranger removed his black coat and folded it neatly over his right arm. "If you trust me, our relationship can be mutually beneficial. It's critical that we work together."

"How can I trust someone who promises something they can't deliver? Is this some kind of cruel prank?"

"Turn around," the stranger asked, which also had a hint of a plea. His tone again was soothing, but not calming enough for Victor to oblige. "Please," added the stranger.

Victor did, but only because he could see the man was not hiding a weapon.

"Close your eyes."

Victor was hesitant but did so anyway, and a second later he heard a faraway voice call to him.

"Open them now."

He did and saw the stranger sitting on a large outcropping of rock a hundred feet away.

"Close them again!" the figure shouted.

Victor did and a second later felt a tap on his shoulder. He spun around to see the stranger standing in front of him. He was not out of breath at all. He was smiling with perfect white teeth, as if he had just had his braces taken off.

"How?" Victor asked as trust, hope and awe are becoming mainstays.

"It's not easy, and there are risks in having to prove myself. Yet always necessary." The figure looked skyward to see tiny specks of black in the sky and frowned.

Victor inhaled deeply then let it out. "You can bring my little girl back?"

"I can. For a brief time. When she is here, I only need to ask her a few questions, then you can have time with her."

"What questions?"

The stranger was thinking and not responding. Victor did not like that.

"What questions?" he asked again.

"Important ones. Very important. The answers are our reason for being here. The correct answers can benefit us all."

"Riddles. I don't like riddles."

"We will reveal as much as we can, I promise."

"We?" That titillated Victor's curiosity.

The figure shifted his coat from his right arm to his left. "I need to prepare first. While I do, I require you to help me. It's essential."

He walked over to the water's edge but was careful not to let the unique liquid touch his bare feet. Victor stood stunned and confused as he swore the man had been wearing shoes just moments ago. His shorts hung loosely over his waist and his button-down shirt was one size too big; those details had not changed.

"It's warm here, like Zianetta-6." He bent down and sniffed the salt water. "I've never seen this before." There was excitement in his statement. He remained bent over, mystified by the liquid, then asked, "Victor, what is it you want more than anything?"

"You already know what I want."

"In a way. I can help you with what has consumed you since her death?"

Victor clenched his fists and the veins in his neck distended. "Anger. Revenge. Retribution."

"There's more. Tell me?"

"I want those who killed my little girl to suffer as she did."

"I need a little more," the sheath probed.

"I want everyone who inflicts pain on others to feel it themselves. Especially the ones who crippled Charlie."

"Keep going."

"I haven't told this to anyone, but after the trial when he was sentenced to only seven years, I waited outside the courthouse with a gun tucked into my waist. I watched him, glared at him as he walked past me. I didn't want to kill him, just make him suffer. But I couldn't go through with it."

"You wanted retribution?"

"Why not? Is it wrong to want that?"

"That is a good question." The stranger stood up and faced Victor. "Very well. I need to make preparations."

Victor again studied the man from head to toe. "Why are you here? I want to know."

"I need to make some observations. I need to learn about many things. You will be my teacher. I will return, soon."

"This time I am not turning away. I am going to watch you leave," Victor said with gusto.

"That is fine. I don't need to hide who I am anymore."

"Then go... ahead... and..."

Before he could finish, the stranger was losing his shape as he saw what appeared to be a swarm of fireflies replacing the man's body. Victor felt a tingling like a mild electrical shock all over his body and it was as if an electrical arc was being sent from the man to him. Perhaps he was standing too close to a live transformer, like those green boxes dotted about his neighborhood. A slight humming tickled his ears, so he stepped back, and it all went away. The stranger was fading until he could be seen through. Then, like turning off the current, he was gone.

A chill went through Victor, followed by a surge of adrenaline. He paid others to audit and analyze, but this time he would trust no one. He had to find the strength and logic within himself to figure out the happenings that he was just a witness to. Patience and calm had to prevail. However, anger and hate would not allow those emotions to take over. Victor grabbed a large stone and tossed it as far into the ocean as he could, the large splash signaling a beginning to the healing.

Or so he hoped.

CHAPTER 9

Tuesday October, 21
4am local time

Naomi's eyes fluttered open. It wasn't as if she was sound asleep anyway. She was like a lioness in the wild plains of Africa, half asleep because her body depended on it, and half alert as if her life depended on it. The cause of the disturbance was a tingling sensation that was strong enough to wake her from her light slumber. She kicked off the sheet and gasped as a figure stood at the foot of her bed.

The figure was slightly aglow, like the faraway glimmer of lightning against the dark sky. In the daylight, the gleam was imperceptible, but here in her room, it was very noticeable. As quick as the lightning in nature, the glow was gone but it left a residue and Naomi knew who it was.

"You are persistent, I'll give you that." She was relaxed now and brought the sheet back up to cover her. She adjusted the pillows to talk more comfortably. "I can't sleep anyway. What do you want?"

"I'm here because you wanted me here."

"I did?"

The sheath nodded.

"I might have," Naomi admitted sheepishly. She touched the phone on her nightstand and the light from her home screen made for a calming atmosphere. "You said you can help me. How?"

The sheath removed her black coat and folded it neatly over her right arm. "I would like your permission to talk to your sister. I have an important question to ask her."

Naomi didn't react to the stranger like the other two times. She had dealt with her anger before she went to bed. Meditation was one of her many studies.

"You are a few months too late."

"What drew me to you was a feeling of loss you experienced recently. The energy from you was unmistakable. I can bring your sister back, briefly. It won't be easy, but it can be done." There was no reaction, so the sheath continued. "Once I get the answer I need, you may have some time with her."

It was hard for Naomi to remain composed after hearing what would normally be classified as nonsense. She could feel her shoulders tighten, but then took in a cleansing breath and her mood softened.

"How much time? Long enough to parade her in front of everyone who was at her funeral."

"Making light of this... it's not uncommon. I understand your feelings, but once we begin, you will understand."

"You didn't answer my question."

"Each reanimation is different. I can give you at least minutes, but hopefully hours with her. The sheath could see Naomi was deep in skeptical thought. "It will all make sense as we progress."

"Progress? What you are proposing is ludicrous."

"An explanation, at this stage, will only serve to confuse you." The sheath recognized the scrunched face and rolling eyes of a skeptic. "However, be patient. Most usually become believers."

"Most? Never mind. I suppose I owe it to Nichala to pursue this baloney."

Then she saw a smile from the stranger that took her by surprise. It wasn't a fake smile, nor a deceitful one. It was genuine. It conveyed legitimacy in the gift she was offering. A sincere desire to help. Perhaps this situation was worth more openness than ridicule.

"You did mention helping each other," Naomi said.

Again, the stranger closed her eyes as if searching for something which was short in duration. Naomi felt strange, like she was being pulled toward the interloper, not physically but mentally. It was uncomfortable in a fascinating way. Naomi had never used a hallucinogenic before, but could this be what that was like?

"Are you... are you trying to read my thoughts!" Naomi exclaimed.

"Not in the way you think. It's..."

"Complicated, I know." The stranger's eyes were open now, and that sensation went away. "What do you need from me?"

"It would really help if you can tell me what you're most passionate about."

After a moment of thought, the obvious response came to her. "Knowledge. The need-to-know new things. I guess I want to know everything there is in this world and in the universe. I have a very curious nature. It's also why I have yet to ask you to leave." She studied the stranger, then said, "But you knew that didn't you?"

"In a broad way, you might say." The sheath shifted the coat to her left arm. "Is there anything specific on your mind that you want to know? We can start there."

"Yes, where are my parents?"

Naomi was taken aback by the stranger's appearance. She appeared to glow ever so slightly, as if on a dimmer switch being turned up gently, then it subsided. Naomi rubbed her eyes as if she were wearing someone else's glasses. The stranger went out of focus, then she was sharp and clear. The entire sequence was so brief that it was more subliminal than realized and filled Naomi's subconsciousness. That was all secondary to the stunning news she was about to hear.

"Take the Sheik Hussein Bridge Road east, then turn south onto the Jordan Valley highway. Drive 2.8 kilometers. There is a farmhouse on the west side near a settling pond. Your parents are there."

Naomi threw off the thin sheet holding her in place and sprang out of bed. She turned the room light on and was near tears. The sheath sensed fear and needed to reassure her.

"They are there, trust me. I answered your question, and I will give you the answer to many more, if that is your desire."

"Okay then, are they alive?"

"Yes."

She covered her mouth and tried to control her emotions. "You wouldn't be cruel to me twice."

"Of course not; that is not why we are here. They are there, and they are alive."

Naomi shifted from one foot to the other as if standing on hot pavement. "Stay here, don't move!" she ordered, then grabbed her phone and darted from the room.

The sheath did so and became an alien sponge, continuously lapping up all the information she could about this species. She could hear bits and pieces of the conversation, as parts were quite loud. *They are there... tip... I want to go with you... tomorrow?* Then she heard silence as Naomi poked her head into the bedroom.

"How many men are guarding them?"

"Four."

"How many weapons are in the house?"

"Six."

"Thanks." She was gone again but returned a minute later. "All right, the wheels are in motion." She sat on the corner of her bed, tossed her phone down, then intertwined her fingers on top of her head. "If this is all true, I can't even begin to thank you."

"You already have. The others will be pleased. I am hoping this is just the beginning of a mutually beneficial relationship."

Naomi was so exhausted she neglected to hear the stranger's words in detail. "I see you are tired. You will have a long day tomorrow. I can return when you need."

Naomi didn't speak, she simply laid back and went quickly to sleep. This was an excellent start, and the sheath was eager to learn how the others were doing and slowly faded away as Naomi was left in the dark once more.

CHAPTER 10

Tuesday October 21
6:58am local time

Joel's favorite couch was getting quite the workout. In his left hand, he sipped from a tall glass of orange juice while eagerly awaiting the 7am rendition of Sportscenter. Normally he would be sleeping off a hangover, but eager anticipation had replaced the need for alcohol.

In his other hand was a pad and pencil, ready to take notes. He would trust nothing to his slipshod memory. He needed a third hand to work the remote so it was the juice he would sacrifice. The first order of business was, yes, to check the date. He turned on the television to his only channel and like clockwork, in the top right corner, in Kaushan Script, he read, *Wednesday, October 22.* So far so good. Then he tilted the Fitbit on his wrist, the one he retrieved and cleaned from behind his toilet and confirmed today's date followed by a fist pump. Right now, the date was all he could get but that would change by tonight.

"Sweet," he said and even sweeter still was Billy telling him that his new iPhone, according to Amazon, would arrive today by 8pm. That was followed by another fist pump.

The first highlight on Sportscenter was a hockey game that was nothing interesting except for a broken finger suffered by one of the Arizona Coyotes defensemen. He went through the scenario of calling the coach and telling him to sit that player out to avoid injury, but he just laughed it off.

Now it was onto the meat and potatoes of his strategy. He studied the highlights and the scores from the entire thirty-minute loop and noticed there was not a lot happening on a Tuesday in October. Nevertheless, this would make good practice for the lucrative Sunday NFL schedule. And as a bonus, he should, by then, also have his new iPad, which Amazon promised by Friday.

He let out a sigh, as nothing was lighting a fire into his plan. Three hockey games, two baseball playoff games and a few local sports scores. Wait, what's this? He almost missed a twenty second scroll across the bottom, at the end of the broadcast, about a soccer game in the La Liga. Soccer was a stupid boring sport that he cared nothing about until now.

He read the scroll aloud, Real Madrid upset by Huesca four nil as eight Madrid players were suspended before the game for disciplinary reasons. Too bad for them, Joel thought then speed dialed Billy as he only had six hours before the game started. While the phone was connecting, he read further that they were all caught in a massage parlor that was raided 4 hours before the game. Not so bad for them, but bad for Joel, as he now only had two hours before the news came out, which would drastically change the odds. His brain was aching trying to coordinate the time change and the date change. His hands were shaking as Billy finally answered after eight rings.

"Billy! Thank God. Were you able to open that account for me?" Joel rolled his eyes as Billy gave him a familiar torrent of complaints about his lack of having his own technology. "My high-speed internet is coming tonight, Billy. I won't have to bother you when my new phone gets here, but for now, were you able to open that account? Fine. I'll wait." Joel nervously drummed his fingers on the table. "Yes, I'm still here." Joel let out a cleansing breath after hearing the results. "Great! There's five thousand in there? Wonderful. What are the odds for tonight's game between Real Madrid and Huesca? How the hell do I know what league they play in!" He had forgotten. He would make it a priority to improve his memory skills. "Try the Spanish league. Yea, I'll wait but hurry."

Joel waited again, but this time worked on a hangnail growing on his left thumb.

"More specific? I want to put the entire five thousand on Huesca to win by four goals. Really? Then put it all on that wager!" Joel had to hold the phone away from his ear as Billy let loose with a flurry of expletives. Most of the theme of Billy's tirade reminded him that he sucked at sports betting and ended with the fact the Joel knew nothing about soccer.

"I do now. Just place the bet. And what's the payout? One million five thousand? Sweet!"

Joel knew this particular betting site, the largest in the world with assets of three billion; they could easily accept and cover such a payout. Joel was considered a lightweight in the online sports betting world as his largest payout ever was a paltry eleven dollars. So puny because his wagers were rarely over a dollar, and most were in pennies. This made the prospects of winning a million dollars leave sweat appearing along his forehead, and even his palms were filling with salty water. Joel decided 'prospects' was not the correct term. He replaced it with certainty, and that caused even more water to spill from his pores, and once he got set up on his iPad and iPhone, not even the sky would be the limit.

"Did you place it? Did you place it! I don't believe you. I'll be over in twenty." Joel fumbled the phone back onto the receiver and, if he sprinted, could be at Billy's in fifteen. He could barely contain the excitement that he *could*, no, that he *would* be a millionaire by the time he slept tonight. If Joel only knew he was setting into motion events that would turn the world upside down forever.

CHAPTER 11

Tuesday, October 21
5pm local time

Naomi pressed up against the dash of the camouflaged vehicle which was nicely hidden behind a stand of trees a hundred yards from the farmhouse on Jordan Valley highway. Her elbows rested on the dash to keep the binoculars steady. They had been parked here for close to an hour, and only five of those minutes had her looking away from the farmhouse. Naomi's eyes were drying out as she was afraid to blink and had no choice but to relax her grip and wipe her eyes on the sleeve of her shirt.

"How many men are you sending in?"

Beside her in the driver's seat was Colonel Weiss, who was the initial investigator involved in her parent's kidnapping and had been very skeptical when Naomi called him less than twelve hours ago. Over the months since the kidnapping, he had painstakingly followed up on tips and leads that never panned out, hours of surveillance that went nowhere, and he was no closer yesterday than he was from the get-go. Then Naomi came along, tells him she knew where to look and without any explanation or evidence to back up her claim.

Yet here he was, about to answer her question.

He pointed to the sky and Naomi could see a helicopter hovering high above the farmhouse.

"Do you know how many resources I had to requisition and how many favors I had to call in to make this happen in such a short time? You better..." he tapped on his earpiece and nodded. "There are four heat signatures inside, two on the main floor, two on the second floor and two more..." he tapped on his earpiece again and raised his brow. "and two more underground about thirty feet east of the house. You may be right, Naomi," the colonel relented, then smiled and nodded. The chopper's new FLIR device was working perfectly.

Her eyes grew as wide as the eyepieces of her binoculars; however, they were welling up causing her vision to blur.

"Alpha team, are you in position?"

"Affirmative."

"Bravo team, are you in position?"

"Affirmative."

"Aerial team?"

"Everything is a go for insertion."

The colonel put a hand on Naomi's shoulder squeezed gently, then gave the order. Through the lenses, she saw three men fire a round of flashbangs, breaking two windows on each floor. Three more soldiers emerged from the settling pond and sprinted toward the rear, easily knocking down the back door. The Apache from above tilted twelve degrees down and aimed its gun barrels in support.

Naomi could barely hold the binoculars steady; she knew what was at stake. The popping sound of automatic gunfire filled the air. Each single pop struck her psyche twice. Once for hope that the kidnappers had been neutralized, and second, wondering if one of those bullets had struck her parents during the violent assault. Seconds later came silence. Uncomfortable silence. Unnerving. The anticipation was too much to bear. She reached for the handle of the door, but the Colonel grabbed her arm and held on.

"Aerial team, status!"

"All primary target heat signatures are down."

Then a few more seconds of silence that was unbearable to Naomi. She tried to pull away again, but the colonel held tight. "Two underground assets remain... lit."

"Get me closer!" Naomi shrieked.

Colonel Weiss started the engine, and they were at the entrance to the laneway in seconds, then he reduced his speed and coasted to the front of the farmhouse.

"Stay here! We wait!"

She groaned and had to close the door shut, as she was halfway out before his order. Her heart was beating out through the thinness of her ribcage. She wiped her forehead and palms with a cloth then tossed it down as a heavily armed soldier emerged from the front door and signaled with a thumbs up!

"All clear!" came through a loudspeaker and Naomi bolted from the vehicle with no resistance.

Ten feet from the front door she skidded to a stop and put a hand to her chest as if putting her heart back into its cavity. Two more soldiers emerged from the door, followed by her parents. They shielded their eyes from the bright afternoon light and looked disheveled and weak. The siren of an approaching ambulance grew louder, ready to whisk them away.

No matter how beaten down her parents were, they both managed a huge smile when they saw their daughter. Their postures immediately elongated as Naomi carefully jumped into their arms, the relief of being rescued buoying everyone's spirits.

It was a long, long embrace, not completely comforting as her parents' bones were easily felt through their skin, and even through their thinner, dirty clothing. The front of her dad's shirt was stained with Naom's tears which suddenly dried up as she wondered if they knew about their other daughter, Nichala. Even more shocking was how did that stranger know where to find her parents.

"Miss, we need to take them now." She heard someone call out. She let her parents go, then turned around, and next to the road, was the stranger she was just thinking about. The sudden appearance didn't spook Naomi, but the colonel motioned for two of his men to intercept and investigate. Their weapons went hot, but before they moved, Naomi called out calmly.

"Wait! Ease off! She's with me, Colonel Weiss. She's with me."

And if Naomi knew anything about the colonel's personality, he would never let this go. How did she know where to find them? He would never let that go.

CHAPTER 12

Tuesday, October 21
8pm local time

"Relax Joel and sit down! You're acting like a jackhammer."

"But I won and it's not there yet. I won!"

Joel was glued to his new iPhone, not because it had been delivered two hours earlier than promised, or that it still had that new phone smell, but because ante-up.com had yet to deposit his winnings. The screen was attached to his face like an alien parasite as he paced about Billy's living room.

"Sit down! Please. I'm getting nauseous," Billy snapped.

Joel finally acquiesced and felt his way to a seated position beside Billy.

"It's just been flagged. Payouts this big are always investigated. It just takes time," he added.

Joel was rocking back and forth, even though Billy's couch was not a rocker.

"Relax! You're acting like you've done something wrong."

Joel's body was suddenly stationary. He looked at Billy with just his eyes. "You think I did, didn't you? You think I cheated."

Billy shrugged and took a sip of his beer.

"This is an opportunity I can't ignore, Billy."

Another shrug. "I don't care how; all I can say is... it's about fucking time you got one right."

"It's not like this company can't afford it."

"Then you are the modern-day high roller of Sherwood Forest."

"You know how I feel. You know the cause that my wife and I were so passionate about."

"Hang loose, brother. I'm on your side. It was hard to get it out of you at times, but I know all about the cause you fought for before you moved here. It's one of the things I admire about you and after all you've put me through since we met, I'm genuinely happy for you." Billy punched him in the arm to see if he was paying attention. He could tell Joel was reflecting and his wife, Kelly was the prime image on his mind. "Listen, anytime you can stick it to the man..."

A gentle smile spread out on Joel's face. "But only if..." Joel stopped in mid-sentence as his peepers grew the size of poker chips. "It's there. It's there!" He held out his phone for Billy to see.

"I believe you. I believe you!"

"I'm. I'm a millionaire!"

"Fucking right you are!" Billy let out a whoop and held up his beer to toast the newest rich dude. Joel slammed his Pepsi into Billy's can of Coors. "Just don't let it go to your head and don't ever forget about the little guy."

Joel did his best to keep from wetting himself. His head was a clean whiteboard ready to be written on. There were graphs, charts and plans in bold red marker. Robin Hood? Joel Hood? Joel's bow was not of arrows but was a stranger with a special gift. As soon as his mind focused on that stranger, he saw a bluish light dazzle him for just an instant through Billy's living room window. Finally, he had the means to continue the movement that was so abruptly halted with the death of his wife.

Other thoughts crept into his mind. Some were realistic, like donating his winnings to charity, others were more daunting like ending global poverty. Yes, Kelly would be proud of him, if only he could tell her all about it!

CHAPTER 13

Wednesday October 22
1:09pm local time

Victor didn't have any pets, yet here he was in the doghouse. Why? Dragging his wife off the resort four days before their trip was supposed to end, was the one and only factor. *Business meeting my foot* was Mrs. Amaya Sierra's response to an obvious lie from her husband. He would smooth it over somehow, but telling her the truth, at this time, would be absurd.

For now, he had to keep this to himself. However, should the stranger follow through on his promise, he would have a serious decision to make.

Which brings Victor to his early afternoon start to the day. The first day of his intricate, ludicrous plan that had no chance of success, had he tried it last week or the week before when it was just an artist rendering, a dream only.

However, that all changed to an actual mechanical reality having had the luck of crossing paths with this stranger. There was no doubt he could pull it off. Of course, there would always be *some* doubt which was why Victor needed to test the stranger's abilities, and why not at thirty-five thousand feet during that flight home.

The incident that spooked him the first time was when he was having drinks with his wife by the pool the last night at the resort. Victor had had the stranger on his mind often since their initial meeting, mostly in his subconscious, yet he could feel the stranger's presence each time, as if they were transferring energy back and forth. He couldn't, or didn't want to, explain it because by the pool, he was breaking the news to his wife about leaving early and their daughter Charlie had come up in conversation, which made Victor think strongly of the stranger.

Suddenly, across the way, on the other side of the pool, there he was. If his wife had been facing that way, she would have noticed him as well. He quickly took his mind in another direction and the stranger was gone. He deduced that the stronger the desire to have him present, the more probable he would appear, possibly at inappropriate times. He also wondered if those small black clouds, for lack of a better term, that appeared each time the stranger came, were somehow related. Either way, he would have to work at controlling his desires.

That would not be easy, as evident by the second impossible incident, the one that removed all doubt, and occurred during their flight back to the United States. In the plane's tiny lavatory, and with his zipper down, Victor had nothing better to do than rehearse his plan of retribution, which involved the stranger. Then came the tingling and the soft glow, followed by the cramped feeling of two occupants when the sign strictly informed a maximum of one. Above the toilet, the creepy stranger's face filled the tiny mirror. The rest of Victor's stream hit everywhere but the toilet.

Now safely back home, and with that doubt about the stranger's validity all but eliminated, Victor was able to relax as he stood on his back deck, admiring the majestic view of the Kings Mountain range. On a crisp clear evening he could see the lights of San Francisco to the north and San Jose to the southeast. His sprawling industrial complex was only ten minutes from his home, at the base of this mountain with Stanford University just up the road from that.

Victor's factory here in Sierra Valley was currently focused on the programming and development of communication satellites for the large cell phone companies, and his new plant in Austin, Texas, was ramping up production of green technologies and would soon be developing a line of innovative green energy products.

He would have lost it all had he committed murder outside that courthouse. The rage that consumed him that day was still burning inside, and now he was grateful for his restraint as the perfect plan to release all that pent up anger had fallen in his lap.

Victor took a couple of spoonsful of his chicken noodle soup and put the steaming bowl on the railing of his wrap-around deck. He tried valiantly to downplay the stranger's importance to the plan he was contemplating because... and as if on cue, he heard the humming and felt the vibration like standing next to a live wire. Victor spun around to see the stranger there, as faithful as Old Faithful. One of these days he would catch him in mid appearance rather than already here. Victor wasted no time and got right to the point.

"I want to talk to Charlie. You promised."

Only Victor called his little girl Charlie, a middle name he chose when she was born. His wife and everyone else called her by her given name, Laila. The stranger wasn't moving fast enough for Victor's liking.

"Well?"

The stranger stepped forward and pivoted, as he was not oblivious to the inspiring view. The sheath put one of his manufactured arms onto the cedar railing and studied the scenery.

"You're not ready."

"The hell I'm not!"

"Your anger will only serve to interfere. You need to be at peace before you see her. Before you talk to her.'

"I..." Victor sighed and inhaled deeply, held it for a three count then exhaled. He did that at times to relieve the stress, then realized the stranger was right. Victor was getting sound advice. "Why are you doing this? Why me?"

"It's mutually beneficial."

"That's extremely vague."

"If I were to explain in full why we are here, it would only confuse you. You need to be clear headed."

"Fine, I will wait."

"All in good time." The sheath was done with the view and turned to face Victor. "What would you like me to do?"

"Okay, let's do this. I need you to break someone out of jail."

"When?"

"Tonight."

CHAPTER 14

Wednesday, October 22
7:17pm local time

Naomi sat on an uncomfortable plastic chair between two hospital beds at The Makassed Hospital in Jerusalem, with her mom on her right and her dad resting to her left. Both were connected to IV's and multiple electronic monitors. The physician in charge of their care just left minutes ago with great news: her parents would fully recover and could be discharged on Friday.

That wonderful news suddenly freed her mind to allow a more concentrated dissection of how her parents were found with the help of the stranger. How could she have known? Was she planted there by the captors as a plot to ambush the rescue team? That was the concern Colonel Weiss had raised, hence the overabundance of firepower. Yet, here Naomi was, her parents alive and still with no explanation as to how the stranger appeared and disappeared in the way she did. Which also left Naomi with some doubts and some thanks, an odd combination.

All this thought brought on a slight bluish glow that seeped out from under the bathroom door and caught Naomi's eyes. Even though she knew what it was and who it was, the sight was hypnotic.

The moth in her was attracted immediately to the blue flame and she tiptoed over to the door then placed her palm on it as if there was a fire on the other side. She felt no heat, just a slight vibration. Naomi was not scared to go in and cracked it open, peaked in, then looked back to make sure none of the staff were in view. She quietly slipped in and shut the door behind her.

"Nice to see you again," Naomi said.

The bathroom was large with plenty of space for the two of them. She took out her phone and placed it on the counter, letting the glow from the screen fill the room with ambient light.

"It appears my information was helpful."

"I don't know how to thank you or even if I should, if you know what I mean."

"I understand. I am glad to be of help."

"Well, accepting you is not coming easy."

"But it is coming?"

"We'll see, but at the moment, I just don't, understand you."

"You will." The sheath held out her arm and rolled up the right sleeve of her black coat.

It was an invitation for Naomi to touch her. Naomi timidly laid her hand on the stranger's skin. It was physically there, which assured her that she wasn't dealing with an illusion or a hologram.

While she, that pronoun would make the figure seem more real, was physically there, the skin did not feel like hers. It felt more artificial, like a doll's outer covering. Naomi would like to take her, or it, down for an MRI or even a simple x-ray to see what was percolating inside.

Naomi wasn't sure how long she should touch her, but then she felt a very mild electrical shock, like touching a metal doorknob in a dry, carpeted room. The tingling spread up her arm, through her shoulder and then up to her head. It was ticklish in a way, and she did not feel it was an attack of any sort. She released her touch and the sheath rolled down her sleeve.

"What did you do?"

"Just a completion of the syncing of our electrical and energy patterns. It's necessary."

"Of what? Is that why you let me touch you?"

"I think you needed some reassurance that I am real, but also to realize I am not like you."

Naomi did not display any look of reassurance. "Please, trust me," the stranger said.

"I'm not stupid!" Naomi snapped back. The word trust frequently gave her a case of mild food poisoning every time someone asked her for it. "It's obvious you are not like us, at all."

This defensive stance had been brought on since her parents' kidnapping. It was a personality trait she never had growing up as a child and wished would go away.

"I'm... sorry. I didn't mean to take it out on you." An apology she had made often, as of late. "This is a lot to take in. A lot to process."

Naomi took a second to calm herself and three deep cleansing breaths helped to clear her mind, which also melted away some of the nerves. She had to stay composed, as she knew there was much more to come.

"Where are you from? And I don't mean from what country."

The sheath walked past Naomi, who cautiously gave her the space to do so. Naomi moved to where the stranger was, effectively changing places.

"I am not from here, as you surmised. I am from a faraway place."

"Come on," Naomi responded flippantly. "Why the riddles? You seem to come and go in ways I can't figure out. You knew where my parents were, right down to the minute details. It's by my nature that I need to know a little more about you and what this is all about."

"It is not my intention to answer in riddles. As you said, it's your quest to know everything that binds us now. In turn, we will help each other achieve what we desire most."

"More riddles," Naomi said under her breath. What was the stranger's desire? What was her motive? She was sure it would be fascinating, far beyond the simple notion that she was here just to help her.

She could have become angry and frustrated again, but instead chose to change her internal dialogue, to take this as a challenge. A mystery to solve. An incredible mystery to solve. A life altering mystery?

She decided to shift to an especially important line of questioning. "You mentioned my sister."

"Indeed, I did. You would like to speak with her."

"Not... yet" Naomi relented then stopped and put a finger to her lips as a sign to be quiet. The light under the door grew brighter. There were voices outside. It was a nurse making rounds along with someone else, a doctor perhaps. If they came in here, she would have a lot of explaining to do.

"I should leave," the stranger whispered.

Naomi shook her head. "Not yet."

Then she noticed the glare from her phone might give them away, so she quietly turned it over. She heard rustling from right outside the door. *What if it's housekeeping?* she thought, and she felt a surge of adrenaline.

"Not yet," Naomi restated, but by only moving her lips and not speaking the words. The thin door rustled then settled down. Naomi was thinking up a fast explanation just in case, but she noticed the light under the door fading, as well as the voices. She let out the deep breath she was holding in, then flipped her phone back over.

"That was close. For now, we should keep you hidden as much as possible. It might not have been wise for you to have shown up at the farmhouse."

"Me showing up will be up to you."

"I understand. You're right, I need to be more disciplined. I can do that." She gathered herself. "Where was I? Right, my sister. You will have to do a lot more to convince me that you can bring my sister back. She's dead. Dead and buried." That might have been a poor choice of words that she instantly regretted, but felt it had an impact. "If you can return her in some alien, spectacular manner, why do you even need me involved?"

"Because there is a considerable shock when a person is reanimated. If their first sight is of a loved one, the interaction goes much better. Your sister will see you, talk to you, and you can comfort her."

"I get it. You've done this before; I can tell. But I'm not ready to see her." That was painful to admit. "I just... I just need more proof, that's all, and I think I have a way to move this along. If you can answer this question, then I will believe you. It's a mystery not only that I have agonized over but the world has also. A mystery that no human has solved to this day," she said with emphasis on the word human.

"Please, what do you want to know? I will have an answer for you."

"We will see. When I was younger, we were on this vacation with my mom's brother and her family in Malaysia. Their vacation was over, so we drove them to the airport. Even today, those goodbye hugs to my aunt, my uncle and their six-month-old are fresh in my mind because it was the last time we ever saw them again. Our flight back the next day to Israel was fine but their flight to Beijing never made it. Their plane disappeared and was never seen again. Their flight was MH370. The complexity and the mystery surrounding that flight makes it a mystery that I don't think will ever be solved."

Naomi paused for dramatic effect.

"So, my question is, where the hell is MH370?"

She was certain that she had just stumped the Jeopardy champion.

"It's lying on the seabed floor, six thousand feet down." There was a short pause, then the sheath continued as if she was revealing a simple weather forecast. "It is one hundred and forty miles east of the Addu Atoll."

"It can't be there, can it? Where the hell is that!" Naomi exclaimed.

She snatched up her phone and searched on Google Maps. *How am I ever going to find out if this stranger is right?* No one has ever suggested, through theory or evidence, that the plane went down there.

"Search there. You will find what you are looking for."

"Then can you be more precise? What are the co-ordinates?"

"1.895 by 74.193."

She entered them and was shocked to find those co-ordinates were right where the stranger said. "I don't even know what to do with this." She kind of did, but her story would be so fantastic that it would be hard to convince anyone to send a search out. "How did it crash? Do you know that as well?"

Naomi had to wait about three seconds for a response.

"The pilot intentionally flew the plane to that location and ditched it into the ocean."

Naomi gasped. "I can't believe it. I know it was one of the possibilities, but certainly not in that area. Why did he do it?"

"His motive... was greed."

Naomi found it odd that this fact would cause a slight grin to appear on the stranger's face, the first show of any emotion since they met. She noticed her teeth for the first time: white and straight. Not perfect but passable and certainly not made of enamel. Plastic, like her skin.

"His wife had filed for divorce. He was filing for bankruptcy. There was certain cargo and certain military papers he would sell for money."

"This is all too incredible. How is all this information coming to you?"

"Electricity and all its components are the most common properties in the universe. Thoughts and images are simple electrical impulses. I can interpret the answers to your questions in a way that you wouldn't understand."

Or won't tell me, she thought.

"This is all too incredible to believe." Despite her misgivings, she still needed to Know It All. "What happened to the people on the plane. What happened to... my relatives? What happened to the passengers and crew?"

"Except for the pilot, they all died of asphyxiation. All of them. They all died before the plane crashed?"

"I... I...."

Naomi could not help but place herself in the seat beside her family. Knowing they were unconscious when they struck the water leant to a small amount of relief. Then another truth was suddenly realized.

"What do you mean except for the pilot? What happened to him?"

"He's still alive."

"What!" Her hands were shaking so much that her phone fell to the floor and landed screen side up. The upward illumination made the sheaths story telling all that more haunting. "How can he be alive?"

She saw the stranger close her eyes like she was a computer collating data. She finished her story with her eyes shut. "Captain Shah caused the plane to decompress but had disabled the air supply that the passengers would use by the drop-down masks." She stopped as if waiting for the next scene to buffer. "Then he set the auto pilot and went down to the cargo hold where it took him several hours to gather the eight million in currency and diamonds and stash it in three large waterproof duffle bags."

"Slow down. Just slow down. You're talking too fast. This is too crazy to comprehend."

"Of course, I apologize." The sheath let the commercial play out then continued at a more dramatic pace. "He also took this blue suitcase with a bunch of important papers which he sold later to the Chinese government. He also goes through all the dead passengers, one by one, taking various things of worth."

"Greed! Fucking greed. He killed all those people, my family, for what, money." She rarely ever swore, but she was so angry. Which also meant she believed the stranger's story. "I want him! The pilot! I want him exposed!"

Again, she thought she saw the stranger smile. But that couldn't be. Naomi must be mistaken.

"What happened with captain Shah?"

"As the plane neared the crash site, he lowered its speed to close to stall and its height to a safe minimum. He opened the middle right door and then pushed the bundles out. They landed near a small boat where three people brought the bags on board."

"Unbelievable! Continue."

"Then at a height of six hundred feet, he jumped out, and parachuted to the ocean where that same boat picked him up twenty-five minutes later."

Her hands still shaking, Naomi picked up her phone and held it tightly. "Where is he? Right now. Where is he?"

"He is living in a place you call the Maldives, on the northernmost island of Uligan. He has a home on a small atoll two miles southwest of there. He is there now."

"That's enough! I can't digest this all. It's too much." Suddenly she felt claustrophobic. "Let me think." She put one hand on her head and moved her hair around, massaging her scalp, trying to clear her mind. "I need time to confirm your story. I have an idea, but when I tell him this story, he'll think I'm nuts, again."

"We have time. Just let me know when you are ready to meet your sister and we will proceed."

If that didn't give Naomi incentive, nothing would. She turned her phone off and the room went dark. She walked past the stranger and cracked the door open just an inch.

Keeping her back to the stranger, she asked, "Why me? Why did you choose me?"

"Because you suffered a loss recently."

"So have many others."

"Some things are best left unknown."

"I can't argue; I'm too overwhelmed to argue."

Naomi stepped into her parents' room and gently closed the door. She knew just who to contact. He already had one taste of her lunacy that turned out to be true. That just might tip the scales in her favor as she tried to convince him of one of the wildest stories he's ever heard.

CHAPTER 15

Thursday, October 23
2:15am local time

Sleep usually comes easy at this time of the morning, for most. Soft pillow, comfortable mattress, quiet surroundings, and a feeling of security. However, for Cameron Mitchell, nothing could be farther from that truth. He did his best, like the night before and the night before that, to get some solid rest. Lying on a razor thin, dirty mattress and an equally thin pillow made deep sleep a chore. Added to his difficulty was the ambient light filtering through the four-inch slit in his cell door, plus the intermittent caterwauling from some of the more insane inmates left him always on edge.

This was the life of Cameron at the ADX in Florence, Colorado. Inside was maximum security and minimal freedom. This facility was recently expanded to a capacity of six hundred and fifty inmates, all confined to ten-by-ten foot, poured concrete spaces of solitude. Cameron's pad was on the second floor. He was only here because he tried to shiv a guard three weeks ago. In a way, he felt honored to be spending the next six months among some of the country's most heinous individuals.

At this exact time, if a guard were to stroll by the outside of his cell, he would see a blueish glimmer seeping out from inside the thin slit in the steel door, and if he were to place a hand on said door, he would feel a slight tingle. And if he were to be outside, he would see small oil slick like black spots visible even in the night sky.

However, on the inside of his tiny compartment, Cameron was facing the cold, cracked cinder blocks, trying desperately to fall asleep. He scratched what he thought was an itch on his back but couldn't reach it. He turned over and rubbed his back on the steel springs protruding through the fabric and felt some relief, then a sense of being watched came over him. It wasn't unusual to sleep though the morning wake-up call only to have a corrections officer roust him, so he wasn't particularly alarmed.

These types of perceptions were necessary for survival in a place like this. Cameron rolled his head casually to the left and his eyes shot open. His entire body tensed as he saw a man standing three feet from him, no uniform, only regular clothes covered by a long black coat. Was it an inmate here to kill him? No doubt the guard he stabbed had let him in. He sat up and took a defensive posture.

The fight or flight instinct was missing one option in this confined space. Cameron had three inches on him but was weak with malnutrition and mentally drained of hope. Against any victory was the thirty pounds the stranger had on Cameron and the thick protective clothing worn by his new cell mate. If he could keep from being stuck too many times… then fake death like the Virginia opossum, he might live to shiv another day.

"Relax, Cameron. I am here to, let's see if I remember, to break you out."

Victor had outlined an incredibly elaborate plan, and his sheath was just beginning to act out the first of many scenes.

"What are you talking about! Do you work here?"

"Of course not. Shall we?" The stranger pointed to the door.

"How did you get in here?"

"Not the same way we will leave." He touched the lock and the metal glowed blue.

Cameron heard a static discharge, the electronic latch disengaged, and the door slid open. He smiled, but then his face went stern. "Is this a set-up? If I step out, will I get fucked up?"

"Follow me, and I promise to get you out of here safely." The sheath walked, carefree, out onto the second-floor balcony and towards the stairway.

"Hey, not so fast!" Cameron whispered.

He soft shoed it by three cells, wondering the entire time where all the guards were. He was wondering about a lot of things, like if he was still dreaming… he didn't think so. He reached the stranger's side, and they walked together down to the mezzanine where there were twelve picnic tables spaced out.

"Stay close. I have a few people to talk to before we leave."

Victor had provided the sheath with a list of names to rouse, and he found those names on a master sheet in the corrections office. Meanwhile, Cameron wasn't happy with the direction he was being led.

"We don't have time for this shit. The exit's over there!"

Cameron thought of going off on his own but knew that could end in disaster. He noticed the stranger counting out loud the cell numbers. The sheath stopped at cell 106, knocked quietly on the door, and after a moment, a middle-aged man with dirty blond hair and glasses revealed himself in the small opening of the door.

"Hey, that's, that's the Oklahoma bomber!" Cameron's pupils were as wide as an owl.

The sheath leaned in. "You're Terry Nichols?"

"Yes, and who are you?"

"I will be back to break you out in two days."

"Who the hell are you? What are you talking about?"

"Believe him. He's breaking me out now!" Cameron boasted.

"Whatever. Get lost!"

"Just be ready." The stranger then walked over to cell 119. Again, there was a quiet knock and an answer. A young-looking man in his late twenties showed his face.

"That's Dokker or Soaker, or whatever his name is, but that's the marathon bomber!"

"Are you Dzhokhar Tsarnaev?" The sheath bumbled the pronunciation.

"Yes, who else would be in here?" he grumbled. "Who the fuck are you?"

"I will be back to break you out in two days."

"I'll be ready," came back the sarcastic response.

"How many more, dude? We gotta scram."

"I'm only to contact three this time."

"This time?"

Cameron followed his rescuer to cell 141, which should be the last one. An excitement grew as he was curious to see who would be behind that door. What presented was a disheveled old man.

"That's- that's the Unabomber!"

"You are Theodore Kaczynski?" the sheath inquired.

"Who wants to know?"

"I will break you out in two days."

"I might need a wheelchair. I'm not doing well," he said matter-of-factly.

"All right, I will let him know."

"Him? Is that the man running this operation?" Cameron asked.

"You will meet him shortly."

"I can't wait." Cameron would learn soon that he would have been better off in prison.

"Let's go."

"Finally. I didn't realize I was surrounded by such monsters. This place is giving me the creeps."

Cameron followed the stranger to the exit without resistance. They passed the central command, and he saw three guards lying on the floor. Unconscious, or dead? There was one more stooped over a bank of controls. Cameron could see himself in one of the monitors, but something was odd. The stranger beside him was blurred, fuzzy, and had a bluish aura encircling him. He shrugged it off, then continued outside.

They were in the main yard now, which was lit up by several spotlights. He took in a refreshing deep breath of humid, free air then stretched his arms high over his head.

"Keep up," the stranger said, and Cameron obeyed.

They easily passed through two heavily fortified gates and were out into the parking lot in no time.

"There's our ride." The stranger pointed to a car parked on a side road behind a stand of trees that was flashing its lights on and off.

"Can you tell your friend not to do that," Cameron groaned. He thought about just taking off but felt he didn't stand much of a chance on his own.

"It's all right, he's stopped. Let's continue."

Cameron followed but grew eyes on all sides of his head. They reached the car, and he noticed another oddity. "Hey, I had a car just like this before I went into the joint." He could see through the windshield a lone figure in the driver's seat of this eight-year-old Toyota. He looks familiar also. Cameron leaned in closer. Perhaps his girlfriend arranged all this.

"Get in," the sheath ordered, startling Cameron as his tone was not as polite as before. He got into the passenger seat and the sheath got into the back.

"Do you know who I am?" Victor asked without looking at Cam. He was on his phone going through his checklist.

"You must be Brittany's old man. I knew she'd come through. Your friend there in the back is a little weird though. If you really want to make some big money and break someone out, you should grab El Chapo. That would be cool. I hear he's in the other compound. He can thank you in a far more substantial way than those other dudes can."

"I am not interested in profit."

Victor reached under his jacket and pulled out a Glock G43 and pointed it at Cameron's head. A small amount of warm liquid seeped into his tattered underwear.

"Why the fuck would you go through all this risk to break me out if you're just going to kill me?"

"I'm not going to kill you."

Cam exhaled the breath he was holding in.

"I will do my best to keep you alive… for now."

More warm liquid soaked his shorts. He casually felt for the door handle, but it had none. Come to think of it, the previous car he owned was missing it too. Victor put the gun back under his jacket and started the car. This could be Cameron's chance. Wrestle the gun away, shoot the weirdo in the back seat, dump their bodies and cheeze it.

Unfortunately, Cameron never had a chance to begin his plan, as he was up against an otherworldly figure in the back seat who grabbed his shoulder with gentle force and an ever-growing surge of electrical energy spread throughout his body and limbs. The sheath was far more efficient than a taser and more precise than a Vulcan neck pinch. He was easily able to paralyze Cameron's body without affecting the systems that was keeping him alive.

"You will make history," Victor stated. The car started on its journey. "You will be the first to experience my full and complete retribution. Memorialized for all to see. A distinct deterrence for those like you."

Cam tried to form speech, but his face was contorted as if he had Bell's palsy. He fought hard because he wanted to plead his case. A small amount of drool dripped out of the corner of his mouth.

"You look just like Charlie did before she died. Excellent."

Charlie! Cameron's body might be paralyzed; however, his memory was working without interruption. He tried to speak, and Victor noticed that.

"Can you allow him to talk?" Victor asked. The sheath touched Cameron's shoulder.

"You! You were in the courtroom! Now I remember. You're that kid's dad. Is that what this is all about. Fucking revenge!"

"Revenge, retribution, eye for an eye. Pick your catch phrase. Oh, and that kid, she has a name. Nothing to you, but she will always be my Charlie."

"Come on, man! Take me back. I'm sorry."

"Oh, you'll go back when I'm done with you."

Cameron didn't like the sound of that, at all. Their car turned onto a football sized gravel patch next to the municipal airport where Victor's private plane was parked. Victor rolled to a stop but kept the Toyota idling.

"Echo, take him over to where I drew it on the plans."

During their short drive here, and even soon after meeting the sheath, Victor was contemplating a name for his new friend. Echo was that name.

"I'll set up the video feed," he continued.

Echo moved the pliable Cameron into position in the middle of the field, about thirty yards from the car. Victor activated the very expensive dash cam that would capture the event for the world to see in 4k color video and crystal-clear sound. He then fetched a wheelchair from the trunk and pushed it in front of the camera.

"This is the chair you put my daughter in. She would have turned 18 next week."

"But I'm paying for that. You saw..." he stopped to suck in some drool then continued his slurred objection. "you saw the prison, the cell I was in. That's my home for the next..."

"Twelve years! My daughter won't be back in twelve years. She's gone forever. Thankfully, this man is going to give me one last time to be with her, just like this is the last time I will be with you." Victor felt good getting that off his chest. He moved the chair out of the way.

"This nice man will keep you company until I am ready."

"Ready for what!"

Victor walked away while Cameron kept pleading for his life. Victor felt no remorse, no pity, no fear. No sorrow, just satisfaction. He then guided the car so that the front of the hood would strike Cam in the thoracic spine anywhere between the t-2 and t-6 vertebra.

Echo signaled Victor to stop, then he got out and joined them in front of the camera. He cleared his throat and prepared to give a speech that would be the beginning of a new era of justice. He looked straight into the camera.

"My daughter was struck and paralyzed by Cameron Mitchell, who was fleeing after a robbery at a gas station. He was sentenced to twelve years. Cameron Mitchell will then be free to live out the rest of his life, completely unfettered, at the age of thirty- four. That is not justice. My little girl..." he was tearing up on the inside but had to keep a cool façade on the outside, "spent the last months in this wheelchair until she passed away. The punishment did not fit the crime. It will now. It will from now on."

"What do you mean?" Cameron shrieked. "I've already had a trial. I've already been sentenced. I promise not to ask for early release. I will serve my entire sentence. I demand you take me back to prison."

Victor walked in front of Cameron and bent down to speak eye to eye. "You will be a part of history. The first of anything is always historic."

"This is nothing but torture! You have no right!"

"This is justice. This is... deterrence." Victor was finished talking to Cameron. His quest for revenge was about to end, and a new quest was just beginning. "Let's get this thing going. Echo, you said when you let go of him, he will have full movement in five seconds."

The sheath nodded.

"You know what to do then."

He nodded again.

Victor backed the car up exactly one hundred and five feet and rechecked his calculations. Nine seconds to slowly get to thirty- five miles per hour, and that should sever his spinal cord but keep him alive. He stepped on the gas and spent the first three seconds thinking, no wondering if this is what Charlie would want.

Five... four... three...

And then to think about how the world will begin to change. Two... one...

Echo released his touch and stepped out of the way. The rest of the contents of Cameron's bladder spilled out just as the sharp edge of the hood slammed precisely into his spine at T-4. A part of his vertebrae splintered into sharp shards of bone, easily slicing through all three maters of his cord like a bowie knife through rope. Cerebral spinal fluid also splattered out as Cameron was catapulted ten feet, then rag dolled it another ten. Victor veered off and skidded to a stop. He angled the car to keep the dash cam aimed at the accident scene. Victor and Echo joined Cameron, who looked like a broken jackknife.

"Can you feel this?" Victor asked after kicking him in the shins.

When there was no response, Victor thought he might have killed Cameron.

"Get the fuck away from me," the body slurred.

Victor felt better.

"In time. In time." He rolled the wheelchair over. "This is your new home... for a long while."

With help from Echo, they pulled him up into the chair. Cameron resisted, but only mildly from his upper body.

"There, perfect." Victor spun the crippled man to face the camera.

"This is a warning to all those who commit violent crimes against humans and humanity. A new era of retribution has arrived. We will be watching." He pressed the remote, which shut off the dash cam. "That went well."

Echo had remained silent during this display, soaking it all in. "I learned a lot today."

Victor was too preoccupied with his next thought to analyze the statement Echo just made, which should have deserved more inspection.

"Charlie, my little girl?"

"I will bring her to you."

Victor felt a surge of nervous excitement. Yet he had to temper it, and fast. He stared up at the full moon shining its spotlight on him.

"I have one more thing to do first. You talked to the three men on the list?"

"Yes, I told them I would be back."

"They won't believe you, but that doesn't matter. I will need two or three days to prepare for them and to edit this video for worldwide distribution."

With his degree in computer science and easy access to all that is tech, Victor had the means to edit and display this video in complete anonymity. Disguising his face and altering his voice would be a simple process. He went to his car and Echo followed.

"I will have her ready to see you then. In the meantime, I will consult with the others on our progress. They no doubt will not be pleased."

Again, Victor failed to probe Echo on what he meant. He just wanted to see his little girl.

"Hey, don't leave me here," Cameron shouted through bursts of spit, most of which dribbled down his chin.

Victor looked at his grotesque appearance. *Just like my little girl. Now you know how it feels,* he thought. Victor felt only a sense of duty. The anger was almost gone, and just in time.

"If you survive the next six months, I will come find you and finish what I started." He dialed 911 on his cell and waited for the operator to answer.

"Florence 911, what is your emergency?"

"A man has been severely injured north of the Florence municipal airport at the old, abandoned gravel field. Send help!"

Victor hung up, then they drove off leaving Cameron spewing expletives. He parked the car and then they both went to his private jet sitting on the tarmac.

"You can leave, now. I will think of you when the time comes. That should give me time to get the proper explosives."

The sheath nodded, and this time Victor watched and felt as Echo made his departure. The sensation of tiny electrodes tickled his body and then the blue light came then faded. Echo was gone, but not the smile on Victor's face. *This was a wonderful day,* he thought. With the best yet to come.

CHAPTER 16

Saturday, October 25th
7:25am local time

Joel was making some entries on his iPad and on occasion would peek at the television, which was so large, he barely had to bring his head up to see it. Seventy inches of 4K glory that was delivered and installed yesterday afternoon. The hamsters in his brain were running wild on food pellets trying to keep up with his scheme as he continuously made changes, hoping for that perfect script, just like the writers of Lost.

He typed in some final points to his overzealous plan then leaned back and massaged his scalp, which was covered with new sprouts. It was time to get back to how he looked before the tragedy. He ran his fingers across his smoothly shaved face then signed back into his bank account using the password 5-3-5-5-9. An easy one to guess, should anyone know his pain.

However, should one know his password, they would see a nice chunk of change in his account, just shy of 5 million dollars. Sure, this was eliminating his poverty, but far from a sane way to eliminate it globally. Sending most of it back home to deserving charities was a small start and was already in the works. Joel wasn't sure how much detail about his plan he would divulge once he was reunited with Kelly, as he did not know how much time he would get to spend with her. Perhaps it was enough to tell her that her dream was still alive.

He decided to spend the largest chunk of their time together telling Kelly, "I'm sorry."

That made him sad, so to lift his spirits he scrolled down to his sports betting app. Joel's last two wagers were especially fruitful. He cleaned up on the Thursday NFL game netting him a cool one point one million. However, that site froze him out after an equally lucrative half million dollar win on a three-goal shutout by the Calgary Flames over a heavily favored Maple Leaf team.

It was his guess that winning on such longshots repeatedly had triggered an algorithm back to the company's betting site, thus denying him any more wagers. Joel tried to mix it up among other dotcom websites, but it seems like they were sharing information about winners like himself. Therefore, he did his best to find stories that would make his wagers appear to be luck rather than potential tampering, influencing, or even bribery.

One such story appeared on Friday morning's telecast which he watched Thursday morning. It was a short narrative that appeared on the scroll at the bottom of the screen about how five of the starting six women of the heavily favored Cel5 Voley La Roya volleyball team in the Argentine league came down with bacillary dysentery. They were subsequently upset by the Bora Juniors. That wager brought in a cool two point five million. The only way he could be found to have tampered with that result was if he had poisoned them himself.

Then there was the thirty second spot that was especially distressing. It was the death of a Belgian cyclist during a road race of the 111th Scheldeprijs. Joel had only ninety minutes to try to get a hold of Augusta Ackermann of Austria to tell him not to race, or at least fall back of the pack on the dangerous curve at kilometer fifteen point two. He spent over an hour trying to contact the manager of the racing team, and eventually managed a connection. No one answered, so he left one of the most preposterous voice mails ever sent. Preposterous to the Belgian cyclist, but who knows, maybe a part of him would take heed.

Of course, curiosity got the better of Joel and he would check on the tour's website to see the outcome. If all those science fiction movies had it right, could saving his life influence the future? What if his warning had saved the life of Augusta and two years later, he went on a shooting rampage? As much as it pained him, Joel decided not to watch any more of those types of stories for that reason and to keep his mind on his main purpose.

Knowing the results of a game before it happened was exhilarating, but now he wondered if just knowing the right lotto numbers to pick, while boring and uninteresting, might be a better way to go. He asked L.J., the name he gave to his new friend, about pivoting to the lotto plan, but was given some confusing explanation about how the frequency of my electrical brain pattern was already coordinated with his and blah blah blah and he would have to consult with the others and blah blah blah. Then some story about the dangers of helping Joel in this way and blah blah blah and some crazy shit about black holes and blah blah blah.

If it was going to be that difficult to change his plan, then why not ask for the ultimate solution? Why not change the world in the way he and Kelly have always imagined. Joel wasn't an economist by any means but why not try to solve global poverty in one fell swoop? So, he proposed that to L.J. and the answer was still to be determined.

The others? Did he mention others?

A little late but Joel just clued into that phrase used by L.J. He didn't like the sound of that. The others? Were there others like him or was L.J. alone and helping others like Joel? More worries to clutter his mind.

Joel was channel surfing through the various sports channels then decided to check out CNBC. Shortly after receiving his iPhone, he asked for a full cable installation ASAP. He was like a kid in a candy store, flipping through each and every channel and checking on the date of broadcast on the guide. Alas, the only channel that was a day ahead was the one the sheath gave him. And by the sounds of it, that was soon to be taken away.

On CNBC, they were reporting on the Dow Jones Futures for when the markets would open in a few minutes. Suddenly they quickly broke to another story that had nothing to do with finance, so it must be important. Joel decided to check out CNN and they were just breaking in on a major news story as well. A story that was so incredible, he leaned forward and turned up the volume to hear a woman reporter standing on the deck of a large ship.

"This is Anna Reunian on board the research vessel Marianas just east of the Maldives island chain in the Indian Ocean. One hour ago, the science team here on board, sent down an ROV after getting information that the missing plane from flight MH370 might have crashed in this location. And we got confirmation just ten minutes ago that they have indeed found the wreckage of flight MH370. It's lying at a depth of six thousand feet. The debris field is relatively small, and the plane is mostly intact, suggesting it impacted the ocean in one piece."

Joel flipped through more channels and just about every news station was covering this event to one extent or another. He returned to CNN to hear even more stunning news.

"We've just learned that the pilot of Malaysian Airlines flight 370, Captain Zaharie Ahmad Shah, has been found alive on a small atoll near the Island of Uligan and has been taken into custody."

Joel's mind went numb, and his mouth ajar.

"We hope to talk to Colonel Weiss, who is in charge of this Israeli led expedition and who sent in the special forces to apprehend the pilot."

"Un-fucking believable," he exclaimed.

This astonishing discovery would easily trump the other incredible story just the other night about a video that went viral. It was the escape of Cameron Mitchell and subsequent video of him being struck and paralyzed. It garnered over fifty million views. The commentary of this worldwide retribution varied from positive to barbaric.

Many were trying to obtain the identity of the poster, including the FBI, who used the viral video as part of their intensive hunt for who was responsible for the attack on Cameron Mitchell. How he got there and who was responsible has still stumped the authorities as their best witness, Cameron, was under heavy sedation after going through extensive surgery. And to add more salt to the Florence Department of Corrections wounds, three more high profile prisoners escaped right under their noses and the noses of one hundred federal agents and law enforcement personnel that had already swarmed the area. It was now all hands-on deck looking for those three dangerous bombers.

Joel pushed his jaw closed then rubbed it in wonder. Three former bombers? The impossible happenings in Florence and Colorado, the improbable events involving MH370, and his own incredible situation. Was there a connection? A connection involving the others?

All this speculation would have to be put aside. He had to prepare for Monday. L.J. said he would bring Kelly to him. Joel turned off the television and was bathed in quiet solitude. He held out his hand, which was quivering. He only hoped for composure when the time came. He only hoped Kelly would forgive him and not only understand but be proud with what he was about to do. Joel got up and felt the pains of hunger. Or was it nerves? He would have some breakfast and pray it was hunger. The nerves would come Monday when he would ask the stranger if Kelly could stay with him forever.

CHAPTER 17

Saturday, October 25
8:22pm local time

Naomi was leaning up against the metal railing of the research vessel Marianas. The second deck allowed her a great vantage point of the action on the lower deck, as well as an eye-catching view over the open water. The sun was low enough to brag about its fiery red glow, which was a part of a nice kaleidoscope of colors within eyeshot.

It contrasted nicely with the new deep blue highlights of Naomi's hair, light brown skin and the green paint of the ship, which was set apart from the large yellow submersible that had spent all day on the bottom of the ocean and was slowly being hoisted out of the water. The final color to round out the palette was the most important of all: an object dangling at the end of one of the ROV's grappling hooks. It was the dull orange of flight MH370's data recorder. It was heavily corroded but had still retained most of its rectangular shape.

Naomi was beside herself with a sense of incredulity. She could barely contain several other emotions, like astonishment, wonder and what else... satisfaction. This discovery of an event that was undiscoverable was the final proof that the stranger, to whom she had given the name Kia, could produce her sister on Monday as promised.

She raised her sunglasses and spied Colonel Weiss supervising the recovery. He was pointing to a man holding the remote. He expertly controlled the claw, which had a secure grip on the vital recorder. The colonel directed him to lower it into a large ice cooler which was filled with fresh water. With the closing of the cooler lid, he turned an equally studious glance toward Naomi, who reaffixed her sunglasses to protect herself from his perplexing stare.

It took a lot of pleading and begging just to get him out here and he reminded her, many times and right up to the discovery of the wreckage, about how much this was costing the Israeli government. So, he wasn't sure what she was hiding behind those dark glasses. And at her elevated position and even from afar, she could see in his eyes that an explanation was about to be demanded.

There was another oddity that caught her eye. It was a slight red aura that surrounded the colonel for maybe three seconds and a brief slightly out of focus image of the colonel as well. Naomi took off her sunglasses to see if they were scratched or dirty, but they were pristine. Was it just a reflection off something, or an illusion made up in her mind after a long and stressful day? Right now, it meant nothing, but she would soon learn the ghastly truth of what she saw.

The colonel left his team to wrap things up and was on the metal staircase heading in Naomi's direction. She knew there was no point in telling him the truth. More to the point, she didn't want to. In a way, she felt like Kia was a new toy she didn't want anyone else to play with.

"Naomi," Colonel Weiss said as he reached the top of the stairs. He joined her at the railing and they both stared out over the calm waters of the Indian Ocean. "I'm not going to ask you how you knew. Although, I will have to put something in my report, not to mention how I'm going to explain this to the press."

Naomi didn't respond, she just smiled and scratched a few itches on her arms and legs.

"What do you think I should tell them?"

"Tell them that the Israeli military just solved the greatest aviation mystery of all time through complex analysis, extensive satellite..."

"Never mind." He cleared his throat. "Are you sure you don't want to share in the credit?"

"I'm good."

"So, what do you have planned for an encore?"

"There's still a Lockheed Electra out there somewhere."

"I love it." Colonel Weiss chuckled. "I'll figure you out, Naomi. One day. I'll figure you out." He turned to leave but just before he went down the stairs, he made one last observation. "What we find on those recorders I think will stun the world. But I have the feeling you already know."

"Goodnight colonel," she simply said.

He disappeared down the stairs just as her phone vibrated. She looked at the alert. "*Interesting*," she muttered. In six hours, there would be another upload of a new video from that anonymous person who posted the crippling of Cameron Mitchell. It had exploded to over two-hundred and fifty million views.

"Live?" she muttered again.

She read on. An actual live streaming of an act of retribution. It was the top story filtering throughout the internet, at least until this one takes hold. The happenings in Florence, Colorado were confounding the authorities, and now the inexplicable disappearance of three of the United States's most notorious bombers?

Did those happenings, a half a world away, have any connection with Naomi's most recent inexplicable happenings? Kia did mention a meeting with the others. At the time, Naomi hadn't paid attention to the word 'others. Yet it must have registered in her subconscious, because she was aware of it now. Who were the others? Was there more than just Kia helping more than just her, or was Kia alone but helping others besides herself?

Naomi might ask, but not until she was with her sister again. She didn't want anything to interfere with her chance to tell her sister thank you for saving her life. Or risk the chance that Kia could make her stay, forever.

CHAPTER 18

Saturday, October 25
11:58pm local time

He chose this part of Texas because he was familiar with it. His company had a large footprint on the outskirts of Austin, and this abandoned piece of property was once considered as a possible expansion site. It was ten acres in size, thirty miles north-east of Austin. There were four buildings, long ago left to deteriorate, but perfect for what he had in mind. It was private and secluded, the perfect place for a live stream event. Walking toward one of the cement buildings was Victor, Echo, and Victor's three guests.

"Welcome, gentlemen, make yourself at home," Victor said graciously.

Tsarnaev looked at Kaczynski, who in turn looked at Nichols.

"I need a few minutes to prepare."

'How long are we going to be here?" the Oklahoma bomber asked.

"Not long."

"The whole world will be after us," Tsarnaev said. He was all too familiar with this after his bombing of the Boston marathon.

"No one knows you're here. No one knows I'm here. I've been very careful."

Indeed, Victor had been. Breaking them out of the prison was a simple enough task for the sheath and flying them here was also routine. He actually enjoyed the three bombers talking and rationalizing what they did. It gave him a lot of insight as to whether he was being too brutal with his acts of retribution. He decided... no.

Watching the three of them having coffee, sitting around a table in his jet, gave him pause for thought. He likened it to watching Gretzky, Howe, and Bobby Orr talking shop. That wasn't fair to those hockey gods, so he changed it to being like watching Mark McGwire, Barry Bonds and Sammy Sosa.

Kaczynski watched, as best he could with his failing vision, Victor and Echo carry some cameras and lighting equipment into the building. Fifteen minutes later, Victor called the threesome in. Mr. Nichols recognized the set-up and smiled.

"What's this? Are we planning on making a political statement?"

"I have lots to say," Dzhokhar Tsarnaev butted in. "The unfair treatment of prisoners, the..."

"Zip it!" Victor shot back. "We will be making a statement, but on my terms."

"I'm just glad to be out," Theodore Kaczynski offered. "But what's with the man in black?"

"He's my... protégé. My conduit, for lack of a better word."

"He's creepy. I don't trust a man who doesn't have an opinion. Those people are hiding something. That man in black, he's not what you think," Nichols observed.

He was right but he wouldn't live long enough to find out.

"He got us out, didn't he?" Tsarnaev added.

"Fellas, come on," the Unabomber said. "In the end, we all have the same philosophies. To spread chaos and fear in an attempt to be heard. We all had legitimate complaints."

"You mean to cause suffering and chaos," Victor added harshly.

"It's the only way to be heard," Kaczynski returned.

"So true. The government works for the people until they're elected, then they work for themselves. Until they come under attack, they exist in complacency and corruption. It's all about the power and keeping it."

"And we didn't need money to do it. Just a few bombs. This power and ridiculous wealth among the few while the rest of us starve will be the death of our civilization," the noted minimalist, Kaczynski, replied.

"We all agree that governments don't work for the people anymore," the marathon bomber added. "They kill innocent people with their wars and their corruption."

"Zip it!" Victor shot back.

While he was gaining some enjoyment from their banter, a few cells in his brain were beginning to agree with some of their points, and he didn't want those cells spreading and putting an end to his retribution.

"Just think of the manpower being used right now to find us. That's power," Nichols said softly.

Dzhokhar got a little woody between his legs just thinking about it, and it grew in size as they saw what was in a crate that Victor opened. The Unabomber was also excited, but he had lost the ability to get hard long ago. Too many bad experiences from the times he had to share a cell.

"Sweet!" Nichols said. "I wish I had this tech back then; I could have done so much more."

"What is it?" The Unabomber asked, his eyes not as proficient in this dim light as the other two murderers.

"Primer cord, and lots of it. He's got something big planned," Nichols noted.

"I'm in!" Tsarnaev replied.

"Have you figured it out yet, lads?" Victor asked.

He finished setting up the spotlight and turned it on. It lit up the interior of the empty building nicely.

"That's a high-speed camera with wi-fi capabilities," Kaczynski observed. "We're going to bomb something, record it, and then post it on the internet."

"Very good," Victor responded.

"Who and what are we blowing up?" Terry Nichols asked.

He rubbed his hands together in earnest.

Victor said quite matter-of-factly, "I am going to blow up three men and a building." He continued to unpack the primer cord and connect it as per the instructions. He then rolled three small cannisters over to the buildings three cement pillars and placed one beside each. "Have you figured it out yet?"

The three men all huddled by the doorway.

Victor wasn't concerned as the trio was deep in discussion. "I'm ready, Echo. If you will."

Echo strolled toward the trio and put one hand each on Tsarnaev's and Nichols's backs, sending out an electrical surge that scrambled the impulses to their extremities. They crumbled to the floor, slightly spasmodic but aware and alert. Victor was behind the camera and had the entire incident in frame. Tsarnaev was first and Echo carried him to the nearest pillar, propped him up, then wrapped the primer cord tightly around his entire body, like wrapping lights around a Christmas tree.

The fear on his face was no match for Mr. Nichols, who saw everything. Both their expressions would make for great characters in a scary movie. Next, he did the same to Nichols, who was wrapped with so much of the explosive cord that he appeared mummified.

"Gentlemen, how does it feel?" Victor asked.

"What the hell are you doing!" Nichols screamed as best he could. "You broke us out just to do this? I thought you were on our side."

"Why would I ever be on the side of killers, murderers? You were both sentenced to death anyway but wiggled out of it. Besides, the death penalty seems to be lacking as much of a deterrent. It's too... painless. There's no shock and awe. We need to be gruesome and grisly to have any influence. You will help with that."

"You can't do this. This is..."

"This is what? My little girl might be alive today if we had this retribution in place." He was only a few feet away from the tied-up men but remained calm as he spoke. He couldn't appear like a madman in front of the camera. "You and those that follow will suffer the same as those you have harmed. Your crime and your fates are linked. Your bodies will be shredded into pieces and shown in high definition to the world."

He looked back and saw that the Unabomber had already made his escape. He wasn't worried. Victor could moonwalk and still catch up to him. He was more aggravated that he would have to explain all this a second time.

"Go get him."

Echo made quick work of the elderly madman and had him tied to the third post in no time. Then Victor centered them into the frame and adjusted the focus. Three orange jumpsuits held in place by red primer cord up against the cold grey support columns. He tapped some commands into his iPad and now he was live. He walked into the frame and checked to make sure his face was blurred. He tested his voice to ensure it was disguised as well, then began.

"As I previously warned, all violent acts will not be tolerated. Punishment will mirror the crime. In case you do not recognize the three men here, we have the Unabomber, the Oklahoma bomber, and the Boston marathon bomber. They brutally maimed and killed innocent people."

"They were not innocent!" That could have been said by any of the three, but only heard by the three.

"These were murderous and callous acts," Victor continued. "This punishment will fit their crimes. This will be an example going forward of the fate of those who have violent desires and carry them out."

"This is torture!" Nichols blurted out.

The paralysis that subdued him had worn off and now he had the full ability to talk coherently and to feel pain. He struggled to free himself, or even knowing if he should. He was not versed in the effects of breaking or tearing primer cord.

"To respond, this may seem extreme, but we need to put an end to violence around the world and find a better way to solve our personal problems. I see this as a necessary deterrent. The world is on notice."

Victor moved a few feet to his left and paused for dramatic effect, then faced the camera again, his hands held together in front. His electronically disguised voice made for an even more sinister tone.

"It is time to begin. As you can see, there is a timer on your screen. I will begin the lesson in five minutes." Victor walked off camera and finished entering the commands on his iPad. "Time to leave, Echo." He put what he needed to keep in a backpack and left the other equipment to continue filming. When the authorities got there, there would only be tiny pieces of plastic, cement, and body parts left. Or just bone fragments once the two large barrels of fertilizer ignited.

They both exited, leaving the trio of bombers to feel the pain they had inflicted on their victims. He ignored their pleas, and one even continued to spew out the conspiracy theories that landed him tied to a cement pillar wrapped in explosives.

He glanced at his watch as they made their way to the car. In three minutes and forty seconds, they would be decapitated, eviscerated, and immolated all in 4K stunning imagery for. He pulled out his iPad to check. Over thirty million viewers with more views to come, once he did the edits in super slow motion.

Broadcasting in anonymity was tricky but doable. A few more taps on his phone and the signal was redirected among a dozen small satellites orbiting in low orbit. Totally untraceable. All of this made possible as the encryption software on his satellites designed by his company were unbreakable.

They reached the car and drove away slowly. As the timer closed in on zero, the viewership rose to 47 million. *Excellent,* he thought, and, in a few hours, he would be landing back at his home.

Twenty seconds to go.

He glanced over at Echo, who said he had to leave him until Monday. He said he needed to consult with the others, then prepare to fulfill his promise of bringing his Charlie to him. Victor was mustering up the courage to ask to have her stay with him, forever.

Ten seconds until detonation.

He wondered who the others were. Were there others besides himself that Echo was helping, or were there others like Echo helping people like Victor?

Three... two... one...

All his rear-view mirrors filled with brilliant red light. Center on his dash, the iPad also showed a flash of light, then ceased to broadcast. On the flight back, he would work on editing the video, frame by frame, which would make his stomach heave and cause him to question his method.

Just before the final scene, the head of the Oklahoma bomber would be seen, frame by frame, ripped and seared from his body and flying toward the camera. The skin of his face melted like a marshmallow put too close to the flame, and his eyes stuck open as if they were still working. Was he dead or were the electrical impulses hanging around enough for him to see his head in flight? It would be a scene that would repulse the world, but would it be effective?

Had he gone too far in his retribution, or was he justified? He only hoped Charlie would understand; that is, if he told her at all.

CHAPTER 19

Sunday, October 26
1:05 pm local time

"Do you see it? There it is again! I don't understand," Sebastien exclaimed. He pushed back his chair and did a nervous spin of two revolutions. "What do you think?"

His co-worker, Julia, was reacting to the same data, only internalizing, thus keeping her cool. She typed a few more commands and called up the image on the control center's large monitor.

A few years back, the European Space Agency launched a satellite to measure the earth's magnetic field. Today, there were three in orbit, and along with a series of ground dishes, they all monitored and collated their observations to these headquarters fifteen miles east of Copenhagen, Denmark. This was a standalone building, plain and drab on the outside but high tech on the inside.

"I don't know, but do you see how similar these readings are from the seventeenth and the nineteenth?" Sebastien saw Julia nod. "Except the electromagnetic pull is three times that of the seventeenth, and one and a half times that of the nineteenth."

"Curious. It's growing in strength. I've never seen anything like it before," Julia added excitedly as her internal emotions leaked out.

"Look at the magnetic lines of convergence. They're elongating towards a point above the Hawaiian Islands. Could be a massive volcanic eruption?"

"Nothing on our emergency channels," she responded. "An earthquake that exposes the molten core?"

"Again, nothing on the emergency channels."

"The cause can't be land based or atmospheric. It must be external," Sebastien surmised.

"Whatever the cause, it's strong enough to move the magnetic compass four degrees. I'm sending out a global alert to all agencies."

Then she grabbed her cell phone and dialed the number of the professor of Geophysics and Seismology at Stanford University. It took her three tries to input the right number, as her fingers were trembling like that after a small aftershock. The seriousness of the event was the driving cause.

"Professor, I am sending you all the data and the password to uplink with our satellites. Yes, the first event was a point two shift and the second a point eight shift and now a four-point shift. If this continues..." Julia was interrupted, and Sebastien could hear an excited professor talking from the other end.

"Yes, if the trend continues, we are looking at a global catastrophe." Julia pulled the phone away and began updating Sebastien. "He has an associate professor stationed in Maui. He's going to wake him up and have him look. He's directly under the convergence."

Sebastien pointed to the room's monitors, as he had some of the online postings up. "People have been posting videos of these strange black lights over Colorado, California, Israel and the largest over the skies of Arizona." Julia's eyes were fixated on the blackish dots of dancing lights in the skies. "Incredible, isn't it? To use black and lights in the same description?"

"It's mesmerizing. But are they lights?" She worked on digitally enhancing the phenomenon. "It's... yes, I'm still here. I can do that now. Hold on."

She put the phone down and asked Sebastien to connect everyone involved via Zoom conference. He slid his chair up to his station and in no time, he had the professor on one screen and his Maui associate, Filipe, on the other.

"Are you getting this?" Felipe asked as he pointed his camera skyward.

Most in this area of the world would be asleep as it was approaching two-thirty in the morning. However, who could sleep with the spectacular, odd, black, swirling auroras that were appearing?

"It's...I'm at a loss to explain how, but it's incredible. Even though the sky is dark..." He paused to adjust his binoculars. "I can see these black spots. They're dancing about like small oil slicks. I can't see through them, but they look like they're trying to come together to form a much larger dark spot. It's weird. I can't explain it!"

"Do you feel in any danger?" the Stanford Professor asked.

"I would sure feel better if they weren't there. Why would you ask?"

"Julia?"

"There is a four-degree shift in the earth's magnetic field. The pull is being generated in an orbital area above your location. My best guess is that if these small areas manage to converge into one, it could cause a major magnetic shift," Julia advised them.

"That sounds bad," Felipe said.

"If it grows large enough..." She stopped short of revealing that she believed that a catastrophic event was possible. It would just be an assumption and it would be irresponsible to cause such panic without more solid data.

"What were you going to say?" The Stanford professor asked.

Suddenly, one of the monitors flickered. "We just lost data transmission from the Jasmin satellite!" Julia exclaimed.

Then the video feed from Felipe went dark. His audio, however, was still working.

"I've just lost power."

"We could see more widespread outages as an effect from the shifting magnetic field," Julia warned. "Looks like we got the satellite back."

"We've got Felipe back," Sebastien said. "Should we notify the major governments?"

"I've been monitoring the local media," the professor interrupted. "They're already reporting on the black spots and the airlines are already on alert. I've contacted our ground radio antennae to focus on that area. We should have some descent data shortly."

Julia studied some more results from the most recent scans and was breathing easier. "The magnetic shift has stabilized. Hopefully, like the other two instances, it will return to normal."

"Do you have any guess as to the cause?" the professor asked.

"We have a conference scheduled in one hour with some leading geophysicists from around the world. At the moment, we haven't a clue," Julia said, the concern in her voice evident to everyone. "And to add an overused catch phrase, it's like nothing I've ever seen before." Even though it was overused, it still had a chilling effect.

Everyone disconnected from the call and both Sebastien and Julia sat dumbfounded. There was nothing they could do but sit back and watch the readings, both wondering if the worst was yet to come.

20 minutes earlier

"It's refreshing to be out of that body," Kia said.

"I agree. Taking solid form is always taxing," Echo responded.

"We were down there a long time," added L.J.

The three sheaths were gathered at a height of forty thousand miles above the surface at a zenith over the Hawaiian Islands. Their three energy spheres bobbed in space like invisible balls in an ocean. This planet's electromagnetic field was nicely recharging them as if they were plugged into a USB port and helping them to regain some of the energy they had expended on the earth's surface. It was impossible to see this relaxation but imagine running a marathon and then soaking in a hot tub. All that was missing were some sprinkles of lavender spa crystals.

"What name did your friend give you?" Echo asked. "He calls me L.J."

Echo sent the familiar energy signature of confusion that L.J. easily understood.

"Joel, that's my pairing, says L.J. is short for Little John. Apparently, this Little John is second in command to a character called Robin Hood, who has a penchant for stealing from the rich and giving it to the poor."

"Interesting," the other two sheaths relayed simultaneously.

"It's a goal of Joel and the one he wants me to bring back, however his original plan would only help him get out of this poverty. He wants me to change course. This requires me to sever our energy bond and create a new one. It might be necessary. What I have given him I should not have but we need these humans to succeed."

"Changing course may have grave consequences," Kia noted.

"We know that one of these three will use the gift we gave them to set in motion events that will stop their extinction."

"And any alteration to that path could upset those events."

"We need these humans to exist for a long time. We need this planet to survive. We have found the means to become free."

"Then you are suggesting that I do not let Joel change his initial plans?" L.J. asked.

"Do you think he will still help us?"

"I believe his change will impress his wife more when I bring her back and he talks to her. That, in turn, should allow her to open up to me when I talk to her."

"Use your best judgement," Kia's thought pattern reached L.J. "What is your friend asking of you?" Kia asked of Victor's symbiotic.

"He desired retribution for the death of his daughter. After that, he wants to punish all aggressions so severely as to deter violence, possibly eradicating it altogether. As always, our goal is to gain their trust. Victor trusts me which will help his daughter open up to him when she is reanimated. He will tell her that his goal of the global cessation of violence has begun, making her trust me when I speak to her," Echo elaborated.

"Total peace could hamper our chances of filling our quota," Kia relayed, and the others absorbed this.

"We will see. So, how is you experience with your connection?" Echo asked.

"She's an odd one, I must say. She strives to learn everything; therefore, she wants the answers to any question she asks me. In return, she will make sure her sister answers my questions truthfully when I bring her back."

"What have been some of the questions?"

"Her parents were kidnapped by a group of radicals, and she wanted to know where they were. Through that, I was able to realize that those radicals, and others with similar violent tendencies, could help to fulfill the quota we agreed to with the solids back home."

"Indeed," Echo said.

"Then she wanted me to solve a mystery, which I did. To me, it meant nothing, but to her and the world she lives in, it was a monumental find. It was priceless to her." There was more that Kia wanted to add, and the others sensed it.

"What is it?" L.J. asked.

"Just how the answers come to me when she asks a question is indescribable. It's like one instant I don't know, then suddenly I do. It's bewildering and intoxicating."

"Be careful, and don't let the bond become unbreakable. Don't get too attached to her. We won't be here long."

"I won't."

"Why did she give you the name Kia?" Echo asked, curious.

"Because from her perspective, I 'Know It All.'"

"Do you think it could be her choices that will be the difference in saving her planet?'

"I don't know who will be the one."

"Perhaps two of them will team up, or all three," Kia mused.

"The decision to interfere and bring them all together is always a difficult one. Even with all our experience, it's hard to know what the right thing to do is," L.J. said.

"Minimal interference has always been the preference; however, we do not need to worry about that yet," Echo added.

"Well, it will all be moot if they already have an afterlife. If they do, we will need to look elsewhere to fill our quota."

"Then let us prepare. Reanimation is always taxing on our bio-electric systems. And potentially dangerous."

With that, they each put up their own barriers, blocking out all outside distractions. How long they remained in a state of recharge could have a serious effect on the planet below. They knew of the black auroras they were responsible for. They also knew of the incredible rare opportunity this planet held that could end the solids hold over them forever, hence the unprecedented risks they were taking. They just had to succeed, which was why they were taking these chances like they never did before.

CHAPTER 20

Monday October 27
11:18am local time

Joel paced nervously, wearing out a dirt trail with his sandals. He had Billy drive him to a secluded mesa with a dazzling view of the Whetstone Mountain range.

The time the stranger promised was nearing. Joel was proud that, despite the momentous event, he was sober. Not even a drop of alcohol to soften the tension. In fact, he had not had a drop of alcohol in three days. He even shaved twice and had on a clean shirt and crisply ironed trousers. His cologne was Kelly's favorite and was hanging around nicely in the gentle breeze.

Looking in his bathroom mirror, an hour before leaving, he saw doubt and misbelief staring back at him.

"Hell!" he thought. "How can she come back? She's dead. I was at her bedside as the doctor pronounced her at 11:33am. I was at the funeral. I watched the casket lower into the ground. My daughters did. We all did!"

Then this skepticism evolved into sadness as that was also the last day he saw his two girls. To take his mind off that sad happening, he returned to the ludacrosity. Even while splashing on his cologne, he wondered if Kelly will even be able to smell this on him. Joel chuckled, because this was funny in an absurd way.

Fortunately, he rationalized, there was a lot of mystery to the man he had met ten days ago. His goofy red bicycle, which he now knew was a mere prop. His long locks and unhealthy pale skin. And the way he turned Joel into a successful gambler? That feat might just sway him to the fact that L.J. could do the miraculous.

Back at the mesa, Joel decided to sit down. He read a list of things he wrote down of what to say. Topping the list was simple, *I'm sorry.* Nothing else after that mattered, as he might only have a few seconds with her.

It was 11:21, which meant he had to pass the time for twelve minutes. Most of that time was spent with wild thoughts and theories about what she would look like. His best-case scenario would be the blue dress he last saw her in, with her long black hair combed to the side, giving him a full view of her sparkling blue eyes. Just like the ones he stared into during their last dance that ended such a beautiful evening.

Then came the dark side of his memories. He remembered the five alcoholic beverages he was secretly drinking while Kelly was mingling with the special donators. He had a rationale for his drinking that evening. One, that he could still function normally and two, these events put a lot of pressure for him to make them perfect for Kelly. Their cause to end global poverty was especially vital to his wife, so he wanted nothing to go wrong. And nothing did, until he decided he was okay to drive home.

Maybe she would appear as he last saw her. Her face bruised and broken, one eye swelled shut due to her side of the car striking the tree. Chest tubes and IV's and bandages and... he had to shove that aside for this special reunion. There was always hope that those images would leave him forever. Then again, a part of him wanted them to remain with him, forever. He could only pray that L.J. had the ability to feel mercy and would bring to him the former.

Joel glanced at his watch; six minutes to go. He wondered where he should look. His nice little secluded picnic type area was surrounded on three sides by a twenty-foot bluff. If he turned around, he would have a magnificent view of the Whetstone Mountains. Instead, he kept his focus forward. Would she be alone, or would she appear from the left with L.J.?

Joel chose this place because he wanted her to feel at home, just like they did back home in the face of the gorgeous Rocky Mountains. This day was perfect as well: a cloudless sky with nothing but a single vapor trail from a passing jet plus he noticed a few oddly shaped black spots high, very high in the sky which he shrugged off. A warm, soft breeze was just enough to stir the radiant heat as it began its daily ascent from the desert surface. Joel was curious if L.J. was responsible for this picture-perfect weather. He would not ask.

There were signs the time was at hand. His heart pounded, his sweat glistening on his forehead so much that he needed a handkerchief to stay presentable.

It was time. L.J. had promised yet how could he possibly fulfill...?

A shadow appeared from around the outcropping and Joel jumped out of his chair. It was L.J. But where? Then another much smaller shadow. It was happening. It was happening! And true to his word, there she was.

His Kelly.

Just twenty feet away.

One percent of his brain convinced him this was a hologram.

However, just like the song, it will be in her kiss.

Kelly looked scared and confused, like she didn't know how she could be here. L.J. let her catch up and then helped her to Joel, whose handkerchief fell from his hand and drifted away. He swallowed as best he could to lubricate his vocal cords, then managed his first words to her since her...

"Kelly? Is that really you?"

"Of course, it is. Joel, I'm scared. What's going on?" Her eyes shifted to L.J.

"It's okay, he's a friend."

"But how?" she blurted out.

She took a few timid steps closer. It was a question he couldn't answer. What he could do was to hold his arms open and allow Kelly to come to him. Their eyes locked and he could see his reflection in the crystal-clear water bathing her eyes. The fear and uncertainty were apparent, yet he would take that over anger.

Kelly was like a fawn born just moments ago. Weak-legged, taking her first steps in life, searching for comfort and safety. She recognized Joel without hesitation. He was the only certain reality. Her husband, lover, and best friend. They embraced and he could feel her body shaking and trembling, but she was real and solid. Kelly was quietly sobbing and that overwhelmed him, but he had to remain calm and focused.

L.J. was ecstatic to see the woman trust Joel. She would listen to her husband and in turn listen to him. It was Joel who ended the embrace as it was time to begin the difficult conversation.

"Honey, you don't know how great it is to see you again! Can you tell me the last thing you remember?"

L.J. inched closer. Her answers were the reason the three sheaths were here. Her answers were the beginning as to whether they stayed or went on their way in search of the next.

"I remember the benefit, driving home, the accident." She stopped as if part one of a movie was ending and the projectionist was changing reels. She was thinking hard about what came next.

"Then I was in the hospital. I recall... I recall the doctor telling me about my injuries and then I remember looking at all the equipment I was hooked up to then looking up at you, but how...?"

Kelly felt her body, tested her legs, and searched the area that was full of rocks and mountains and sky.

"This isn't where I should be. I was dying, I was in a hospital."

Joel could easily tell she was agitated. He held her hands as tenderly as he could. "Do you want to sit down?"

Kelly nodded and took a seat. Joel pulled him close to her. He could see her breathing ease and felt he could reveal more. Meanwhile, L.J had moved behind them and taken the role of kibitzer.

"I feel better. Joel, how am I here?"

"Where to begin? Everything you remember is true. The reason you're here..." Joel bowed his head, ashamed to look her in the eye. Then he thought, *how dare I not.* He lifted his chin. "is because of me. I should not have been driving. I am so sorry, Kelly. From the bottom of my heart, I am so sorry."

He was as heartbroken today as he was when he said it at her bedside. He was about to drop his head again, but Kelly placed both hands on his face and gently lifted it up.

"It's all my fault," Joel continued. "A day hasn't gone by where I wish I could do it all over again. I begged you to forgive me, but you were gone. A day hasn't gone by wondering..."

"If I forgave you?" Her eyes were caring and genuine, just like the first time they had met. Just like the first time they fell in love. "Of course, I did. I heard you. I forgave you without hesitation. I love you, Joel. Always."

"I... I didn't hear you." The main emotion washing over him was tempered relief. "I should never have doubted you. I shouldn't have had to hear it to know."

"I did forgive you. I can still hear myself saying it. I don't know how..."

"It's okay, honey. It's what I have longed to hear. I've wasted so much time." His growing smile was infectious as it spread rapidly to Kelly. However, there was still an alien elephant hanging nearby, and L.J. made himself known.

"Joel?" he asked, not as a boisterous elephant, but as a soft dove. "We need to know."

"Listen, honey, do you remember anything after you..."

"After I what, Joel?"

"After you closed your eyes in the hospital."

"I remember it became dark. The light in the room went out. It got quiet. Then I was standing next to that man."

"You don't recall anything after the darkness?"

Kelly shook her head, feeling like she had given the wrong answer.

"No experiences? No memories? No light? Not even a dream?"

Again, she shook her head. Her face showed sadness and confusion.

"What are you trying to say. Joel? Do I have amnesia? How am I walking? I don't remember my rehab or my recovery. Joel?"

"That's because you never woke up. Ever. You died in the hospital."

Kelly withdrew her hands and recoiled into a protective posture; her arms folded across her chest. "Why would you lie about such a thing! Why would you joke?"

Then she realized he wouldn't. He would never be that mean. She was deep in thought, going through all the information she had and coming to one conclusion. It must be true!

"Please, can I have your hands again?'

She did so. They were warm and real. Just like before. This was the real Kelly to him. No duplication. No hologram, but her flesh and blood. Now more than ever, he wanted her to stay with him forever. Unfortunately, the decision would not be his.

"Look into my eyes, Kelly."

She couldn't, not yet. Instead, she scanned her surroundings. There was the odd man who brought her here. Not only was he odd, but he was giving off an unusual vibe. It was mystical for lack of a better description. Which might sway her into believing what Joel was going to say.

"Please, Kelly. Look into my eyes."

She did so.

"You did pass away. Your injuries were… there was nothing the doctors could do. I am telling you the truth. Since then, my life…" he stopped himself. It wouldn't be fair to make her sad. "Let's just save that for later. My friend brought you back so we could have this moment together, and to find some answers."

"What answers? I mean, what you're saying is hard to believe. I still remember my life, all of it. From my point of view, there has been no passage of time from the accident to now."

"Then you do remember clearly the night of the benefit?"

"Of course, like I said. Even down to the exact amount we raised from the donations."

"Do you remember the date?"

"Yes, April third."

Joel bit his lower lip, then took out his cell phone. He handed it to her. She smiled as the screensaver was of her and her two daughters from high atop a trail they hiked last summer.

"Look at the date."

He saw her eyes shift to the top of the phone then her hand began to shake.

"Hey Siri?" Joel asked. "What is today's date?"

It is Monday, October 27th.

That was the final confirmation.

"Then it's true!" Kelly cried. "I don't understand how this is possible."

"My friend hasn't really told me how or why for that matter. Just believe that you're here. We are together. Again."

Kelly squeezed Joel's hand.

Joel turned to L.J. "How much time do we have?"

L.J. looked to the sky then said, "I can keep her, as she is, for a little longer. Please continue."

That wasn't as comforting as he had hoped and too vague for his comfort, yet he still decided to take a little time to organize his thoughts. He had all but eliminated the thought of asking L.J. to keep Kelly around forever. It would not be possible to explain to the hundreds of people who were at her funeral, to the doctors who pronounced her dead, and to the foundation, who set up a donation website in her honor. How could he explain her existence? She would have to live in seclusion. What about their daughters? It wouldn't work.

Yet, he had not eliminated the thought totally, which left a small chance he still might ask. He felt a little selfishness was warranted.

"Joel?" Kelly asked. "You have a lot of things on your mind. I know you all too well."

"I have a plan. I've been working on it since he made this all possible."

"About what?"

"About what?" Joel repeated.

Again, he was lost, this time in her voice, lost in her familiar tone and her usual facial expressions. Everything is as it was before.

"You said you had a plan?"

"Yes, I'm so excited. It will be the solution to a cause we've been fighting for since the day we met. An end to poverty around the globe."

"Really! That would be incredible. We were able to make a slight difference, but nothing on the scale you are saying."

"This man is going to help me and don't ask me how, but you're here so I know he can do it. In fact, there are things, miraculous things I've seen him do since we met, that I don't ask, I just believe. I hope you do that. Just believe."

Kelly nodded and looked hopeful.

"L.J., now don't scoff, is going to allow me to take all the wealth in the world and distribute it evenly among the world's poor. That's roughly nine-hundred trillion dollars and share it with the three and a half billion people living in poverty around the world." He knew from Kelly's pursed lips that she was a tad skeptical.

"If I ask him, he will do it." Then he leaned in and whispered, "And he hasn't asked for much in return."

"What does he want?"

"Just to ask you a question."

"Why is he doing this?"

"I...didn't ask."

"Shouldn't you?"

"I... didn't want to risk losing this opportunity to see you." One last time, he was about to say, but held it in. "This will be the pivotal point in human history. Think about the possibilities. Remember Anthony?"

Kelly nodded. Anthony was being honored at their last benefit. He was a farmhand who worked sixty hours a week, struggling to care for his family.

"After I'm done, Anthony and the CEOs of the world and the top athletes and the entertainers and the politicians, they will all be equal. Remember Rachel Brown, the line cook? She will have the same access to everything that Gates, Federer, Rinaldo, Lucas and Bezos have. They will all have the same net worth."

"You can make that all happen?"

Joel nodded and was brimming with confidence. He was also taking all the credit.

"Remember that village we visited outside Monrovia? The people struggle to grow crops, to get clean water and to provide health care? How hard everyone worked just to survive? All that misery? Soon they will share the world's wealth. Putin, Trump, the Sultan of Brunei. All equal access to medicine and education. The Royal family? All their wealth shared to all who need it. No more elitism, no more favoritism."

"And he can do it?!" Kelly asked and exclaimed at the same time.

"Once he finishes his talk with you, he, we will make it happen."

"This will be an historic event. However, you know there will be resistance. There will be push back."

"Of course, but we have the numbers. We are ninety-nine percent. We will simply change the perception of how we view the world and the privileged now will just have to get used to the notion that our contribution is just as important and essential as theirs. They will adapt. They will have to. But..."

Joel knew what Kelly was going to ask and some of the joy of the occasion wafted away.

"...will I be around to see it all?"

"I... I don't know." Was all he could muster.

"I might be able to answer that," L.J. interrupted. He put a hand on Joel's shoulder. "I'm sorry to interrupt but it's time."

He circled around to have a more intimate discussion with Kelly. "Kelly, can you describe for me, once more, what you experienced after your eyes closed in the hospital with Joel to now when you opened your eyes standing next to me?"

Both Joel and L.J. could see her straining to give an accurate response. "I don't recall anything. From then to now, it's like there has been no passage of time."

"Even though Joel has shown you that six months has gone by since you passed?"

"I can't explain it, I can only tell you the truth."

"I'm sorry, but I must be sure that you've experienced nothing that could be interpreted as dreams."

"Nothing."

"No sense of an existence, either physical or spiritual?"

Kelly shook her head. The disappointment was not only Kelly's, but Joel's as well.

"That's very disheartening to learn," Joel said. "That we simply cease to exist."

"I can change that," L.J. said matter-of-factly. However, to Joel and Kelly, that statement packed a wallop. "Please, each of you take my hand." Joel was more than eager to take L.J.'s open hand. Kelly was a tad more reticent. Joel gave her a calming wink and she followed suit.

"Joel?" Kelly asked.

"L.J.?" Joel also asked.

"You're safe," L.J. answered them both enthusiastically. "We're going for a ride."

"Where?" they asked in unison.

"To a new beginning," L.J. responded to Kelly. "And to a possible new hope for all of your humanity," he added at Joel. "Close your eyes, please. This part can be a bit vertiginous."

Neither of them knew what that meant, yet they had no qualms about doing as they were told. They clinched their eyes shut then felt the start of a tingling, beginning with the fingertips, then spreading as if all their blood vessels were low voltage wires. A sense of euphoria accompanied the electric charge, like being given a safe dose of blotter.

They could feel themselves gaining altitude, like riding in an express elevator at its fastest setting.

"Joel, what's happening?"

"Don't be afraid!" L.J. said without delay.

Joel heard Kelly's voice clearly, yet he shouldn't be able to. His senses conveyed to him a fast ascent yet there was no wind or temperature change. It was, in a word, exhilarating.

"Where are you?" Joel asked. It was a strange question with an even stranger response.

"I don't know, Joel."

"Just relax and enjoy the ride. We will arrive shortly."

"Arrive? Arrive where? Should we open our eyes?" Joel asked.

"You can, but you won't see anything. We are in the transition phase."

"From where to where?"

"From a physical dimension into one of thought and energy."

"Is he suggesting what I think?" Kelly said.

"You understand?"

"I… do."

"Your wife knows, Joel. And when it is your turn, you will also."

"My turn?" Joel asked.

"Relax, honey," Kelly conveyed softly. They had transitioned to the point where the spoken word was no longer available.

"Where are you, Kelly? I can't see you anymore, but I can hear you. I want to see her!"

"Please, Joel, you are safe. We will arrive very soon," L.J. said with his thoughts, which were sent only to Joel.

L.J. was an expert marksman when it came to aiming his thoughts at a specific target. He also knew from vast experience that this transition from a solid to electrical energy could be difficult. Some even described it as terrifying. But with help from mentors like L.J. and the others, this transition can also be transcending.

Kelly and Joel felt their ride slow, like reaching the apex of a roller coaster. The entire journey from the earth's surface to their parking spot in orbit took a mere twelve seconds. They both waited for the requisite drop, but it never came, then accepted that this ride had come to a complete stop.

"Kelly?"

"I'm here. I can hear you. I can feel you and see you, yet I can't see you. It's... incredible."

"L.J.?" Joel urgently asked.

"Kelly understands. She is free of her physical body. Her memories, her experiences, even the natural life she knew before her death, are now encased in a contained sphere of electrical energy. An existence where she can communicate with others like her and travel wherever her thoughts take her. You, Joel, because your life has not ended, are inside my sphere of influence. I must return you shortly. The risk is too great should you escape my influence. It would be... catastrophic."

"Do you understand now, Joel?" Kelly asked.

"I think so," Joel said, the vocals now being carried as electrical energy. He had yet to develop the skill to focus his thoughts so both Kelly and L.J. were effectively eavesdropping. "L.J.? This is why you're here?"

Joel was awash with the sudden realization as to the enormous potential being put forward by L.J., which helped cancel out the vertigo, as he had just learned how to see without physical eyes. Joel looked down on the planet earth without a platform to stand on. He floated like a helium balloon, gently bobbing as if the space around him was an ocean and the solar winds were the breeze.

He was overcome with joy and happiness for his wife and a relief for a guilt that was freed from his soul.

"This will be life after death?" Joel asked.

"It is for Kelly. As for all humans? Time will tell. There are still two others. If all goes as well as it has here? As I said, time will tell," L.J. said.

"How are you feeling, Kelly?" Joel asked.

"My feelings are indescribable. Really, just look below at how beautiful our planet is. And our thoughts! I can't just hear you, but I can also feel your emotions. It's utterly amazing."

"I'm so happy for you."

"This is just the beginning for her," L.J. said. "Once she hones her skills, once she has mastered the ability to control her thoughts and energies, the universe will be hers to discover. For all of eternity."

This was a wonderful time to let them explore and a last chance to be together. L.J. did not do this often but felt this was a special occasion. The sheaths needed this planet to survive, and they needed Joel and the other two to put complete trust in the sheaths and their cause.

"Would you like to check out the possibilities, Kelly?"

"Really? Of course," Kelly responded quickly.

L.J. liked the fact that she was adapting well.

"You will make a great ambassador. You will be a pioneer and a mentor to help those that follow. You will help them adapt to their new existence."

Joel was feeling pride and Kelly was attuned to it. "Can Joel come with me this one last time?" She pleaded and L.J. agreed, so she asked Joel. "Joel, will you come with me?"

"Lead the way," he thought just as fast.

"Where would you like to go. A quasar? A Nebula? How about a binary star?" L.J. asked.

"Joel knows where I want to go. The rings of Saturn."

"Then let your thoughts be your guide."

L.J. was surprised how little preparation Kelly needed. Within seconds, Kelly's energy sphere was a few hundred thousand miles from the planet Saturn, with Joel riding shotgun within L.J.'s own sphere.

"My God, Joel! This close, it's... spectacular."

They were both staring with stunning clarity at the incredible gas giant, so near it was as if they were standing a few feet away from the largest and clearest OLEG television.

Joel was in such awe he could hardly believe he was here as well, brought millions of miles in the blink of an eye. "Kelly, it's amazing. Thank you for bringing me here."

"My pleasure, honey." There was a small drop in her energy.

"Why the sadness, Kelly?" Joel realized.

L.J. knew why.

"I was hoping to immerse myself in the rings. I've done it so many times in my dreams it would be a shame not to take advantage."

"With practice your aim will improve, but you did well for your first time. In the future, every point in the universe will be yours to discover. Only, do not venture into my star system. That is one place you must never go."

"Understood," Kelly agreed. She was so enthralled by the possibilities that lay ahead that it never occurred to her to ask why. "But what about you, Joel? What will happen to us?"

Joel was not able to sense emotion and thought as easily as L.J could. It was not his time, however, a lifetime of interaction with his wife made it easy to understand her tone.

"When it's Joel's time, he will find you, if that is his wish," L.J. offered with kindness. "It will not be difficult."

"But you will be alone until then. Travelling alone."

"She will meet other spheres. As big as the universe is, and we have been at this a long time, the odds are in her favor for crossing the paths of the many. Especially in the most popular regions."

"I would feel better if you could stay with her in the beginning," Joel asked.

"I will spend some time initially with her. But don't worry, as I said, she will meet others, and they will help her if she needs."

"Do you feel better now?" Kelly thought playfully.

"I do."

"Then it's time to return you, Joel. I can't hold you in here with me much longer. I can't risk your energy escaping."

"Can I have one last chance to hold her?" Joel pleaded.

"It's not wise to return her to her physical body. She's adapting nicely. She's strong. Eternity is within her grasp."

"Please L.J.," Kelly interjected, her thoughts aimed only at L.J. "I will be fine. It's important to Joel."

There was a lengthy silence as if the quiet vacuum of space had leaked inside. Suddenly, Joel saw the glorious sight of Saturn grow smaller and an instant later he was standing in front of his wife, on the same spot, on the same mesa that they left from. Just like a drone returning to its home point before its battery ran down. This time, L.J. was content to be an observer in the background.

Joel's stomach was in knots, just like their first date. The two of them, standing in front of her apartment door, neither knowing what to say or what to do. That was their first date. Now, this would be their last. They held each other tightly.

"I am so sorry," Joel began, with a whisper into her ear, this time keeping himself together.

"I never, ever blamed you. It was an accident. I loved you before with all my heart and I love you now with all my heart. Just, please, somehow, say good-bye to the girls for me."

That did it: Joel began to cry, but the next words from Kelly lifted his tattered heart.

"When the girls came to see me in the hospital, they told me about how they felt, about you, about the accident. They were hurt and they said it would take time but if you go to them, talk to them, they will forgive you. I know they will."

"I've been a fool for too long. I've been wrong too many times. I will talk to them. It's long overdue. And I promise to find you, out there somewhere, when the time comes, and I will tell you all about them and their lives. L.J, will she be able to visit earth and see the progress for herself?"

"It's not easy for a species to re-enter from where they once existed, because of the contradiction, but many do succeed. With practice and discipline, it will be possible for her."

"Wonderful, but just make sure Joel, that you don't look for me for another fifty or a hundred years."

"A hundred?"

"A hundred."

They both chuckled and Joel added, "You will be proud of our cause, and you can go knowing we have changed the world. If you can return from time to time, you will see the changes. We did it, Kelly!"

"We sure did."

Joel felt the warm lips of her kiss, then suddenly felt his arms start to loosen their grip. He knew it was time for her to leave. They held on as tightly as they could, but her physical body was slowly losing its substance.

"I love you, Kelly."

"I love you too. Be happy, always."

These were Kelly's last words as she vanished from his hold. He looked around and saw L.J. nod. Joel wiped away a few tears as L.J. approached.

"I will be gone for a few days. I will stay with her and ensure a smooth transition."

"Thank you, for everything."

"This is just the beginning, for both of you. and for all of us. I will be in touch."

Then he was gone too, and Joel stared skyward. He took in a huge breath, then let it out in force, feeling invigorated. He had a lot to prepare for as he was about to change the world. However, first he had to muster the courage to make some phone calls. He had two relationships to heal.

CHAPTER 21

Monday, October 27
8:32pm local time

"Whatcha got?" Sebastien asked.

"Another shift in the earth's magnetic field," Julia answered with a hint of concern.

"And?" Sebastien guessed she had more to add.

"There was an earthquake, four-point eight, just south of San Diego California."

"Home of the Padres."

"What?"

"I like American baseball." Sebastien could tell she was slightly annoyed. "Never mind, Julia. Please continue."

"The minor shift occurred over Whetstone, Arizona and the first shift occurred over the Hawaiian Islands, and the quake just so happens to be in line with the two."

"Correlation of causation?"

"What do you think?" Julia responded, then rolled up her sleeves and engaged the large monitor. "Take a look at that!"

Sebastien steered his chair over to her station.

"These have been popping up online," Julia said.

They were both in awe at the videos showing these black auroras dancing high in the Arizona sky, and in daylight! They were dark and opaque, in sharp contrast to the blue sky, which is what made them stand out.

"Now look at this!" Julia used a split screen to add a new image. "The International Space Station was in the area and was able to capture this."

Sebastien's jaw fell open as he noticed blackish lightning flashes from space that could easily be discharges from those spots. They lasted for a short duration, stopped, then reappeared a brief time later.

"Then wait," Julie advised. Before orbiting out of range, the station captured one final array of those blackish special discharges. "That last jolt, as well as the ones before, are where the convergence of that new magnetic pull is. As if they were drawn to that electrical discharge."

"And now?"

"Back to normal, just like the previous one over the Hawaiian Islands. It's just playing havoc with air travel and anything depending on a magnetic compass."

"I don't like the trends I'm seeing," Sebastien said, nodding to Julie's laptop. "The constant stretching and relaxing of the magnetic field. This is a new phenomenon. It appears to be like pulling and twisting on toffee. Eventually the field could break or snap."

"Let's hope these are rare anomalies."

"I don't want to be unprepared in case they aren't. Get that professor from Stanford on the horn again and send him all our data," Julia ordered. "He'll know what to make of all this."

Julia got up and went to the window. She couldn't see past her own reflection, which showed the grave concern on her face. They had to find the cause, but how? It's nothing like they ever dealt with before!

CHAPTER 22

Tuesday, October 28
7:08am local time

It was a glorious morning in many aspects. Over Victor's left shoulder was a stunning sunrise, and over his right was a spectacular view of Mount Safa, the holiest of places for the Muslim faith. He chose this place to honor his wife, who is Muslim.

The air was crisp, despite the desert setting, and calm and quiet, which bode well for what Echo promised, and that was his Charlie. Victor didn't know how he would bring her, and he didn't care to know. He just wanted to see her again.

Victor had flown into the Makkah Airport about eight hours ago and drove here to the spot he picked out from memory. It was an adequate spot with rolling hills and a large flat area of ground and considering the sparsely populated areas to the north or west, this was a smart choice.

Victor's business travels often brought him to this area of the Middle East, so familiarity bred comfort. This was also where he had met his wife of twenty-seven years. Their only daughter, Charlie, was born close to here, and even though Victor was a catholic atheist, she was raised Muslim. This leant to many an interesting debate, but were debates only, as respect for one another's beliefs always won out.

It was their strong religious belief that gave him hope. Hope that when Echo brought her back, she would regale him with fascinating adventures of her existence after her death. Charlie and Victor's wife were true believers of various interpretations of eternal existence, of heaven and delight and beautiful gardens devoid of suffering. He was certain that Charlie would bring him proof of heaven. Then, that would lead to the existence of a hell, a perfect place for the one who did this to his little girl.

Yet, what was that one question Echo wanted to know? Victor had a sense it was to question just such an existence. Why else would he bring her back?

Victor adjusted the two chairs to better face each other, tucked in his shirt and...

"My God!" he gasped as Echo came into view, holding the hand of Charlie.

She looked perfect for lack of a better word, just like the day before her accident. Unfettered by her paralysis. No wheelchair. Healthy, but not happy. Her expression was a mixture of confusion and fear. He needed to step in fast and explain to her as best he could. This could take some time and time was one thing he wasn't sure he had a lot of.

"Dad?"

That did it. He could barely hold it in, and hearing her voice brought down a few tears as he ran to her and grabbed hold of each hand. No hug yet; he wanted his little girl to accept who he was first.

"Yes, Charlie. It's me. Your dad."

"I...where am I?"

He now felt comfortable enough to give her a hug and she welcomed him into her arms. This went a long way to settling them both down. Victor brushed back her long black hair and gave her a kiss on the cheek. She still had that youthful light brown skin, flawless now, innocent brown eyes, and that summer dress. The same one she wore on her last birthday.

"Thank you," Victor said to Echo. "For bringing her back. Just like I asked. And Charlie, I have a lot of explaining to do."

Echo left them to get re-acquainted but kept within earshot. For the next twenty minutes, he observed a plethora of emotions while Victor did his best to explain something that was impossible. Then a confirmation of the date did the trick as she had so much trust in her dad that his truth won her over.

Echo knew from experience when to step in. He gently tapped Victor on the shoulder.

"May I?" he asked.

"Of course," Victor agreed.

"Charlie, I need you to answer your father's questions and mine as best you can. It's important."

She nodded. Victor smiled.

"Charlie," Echo began, softly. "Can you describe to me what you remember right before you woke up beside me?"

Please, Charlie, please tell us of beautiful gardens and heavenly surroundings. Please tell us of meeting God and all the joy that followed your death. Talk about a physical existence free of pain and filled with wonderment. Victor desperately hoped she would talk about such things. Echo wanted the opposite.

Charlie took a deep breath as she searched her mind for the answer. "I… remember the candles, and the flames and people singing. It was my birthday. I also remember clearly that uncomfortable... prison I was in," she added, referring to her wheelchair. "The constant pain. At times wishing I would die. Then I recall becoming dizzy, and then the ride to the hospital."

Victor wanted to go to her, but Echo put out a hand. Victor wanted to ease the struggle she was obviously dealing with as the truth came out, but Echo didn't want Victor to distract her or to influence her recollection.

"Again, I was back in the hospital. Angry, confused. Helpless. You were there, dad, and mom also. You were both crying, and then my eyes closed."

"And then?" Echo asked.

"Then being here with you and my dad."

"Are you sure, honey?" Victor prodded. This couldn't be. The religious ramifications would be historical. Charlie was a devout Muslim. Prayed, studied, believed. How could she experience nothing but darkness and non-existence?

"I'm very sure. It's as if no time has passed. From back then, to here now… no time has passed. I wish it weren't true, dad."

Again, more pain on his little girl's face.

"How could everything I learned about my afterlife be wrong?"

"Echo?" Victor asked. "Could her experience be unique? Or could it be the fate of all Muslims after they die?"

"From my vast experience, she is recalling an experience not just for that one belief but is a likely scenario for all your species. She has at least confirmed, to me, that she had experienced nothing after her passing."

That statement sent him into the state of denial. Victor searched his daughter's eyes and found a growing acceptance rather than a strong denial.

"That would be a devastating revelation. It would mean the loss of hope for millions. Are you positive?" His question was meant for Echo.

"The other two will verify what your daughter has said. But I can correctly say she is speaking the truth. Yet, it's not the loss of hope but could be the beginning of something all encompassing."

Victor expected to see sadness or negativity on Echo's face, yet he saw positivity. Why would this alien be okay with us having no existence after death? Based on the brief time he has spent with this unusual man; he came to one startling conclusion.

"You're here to offer us all hope, not just my daughter. You're here to give us an existence after death that we all hope for!"

"There is nothing I would want more, dad, but can he do that? It seems impossible," Charlie added with skepticism.

"There is nothing wrong with dreaming of an afterlife, but we are here to reward those that deserve, an incredible journey. Let me show you," Echo responded. "Each of you take my hand."

"I'm... not sure." Charlie hesitated.

"It's crazy, but I trust him. I just trust him."

Charlie saw the familiar face of a father she never had doubts about. If he said to trust him, she had no reason not to as well, and they did as Echo asked and joined hands.

In the blink of an eye, two spheres of excited energy were whisked away and in orbit above earth, about to embark on a spectacular journey of Charlie's choosing. Charlie in her new home, Echo and Victor inside their own duplex. Echo spent some time explaining and Charlie spent a lot of time controlling her emotions and trying to make sense of the unbelievable potential that Echo was granting her. Victor was okay with letting Echo be the teacher, and now it was time for Charlie to take the training wheels off her bicycle.

"Where do you want to go?" Echo asked.

"I think I know where she wants to go," Victor thought.

Charlie had always had a fascination with meteor showers and comets.

Any chance she got with her dad, even at four in the morning, the two of them would drive out to the country, binoculars in hand, and watch the sky show. Which meant there was only one choice, and she picked the standout of all comets: Halley's comet.

Charlie meandered her sphere in search of the famous comet. Concentrating her desire was hard at first, but she was driven as always to impress her dad and she found her target in a relatively short period of time. Forty-five seconds was all it took to reach the comet. In time, she would learn how to expertly steer that bicycle in a straight line.

Once there, they hovered a few hundred feet away. Charlie was having some difficulty at first keeping her sphere's speed to match the seventy-five thousand miles per hour of this hurtling wonder, falling back, then catching up. Falling back, then catching up. Victor genuinely enjoyed watching his daughter learn this new craft. He felt confident she would master it in no time at all.

It was hard not to be inspired by this icy rock. The tail was but a whimper, being so far from a heat source, but that made the surface that much more vivid. She dropped to within thirty feet and had the best 3-D view ever of sharp rocky terrain near the rear of the comet and smoother crevices near the leading edge. It was crystal clear as if studying a rock during a hike on earth. No birds to distract her, no winds, mosquitos, or weather to disturb her experience. It was as if she were wearing a pair of noise cancelling headphones.

She pulled her sphere away slowly and panned around. As a bonus, she was able to glimpse Neptune as a faraway backdrop. Not bad for her first attempt. Charlie vowed that once she became more practiced, she would venture farther. The Galaxies were also a favorite of hers, so without a doubt, the Andromeda Galaxy up close was a priority. At two-and-a-half million light years distance, it was easily within reach.

Echo would need to spend some more quality time tutoring her before any of these jumps could proceed. There was a noticeable reason for this. Whereas Joel's wife took to it right from the get-go, Charlie wasn't as taken to it. One reason was that this afterlife was not as her religion taught her, and she was struggling to accept it. However, this first amazing trip went a long way toward that acceptance.

They returned to the base of Mount Safi, the last time for Charlie. Echo made sure to reassure Victor that Charlie would flourish, and that comforted him greatly. It was an all-around great morning. Victor took Charlie by the shoulder and the two went for a last slow stroll.

"Where are you off to next?" Victor asked.

Charlie smiled and bowed her head. "Anywhere I want. I'm still trying to wrap my head around all of this, but I am believing in it, so, I'm going to go anywhere I want."

"Echo will help you. He will help us all." He lifted her chin and nodded. "You haven't answered my question."

"Well, one place I won't go is Echo's home. He was quite adamant that I stay away. Other than that, I think I might go check on my friend Andromeda."

"Baby steps first?"

"Fine, dad, baby steps first." They laughed together. "He did say I would meet others during my travels that could recommend other places to go. I don't quite know how, but he said he would show me."

"Incredible, all of this, isn't it?"

Charlie nodded. "So, what's next for you?"

Victor wasn't sure if he would divulge all that he had done. The retribution, the vengeance. The violent retribution. He decided to tell her of his next act as if it was his first and see her reaction.

"Remember the friends you met in Syria when you were seven and we were there for my work? And then later learning they were killed in that government-led gas attack?"

"Of course, dad. I cried for months. It still hurts."

"Well, I plan, with Echo's help, to have a private chat with the Syrian leader. Send a little message to the world that his actions are unacceptable." He wasn't about to go into all the gory details. "I want to put an end to all the suffering at the hands of such bad men," he said simply.

"The would be a wonderful thing, and based on what I've seen, I believe you. Just be safe when you do it. I don't want to see you for an exceptionally long time. If you know what I mean."

"I do."

Victor could feel her shoulder start to soften, and her entire body appeared to be fading. It was time to say good-bye. He pulled her in, and they embraced with the love that only a father and daughter could feel.

"I love you, Charlie. Be happy, always." He gave her a kiss on the forehead as she dissolved into nothingness, only seeing her lips move but not hearing her final words to him. Yet, he knew what they were.

"I will be back in a few days." Echo said, startling Victor.

"Of course. I have some preparations to make anyway. Take care of my Charlie."

Echo vanished as sadness overcame him, but that was soon replaced with resolve. He had a challenging task ahead, but not impossible given the tools at his disposal. He knew where he could get Sarin gas and Chlorine gas, but Mustard gas was proving elusive. He already had a spot picked out for his live feed. The chamber he was going to put the Syrian leader in was there, so all that was left was for Echo to pick up the maniacal killer.

Victor was understandably nervous, so much so that he had to rely on his meditation to calm him down and keep his heart rate in check. There were lots of uncertainties ahead. How the world will react could be unpredictable. There was also the uncertainty of guilt. He had no qualms about gassing the Syrian leader in front of a live audience. His guilt was proven and the evidence solid. But what of the others? The Russian leader could be next on his list, followed by the North Korean leader. Yet the evidence of their atrocities was not as easy to find. If only he knew someone who had all the answers. They would make a formidable team.

He began the long trek to his car, all the while checking his phone for news updates. One he noticed really caught his eye. CNN was reporting the finding of wreckage belonging to Amelia Earhart. *That's odd,* Victor thought.

No, not odd, but suspicious. MH 370 and now Earhart? Victor's friend Echo? The others he mentioned. These were not coincidences. No doubt he was not the only one with a new friend. He needed to find the others.

But how?

He had the resources. He would find a way.

Victor reached his car but before getting in, he looked up and saw the remnants of black auroras in the sky fade away.

"Good-bye, Charlie. Take care."

CHAPTER 23

Tuesday, October 28
3:30pm local time

Naomi sat on her front porch in an old rickety wooden chair. She wished it were rocking in nature, as it could help with her nerves. This was a bittersweet moment, as seventeen weeks ago, at this time, she had seen her sister Nichala for the last time. Such a contrast from the horror back then to the relative peacefulness that she was enjoying today. Of course, any sharp, distinct sound would ignite any PTSD symptoms she still had from that event. Thankfully, these moments were becoming manageable.

Despite the calm, she drummed her fingers on the ragged wooden chair, which turned to a tight grip as two figures appeared.

"I don't believe it!" she whispered.

Naomi scanned the dusty street and saw no-one else. The pair was walking slowly, drawing closer.

"It has to be her!" she exclaimed with more effort, yet inside said, *how could it be her?*

She was wearing the same clothes as the last time Naomi looked up at her, when the trap door had closed. White sundress, casual sandals and her long black hair tied in the back. Nothing at all like she appeared at the morgue when she had to identify her sister's body. Again, she cursed herself for bringing that image into her mind.

The two figures blurred until Naomi wiped the tears away, and they returned to their crystal-clear form. Naomi stood and let Kia bring Nichala to her. She looked scared and confused, yet uninjured and unhurt. She looked perfect.

Nichala was a devout Jew who believed in all that her religion taught her when it came to life after death. Naomi was more skeptical. If Nichala had returned with incredible tales and experiences, Naomi would owe her a huge apology.

"Naomi? Is that you?" Nichala asked.

"Yes. It's me. You look... amazing!"

"I don't understand. What's happening?" She looked around. "Things have changed. Where is..."

She couldn't finish her thoughts as the confusion overwhelmed her. Kia stepped back to help her feel at ease but stayed close enough to overhear. Naomi took Nichala's hands and locked her eyes on her sister's face, then brought her in for a tight, comforting hug. She knew exactly what she wanted to say and got right to it.

"Nichala, I want to thank you so much. You can't believe how being able to talk to you and to say thank you just fills me with joy and relief. Thank you for saving my life." Naomi felt some of the tension leave Nichala's body.

"I would have done anything to save you. I'm so glad and relieved to find out you survived." She then pushed Naomi away, slightly, and most of the tension returned. Nichala gave her own body an inspection and added, "And I survived as well? But something doesn't make sense."

"How so?" Kia asked. *How so? What a stupid question,* she thought.

Nichala eyed the stranger suspiciously but answered the question anyway. "It's too quiet. No gunfire. No bombs. No trouble. The last thing I remember was putting you in the hole, then some men came in and they..." Fear grew in her expression.

"It's okay, Nichala. Why don't we sit?" Nichala nodded and Naomi slid the better of the two wooden chairs close to hers and they sat down facing each other.

"What I remember vividly was being attacked. I was beaten, Naomi, it hurt so much. Over and over. Then I felt my arm being broken, my dress..." She didn't realize she was clutching her sisters' hand so tightly that it was turning white."

"Nichala! I'm so sorry."

She had to keep it together for what was to come.

"Then?" Kia asked softly.

Nichala patted the back of her head. Felt around for some remnant of a scar or traumatic injury.

"I heard a gunshot, so close to me, then an incredible pain in the back of my head and a split second later, there was darkness. All I had enough time to say to myself when I faced where you were was *goodbye*." She paused for an instant as her brain was attempting to explain to herself how this could be possible. She didn't have the answer, so continued hoping someone else did. "Then I was standing next to her. I must have dreamed it all. What happened?"

"I need you to look into my eyes, Nichala."

She did.

"Do you trust me?"

"Of course. What I don't trust is myself. Do you know why I experienced all that horror, but I have no evidence that any of it happened? I don't feel any physical pain, yet it's still clear in my mind."

"What I am about to explain, you will find hard, no make that impossible to believe. First, this is Kia. She is a... friend of sorts. She wants to ask you a question before we continue."

"Thank you, Naomi." Kia acknowledged Naomi with a nod. "Nichala, do you remember your entire life up until the pain in the back of your head and the darkness that followed?"

Nichala nodded.

"Then you remember only standing next to me?"

"Yes."

"No dreams or experiences after the pain and darkness?"

"None," she replied after a brief moment of thought.

Naomi stepped in, as she was uncomfortable with the anguish on her sister's face. If her sister's recollection was accurate, how would she react? It was time to find out.

"Nichala, you were not dreaming. It all happened. Putting me in the hole. The attack. All of it. I know it sounds impossible, but I want you to trust me. I hope you will believe my story. Here, look at my phone." Nichala took it with a shaking hand. "Do you remember the date they attacked our village?"

"Of course. It's all as clear as you are in front of me."

"Now look at today's date."

Nichala glanced at the screen but didn't really look at it. She was afraid. She looked up and Naomi nodded. Nichala then studied the date and her face turned ashen.

"It was not a dream. I know you came from then to now in the blink of an eye, but four months have passed. You died in that attack four months ago, and four months ago you saved my life!"

"How is that possible? This is hard to accept," Nichala eventually said. "But you have never lied to me before, so I must believe you. You would never do anything to hurt me."

"It's all true."

"But..."

"But how is this possible? I would like to introduce you to my friend Kia. She brought you back. She made it all happen."

Nichala turned and made more of a concerted effort to study this unusual stranger. She looked like a human, a little pale, but nothing mystical. She had a smile that showed genuine care, yet her eyes hid a secret. Then she looked at Naomi and there was this unspoken sisterly bond where spoken words were at times unnecessary. They could share the same feeling without it being known to others. Naomi was sharing honesty.

"I do believe you, Naomi. The more I see with my eyes and the evidence around convinces me that months have passed. But you know what really made me a believer?"

"What would that be?" Naomi asked as a softening appeared on Naomi's face; it was good to see.

"Your dress is different from the one I left you with just a moment ago, but the odd clincher is, since when did you have blue hair? A moment ago, it was a different color!"

"You were always a detective at heart."

"Then why didn't I experience something after I died? All my studies, my beliefs, everything I prayed about every day, it's all..." She paused to find the correct word. "...it's all wrong. I pray it is only me, because people need hope that there is more."

If it was indeed true that humanity held no afterlife, it would throw religious studies into chaos. It could cause mass depression and much worse. She needed Kia to have an ace up her sleeve.

Kia stepped in as if on cue. "It's not just you. We have abilities to sense energies that form after death. Some civilizations already do have an afterlife. Each is different, unique and wonderful. Our initial assessment was that there is none here, but we need corroboration. We needed proof. I brought you back to determine if you have continuation after you die. It is essential that we get that proof, and this is the only way we know how. It's complicated and can be taxing on our own energies, but very, very essential."

"Then you are here to..." Nichala put a hand up to her mouth and gasped. Naomi was equally shocked, as she was never sure of Kia's motives until now.

"To give humanity the gift of an afterlife, if there is none."

Naomi's skin burst out in a field of goosebumps that were no match for the humid air.

"Let's go for a journey, and I'll show you what eternal existence will be like." She turned toward Naomi. "You can join us and be a witness. Take one my hands, each of you."

Nichala searched Naomi's face for assurance, and it was there. With all their hands connected, they all dissolved into nothingness, and seconds later Nichala was high above the cloudless country of Israel in her own bio-electric protective sphere, and as for the other mortals on planet earth, more of the black auroras appeared in their wake, to be viewed and shared.

Nichala's life's experiences and awareness's remained intact. Meanwhile, Naomi believed she was witnessing the breaking of every law of physics. Then again, she wasn't a physicist, so acceptance came easier. Nichala used her bubble as an aperture, letting light in and creating vision, while keeping all that could harm her out.

"Are you ready to go?" Kia sent the thought to Naomi.

She was more than ready. There was a twenty-minute tutorial during which Nichala practiced controlling her emotions and focusing on her desires, then she was ready to go.

"Let your cravings be your guide," Kia added.

"You will stay close?" Nichala asked. She got the comforting acknowledgment.

Meanwhile, Naomi was just as green and in just as much wonderment as her sister. She had no choice but to relinquish control and become a passenger on the greatest ride ever designed.

"All right, here goes." Nichala visualized her destination in her mind and, once again throwing physical properties in limbo, her energy sphere was gone and in the blink of an eye appeared again, four-hundred and fifty-eight point two light years away.

Both spheres were hovering just outside of this Tri-Star system. Nichala was downright pleased with her first attempt, which was a short transit stop on her way to the brightest star, Polaris A. The north star. The star of hope and inspiration to her people.

"Incredible!" Nichala voiced her thought, which was easily heard by Kia and Naomi. "Look! Planets." She began to count the points of light around the star. "Six... seven planets! I can't believe it. Let's go check them out!"

"No!" Kia thought strongly, then softened her energy. "I mean, hold off for now."

"Why?"

"Nichala is more than welcome to explore but as for Naomi, what you might see there should not go back with you."

"Are you saying there is life there?" Naomi blurted out only milliseconds before her sister was going to ask the same thing.

"I don't know. What I am saying is that you can go, Nichala. However, Naomi's life still has many years ahead. Some knowledge is best left to explore and discover when the time comes."

"But I want to..." Then Naomi thought it over. "Perhaps you're right."

"I promise, sis, I'll fill you in when the time comes. In a hundred years, I hope. And with a lot more stories to share."

Kia could sense the close bond between the two. It made her happy. Unfortunately, the time had come for them to depart.

"We should leave," Kia informed them.

"Can we say good-bye in person one more time?" Naomi pleaded.

"Yes, but not for long. The process of maintaining someone who has been reanimated can be dangerous."

Without delay, Kia and Nichala's desire to be where they wanted enabled them to bypass hyperdrive and snub their nose at the complex Einstein-Rosen bridge, simply by just using the more powerful energy of the mind. Instantly, they were back on Naomi's front porch. They were physical bodies now, hand in hand, their eyes tearing up, locked and pupils wide open.

"There is something I want to say that I said at your funeral, and I can hardly believe I have been given the chance to tell you again in person. I am the women I am today because of your sacrifice. You gave me this gift of life and when I wake up every morning, I look up to the heavens and say thank you. And now I know you will hear me every time, if you want."

Nichala squeezed her hand tightly. "You are welcome. You are my baby sis. It was an easy decision to make. And now, I have a lot of new places to explore, and you know how much I love to travel." She smiled, more to the fact that she sensed a wave of relief exiting her sister's body. "What's ahead for you, Naomi?"

"Kia and I have a lot to talk about, and I think you will enjoy the changes because I don't want what happened to you to happen to anyone else. And with a little luck from Kia and the others, we are well on our way to making that a reality."

That was cryptic as well as uplifting, also enlightening to Kia. Nichala did not feel it required any explanation.

"Well, be happy always in whatever you pursue."

They hugged and Naomi felt her grip slipping away. Nichala began to transcend into non-visible energy. All Naomi could see was her sister's lips moving, and she knew exactly what she was saying. Then she was gone like dandelions in the wind. Gone, but not forever.

"I love you too." Naomi said aloud, pushing her voice up to the sky.

Once alone, it really hit her the scope of what she just experienced. The thought of an afterlife such as what she just experienced could change the feelings and beliefs of every human being. Giving us all what they truly needed.

Real hope!

Knowing that we could retain the memories of our lives for an eternity would have a tremendous positive impact in the face of such a difficult world to live in.

Yet, why wasn't that enough for Naomi? She couldn't just let it be. There was more to this strange alien than meets the eye. A lot more, and she had to know it all.

Naomi had some questions, tough questions, for Kia. One was motive. That was burning away at her from soon after they met. Kia may have been a gift horse, but she had every intention to look her in the mouth.

It was her obsessive curiosity and the need-to-know things that drove her, and one of the things gnawing at her was why Kia would put herself in the position to have to answer any question put to her. That would certainly make this unusual alien open to vulnerability. And where are the others Kia mentioned? How many other aliens were paired off with other humans, and where were they?

She just had to find the truth.

"I will be back shortly." Kia stepped in.

Naomi's interrogation would have to wait.

"We will talk, I assure you."

Naomi believed her as Kia slowly faded away. The sight of someone dissolving, whether it be human or alien, would never get old. It was a talent that could win any competition. She was alone on her stoop, then went inside and turned on the television. She turned the notifications back on her phone and it was blowing up with reports of specific stories she was following, one was of particular interest.

Was he one of the others?

She was referring to a news item that was currently on one of the local stations out of Jerusalem.

"Unbelievable!" she exclaimed. She read the banner running across the bottom of the screen. *Whereabouts of Syrian leader unknown.*

Naomi was connecting the imaginary dots with an imaginary permanent marker. Confirmation would come when Kia returned, but would it be in time to explain what could turn into a catastrophic world event?

CHAPTER 24

Tuesday October 28
8:17 am local time

It was abnormal for this trio to converse in the form of the species they were here to help. Back on the sheath's home world, they did have a physical form which was necessary to serve the solids and to better construct a working civilization. However, it was quite a different form from the humans living on earth. Back home, Kia and the others had bodies that consisted of four upper appendages and a tri- pedal lower half. Co-ordinating all that movement was an elongated head with multiple eye sockets, an appearance not unusual among the thousands of species they had helped. Placing their bioenergy into these human appearing bodies did not absolve them of feeling pain. They were experiencing some discomfort right now, as this unique environment held many dangers to them.

These three human body shapes consisting of Kia, Echo and L.J., were each resting on one of three flat stones with a spectacular view of the north rim. Below, and about a mile down, was the Colorado River, which had carved out this amazing view they were enjoying.

"Breathtaking, isn't it?" Echo said, his lips moving as if he were human.

He was not bothered by the shining glare of the rising sun, as his eyes were for appearance only. He could see in amazing detail, but in his own alien way. Echo touched his soft body, which was not real like Victor's, but close enough for their purpose.

Kia's lips began to move, and speech was about to be formed. She was becoming good at mimicking human traits necessary to blend in. "Is anyone sensing a shift in our original thought? Is this civilization still on course for extinction?"

Echo nodded.

L.J also agreed, and added, "Which means nothing that any of our companions have done has changed this planet's future."

"Yet." Echo pointed out. "One of them will; it's only a matter of time. It's always just a matter of time."

"Then what had your symbiotic created?" L.J. asked of Echo.

"He's created a series of retributions to atone for the death of his daughter. That initial act has manifested itself into an obsession. Just recently, I helped him obtain an important and brutal world leader. When I return to him, it's his desire to expose him to the same gruesome death that befell his victims. It will be witnessed by the entire world. Victor claims it will be a strong deterrent and a stern warning to others who torture and kill."

The trio felt an eerie similarity to their own situation. The solids, their nemesis, their enslavers, were equally gruesome.

"Do you think that could be the event?" L.J. asked.

"Victor wants this leader to die in excruciating pain and in such detail and clarity that it will put the fear of God, as he phrased it, in others with the same evil goals. Make them think twice."

"That could be the incident that will set into motion the events that save this planet."

"And when that happens, that spectacle will reach us and leave us with no doubt; however, my companion doesn't plan to stop there. He is going to give a global warning that other world leaders will be judged and sentenced to similar punishments as a deterrent not to murder or mistreat those who put them in power."

"Victor could be the key."

"He will act swiftly. He mentioned some names of others he wants to punish; they mean nothing to me, but to Victor, they mean everything."

"That could help us in the short term, but could be problematical in the long term," L.J. pointed out. "Victor's plan could produce some food for our enemy in the short term, but if he succeeds in spreading peace, that could make it hard to fill our quota."

"Then again," Echo surmised, "these countries that suddenly are without those world leaders, as evil as they are, could lead to some panic and instability."

"My Joel's plan could be in contradiction to Echo's companion."

"Then if Victor and Joel were to ever meet before their plans unfold, there could be conflict, perhaps leading to an unbalance."

"We must continue to let events unfold as usual. We are joined to each of them, like solder and wire. We follow their rules, follow their commands and the event that saves their planet will follow as well," L.J reminded them.

"You're right as usual. However, we do have the tendency to play the 'what if' games from time to time," Echo added, then turned to Kia. "You are quiet. This is not like you. Is your companion giving you worry?"

Kia stood then walked closer to the edge of the rim and stared down a mile into the deep canyon below. "She's a unique individual. While what she wanted, on the surface, does not appear to have the ability to alter humanity's course, she does have a vision about how humanity has the best chance to succeed long term."

"You have become close with her?" Echo inquired. "And by close, I don't mean by the usual electrical connection. By close, I mean you have become her friend."

Kia turned away from the spectacular view. Echo and L.J. could see the answer written on her face. It wasn't obvious at first as they did not have much experience in reading human facial expressions and Kia did not have much experience in generating them.

"We should not get close to our companions," Echo reminded her sternly. "We give them an afterlife, and they supply our enemy with food. They are simply a means to an end."

"And it wasn't wise to have granted your Naomi her desire to know-it-all, Kia."

"Why did you allow it?" L.J. insisted.

"There have never been secrets between us before." Echo was trying to get Kia to lower her barrier. "Since we lost the war to the solids three hundred million cycles ago, we have always been open and transparent. We have always shared one goal, and that was filling our quota. Knowing each other's thoughts is integral to that goal."

"That's changed, hasn't it Kia?" L.J. asked.

"I… I am tired of the deception. The motivation to continue with the deception is waning," Kia finally revealed.

"Is that why you agreed to Naomi's wish? So that if she asked, you would have to reveal the truth to her?"

"It could be that my judgement is waning as well. I did what I did. It is done. Once I agree to the desire and the bond is made, there is no breaking it."

That answer did not sit well with the others.

"My bonds are always unbreakable. You may have a different way, a dangerous way," she added, referring to LJ. "But I don't want to change a way that has kept me at peace since the war ended."

"If you go against us, if you decide to end our partnership, our enemy may consider this an abrogation of our treaty. We need you with us. Filling our quota without you will be difficult. If we fall short of that quota, they will want an explanation. They may retaliate against us. They may even have the ability to retaliate against these humans, here on their home."

"I don't believe so." Kia shook her head. "The solids have become so dependent on us supplying them with the food they need to survive that they have abandoned all their desire to explore space past their own star system. It would take them an awfully long time to renew their technology, and then a very long time to reach this planet. In their current dependent state, I don't believe they are a threat to these humans."

"I would have to disagree," L.J. said.

"I also disagree. We don't trust our enemy. You know they have wanted our abilities since the war began. You know they must be trying to duplicate it. This planet is so fragmented that should the solids come, these humans would offer little resistance, no matter how weak the solids' attacks would be."

"And you know how vital our success here is. More than any other civilization we have helped before," L.J. reminded her.

"Naomi, especially, and the others could be the ones to help unify these humans. We all know how important unification is in the longevity of a civilization."

"Our enemy is not so unified. Naomi and the rest of these humans may be able to defend themselves," Kia reminded them. But not in their current state; she kept that to herself.

"If you would lower your barrier, I would know if you really believed that."

Kia's mental barrier was set to impermeability, a fact that was uncomfortable with L.J. and Echo.

"From what I have learned, as it is today, it will be impossible for hundreds of bickering, divided nations to agree on how to unite against a common enemy."

"Naomi is… I think she's special. She will unite with Joel and Victor. Together, they will change this world. There is something special about her that I can't explain."

"You wouldn't have to explain if you would let us in. If you would let us help you to explain." L.J.'s tone was as stern as ever, yet Kia would not lower her mental screens.

Kia would not budge and continued her communication using human verbal speech. "I'm sorry but time has allowed my conscience to expand. Have you thought, really, really spent time contemplating the cost of keeping our civilization alive?"

"The costs are minimal," Echo responded quickly, which answered her question just as fast.

"To us they are minimal, but what of those we send to the solids for slaughter?'

Her words had an impact. Echo tried to debate her, as his belief that they were doing the right thing was taking a beating.

"It is only the evil and the malicious, those who do not deserve an afterlife in the first place, that are slaughtered by our enemy. It's helped to maintain a treaty that has withstood the test of time."

"Do not those undeserving, deserve better than what they have coming to them." She was now easily able to move her facial muscles to show sadness and determination, which was learned from Naomi, but also remembered from what they once were in appearance.

"Kia, this place is perfect. It could be decades or even centuries before we come across the next violent place. Here, these humans can supply our enemy with enough food regardless of how long the next drought lasts," Echo reminded the others. "It's also why we are taking extraordinary chances here to help them."

"And you know what could happen if we run out of evil."

"The good ones, those who have hope of a wonderful long-lasting peaceful afterlife, will be sacrificed. They will experience enslavement and torture. Is that what you want?" Echo continued; his strategy obvious to all.

"Bottom line?" Kia asked.

"We do what it takes to succeed here. Success here means not having to re-evaluate your conscience."

"That is easy to say when I am a mass of bioelectricity, but having taken their form, I am finding it hard not to take in their morality," Kia explained, her voice loaded with guilt.

"Taking physical form comes with many risks," Echo agreed. "But again, I remind you, the opportunity to end the war and to end our slavery is here. This place holds the one substance that can defeat the solids. We have yet to find it anywhere in the entire universe, we may never get another opportunity like this… ever!"

"We need to be in this together, all of us. Are you with us?"

Kia turned from worry to sorrow, which the others could see but not feel. Since L.J. and Echo's barriers were down, they could communicate with each other without Kia eavesdropping.

"If she leaves us, she could bring the war back upon us," Echo thought fervently.

"We couldn't defend ourselves back then, and nothing has changed in all that time." L.J's thoughts were sent piggybacked with regret.

Six hundred million earth years of acquiescing to the quota. Not one minute ever fighting back. Not one minute ever spent standing up to their enemy. Not one minute questioning the treaty they had agreed to so long ago. A treaty that kept the bio electric sheaths alive.

"You're right. We have no defense. We would be tortured to make up for the shortfall. That must be incentive enough to continue as we always have?"

"But these humans-"

"Don't! Don't let Kia influence you. Don't let these humans influence you. We cannot tell them the truth."

"How can it not be a factor? Aren't you moved by their appearance? Aren't you moved by the civilization here? It's like none other. The beauty of this unique world is beyond comparison. The potential to have something great here..." Echo put up his barrier quickly as their conversation was stirring up feelings like those of Kia's.

Kia was about to end her silence, which was great timing for Echo, as he did not want to explain why his barrier was up, even if it was just briefly.

"I won't interfere," Kia finally said. "I understand what's at stake." She revealed this with her barrier down, solid proof to L.J. and Echo of her commitment to the cause. She watched the other two dissolve. Echo went on his way back to Victor and L.J. to his companion Joel.

Kia turned back to the spectacular view of the north rim and took pride in her newfound morality. She also took pride in easily learning one common human trait.

She was learning how to lie.

CHAPTER 25

Tuesday October 28
9:47pm local time

Naomi was being attacked on all sides… by uncertainty. She wanted answers and Kia was soon to return. She wasn't sure whether to confront, demand, or ask compassionately for those answers. Then there were the breaking news headlines filling multiple channels on her television screen. Then even more unnerving was the upcoming live stream on her laptop. Viewership had surpassed the one hundred million mark and was climbing with each passing second.

"What the hell is going on?" Naomi whispered.

Was that going to be her first question for Kia? If it was, she would have to be more specific.

The blackness of the live stream transitioned to that of a tall, thin man, his arms stretched high over his head, his hands tied by a rope to a hook which was attached to the ceiling. The beleaguered man was not dangling as his feet were resting flat on solid ground.

Naomi was hypnotized by this curious event. Whatever camera that was capturing this scene had changed from a wide angle to suddenly focus in on the man's face. There was no audio, yet it was clear the man was red-faced with terror and yelling out something, perhaps pleading for his life or for mercy. If there was audio, he would be heard screaming out defiance and his innocence. Victor wanted no one to hear the words that might be an enticement of his followers to exact revenge, so only Victor's voice would prevail. A voice that would be disguised, mechanical and frightening. Naomi slid up the volume to hear the short and succinct manifesto.

"This is a warning to all the world leaders who commit atrocities on their population. It will no longer be tolerated. Do right by your people, or I will come for you!"

By now, the world knew who the subject of this torture was. The Syrian government had been silent about their leader's kidnapping until now and had decided against posting any reward for the safe return of him. That spoke volumes. Even without the monetary incentive, hackers from every corner of the globe were writing algorithms to search for the source of the transmission.

Victor, however, was confident that his multi-layered firewalls would thwart any attack on his systems. Not one hundred percent confident though, so it was time to get on with the performance.

Naomi rechecked that she had turned up the volume and now she was hearing a distinctive hissing sound like that of a valve being opened. Known only to Victor and Echo, Sarin gas began filling the room of the Syrian President. Then Victor started to type a narration on his keyboard, to ensure the five hundred million viewers also knew who this man was and what was happening to him, thus leaving no doubt. Then he added in a statement that Chlorine gas was next to be added to the small room.

Major news networks like CNN, Al-Jazeera, Xinhua News Agency and the BBC were fixated on this historic, ratings-grabbing event. The image panned out to show the leader's body begin to convulse so much so that the ropes were eating away at the flesh of his wrists and ankles.

Victor was manipulating the focus to maximize the grotesqueness. He zoomed in on the President's face, whose skin began to mottle then sag as if he were made of wax under a scorching heat lamp. Blood began to drip slowly from his nose and ears, and the whites of his eyes were beet red. Victor seized the opportunity to activate the microphone.

The Syrian leader was screaming in agony but couldn't form words as his tongue blossomed like exploding popcorn. Then his shrieking stopped abruptly, as air could no longer pass over his vocal cords. Four of his teeth had no more anchor points and slid down to his chin, then clanked on the concrete floor.

Victor looked down at the killer's vital signs and rubbed his chin. The small heart monitor he had placed on the president's chest was still recording a faint and irregular heart rhythm, which meant he was still alive and suffering at a vomit inducing pace. Victor could only guess the concentration levels of the chlorine and sarin gases and based on what he was seeing, he might have overcooked the mixture.

He put a hand on Echo's shoulder and smiled as he noticed the president's eyes begin to emit a vapor like that from boiling water. Those same eyes had seen a thousand similar deaths. A well-placed mirror meant the last death he would witness would be his own as his eyeballs exploded, sending fluid and tissue out like a geyser. The graphic content would be blurred by the networks, but the scene would be shown unedited everywhere else.

Meanwhile, all through this horror show, brutal leaders from around the world were sprouting bodyguards. The North Korean leader hunkered down in a lavish underground bunker with twelve of his elite guards standing ready for any kidnapping attempt.

Victor's laptop was showing that some hackers out of... he typed a few commands... out of China had breached ninety percent of his defenses. That annoyed him enough to consider sending Echo in that direction. Victor had to temper his zeal for random acts of retribution. It was the world leaders that required his full attention, and the guilty ones at that. Proof of their guilt was an essential part if he was to garner any support for his acts, and when this was wrapped up, he knew just the right person to approach to get that proof. Just the right person with all the answers.

First things first. It was time to wrap things up.

The man's arms had already dissolved so much that he had slipped through his restraints and was a mere puddle of goo on the floor.

"What the hell is going on?" Colonel Weiss said, startling Naomi who did not notice him come in. "You should really lock your door."

She moved her eyes to acknowledge him then went back to glare at the craziness on her screen. "Why ask me? Oh, and come in," she added as the colonel was right, she should have locked her door!

"Because you seem to have the answers to everything." The colonel shot back. "I mean, world leaders are on edge, black auroras are showing up, magnetic fields are going haywire one second, then fine the next."

Naomi gave a bored shrug of her shoulders which aggravated the colonel.

He leered at her, then continued. "I think you could have the answers if you wanted. Or maybe you already know."

"What are you talking about? I don't have a clue!"

"Well either you or your friend knows something."

"Friend?" Naomi tried to act cool, and bored but was worried about where this was going.

"You don't think I've had you under surveillance since that MH370 finding? Information is power, and you or the company you keep know things that are… unknowable. Which makes you powerful."

"Well now I also know you're following me." Naomi raised her eyebrows as if to show off. It was an attitude she regretted displaying. "Listen, Colonel, if the men of this world weren't so violent," she emphasized the word men, "and world leaders so corrupt and violent, you wouldn't need me to solve these mysteries. And a fragmented world makes it impossible to solve our problems. They all deserve what they are getting. We need more cooperation and peace and less... of you." She turned the volume down on the television. "You know, colonel, if honeybees worked like humans, we would never see a drop of honey."

"You, my dear, are an idealist."

"The fate of humanity depends on cooperation and unity, so I've been reminded. Instead of bothering me, you should investigate that." This time she did not regret antagonizing him, as she could not help herself.

"I can see this is going nowhere. I was hoping to return to the Israeli President with some answers. You see he is nervous, which translates to me being nervous."

"I'm sorry to disappoint you. One thing I can offer that you should consider: any leader of any country that suddenly strengthens their protection is admitting guilt and painting a target on their back. It will only show to whoever is doing this that they have something to hide."

Naomi saw Colonel Weiss shift from one foot to the other. He then took off his beret and rubbed his dry forehead.

"I'm just following orders, Naomi. I will ask you one last time. Do you know who is doing this?"

She walked over to the kitchen and responded with her back to him. "I really don't. Would you care for a beverage?"

"Thank you, no. I should be going."

Naomi was back at the doorway to the living room with a glass of water in her hand and then the colonel turned to leave. At that precise moment, came a flicker of blue light that lit up the interior of the small kitchen, but only for an instant. Fortunately, there was no reflective surface in view of Colonel Weiss's eyes. "Good evening, Miss Danieli. I'm sure we will meet again."

Thankfully, he left, and Naomi tiptoed to the front door and cracked it open just a sliver. The colonel must have been royally pissed as he was already gone and out of sight, and she could finally let out the ten gallons of air she had been holding in. Her relief was short lived as she saw Kia walk into the living room. Naomi had just endured one interrogation, which at least put her in the mood for the next.

"Where have you been?"

"In discussion with the others," Kia responded.

"Others like you?"

"Yes, two others."

"I knew as much. Then I must assume there are two others like me?"

Kia nodded.

"I think I know what one of them is up to. Not sure about the third." This was more of an observation rather than a Jeopardy style question. "One thing I don't understand is that you've opened yourself up to an incredible vulnerability." Naomi was a bit harsh in her tone but then noticed a general fatigue on Kia's face and body. "Why have you done that?" she asked more softly.

"Because it's time. This really is the perfect time."

"Time for what?"

"To reveal the truth. To tell our story." Kia straightened her frame as if she had an actual vertebra. She held her arms out openly. "Let's take another trip!"

Naomi was immediately intrigued, as it was an offer she couldn't turn down. She knew she was in for another amazing adventure and placed her hands in Kia's. The essence of Naomi was instantly converted into electrical energy. Safely inside Kia's sphere of influence, they were whisked off the planet's surface. In three blinks of an eye, they were high above the earth, watching it grow small.

"Where are we going?" Her body felt like a live wire, surging with thousands of volts of current. That would be most deadly were a human to be in contact with a thousand volts, but in this non-human spectral state, it was natural. It took until reaching the area of Neptune, about fifteen seconds, to reduce her excitement to that of a trickle charge.

"Are we there yet?" Naomi said jokingly, then asked, "Where are we going?"

"Home, Naomi. We are going home!"

"Where you told my sister not to go?"

"Yes. I will take you there as slow as it takes to answer all your questions."

Being in Kia's bubble for the second time was less nauseating than the first. It was not easy imagining an unseen barrier protecting her energy from dissipating into the cold vacuum death of space. Once she felt more at ease, it was time to begin to learn the truth.

"I don't know where to start." Naomi confessed. "I was hoping to be more organized. I went over to myself every question in a certain order earlier, but now my mind is a jumble. Let me start with some simple questions, like where is your home?"

"It's thirteen galaxies distance from yours. Within that galaxy is a binary star system. We are a part of a civilization consisting of two planets orbiting the smaller of the two stars. Our neighbor owns the larger star, and they live on three of the only four planets in that system."

"You say neighbors with a lot of pain, I can sense it." Another skill Naomi was learning.

"You will soon know the pain as I know it. I don't want to keep our secret anymore."

"You've asked, begged, perhaps ordered everyone you've helped never to visit your home world, not just my sister, in order to keep that secret?"

"You will see why, shortly. And I must warn you that what you'll find will be depressing. Some of it will make you angry and horrified. It may be peaceful and quiet from this far away, but you need to prepare yourself. You could find it gruesome and unimaginable."

Just like earth is from here, peaceful, and what earth is or on its way to be... Naomi observed.

"I've been through a lot myself. I want to see. Let's keep going." Naomi felt the sphere speed up even though she had no points of reference to prove the sensation.

"Some of our history I am both ashamed of and embarrassed to be a part of. I do ask that you reserve any judgement until after you have seen and heard the entire story."

"Yes, of course."

"About six hundred million years ago, by your calendar, it all began."

Naomi found the number mindboggling. Being alive in one form or another for that long was astounding.

"The ones we share this binary system with are called solids. They call us sheaths."

"Sheaths?"

"It's a simplified term. We use these sheaths or casings to contain our bio-electric energy. It allows us movement."

"What did you, or do you, look like on your home planet?"

"We have four upper limbs like yours but longer. Wider hips. Thighs rotated more externally. Arms longer and closer to the midsection. A bulbous head larger than yours. We have multiple eyes and ears that are larger than yours which we use as sensors to help coordinate our movement about our environment."

"My compliments to your designer. A very useful shape." That response was said after she imagined how much more could be done with their bodies than ours.

"We use these bodies to construct our civilization."

She wanted to ask to visit Kia's home but not yet. "What do these solids look like?"

"Why don't I leave that for you to see for yourself. We will be there soon," Kia said. "One thing I can say is that there is one major difference between us and them, and that difference is what brought about our war with the solids."

"It all has to do with this afterlife you give to others, doesn't it?"

"Yes, and it has everything to do with our special abilities. The special abilities we have, and the solids wanted. For as long as our history is recorded, we have had immortality. Our memories and all the essences of our life experiences are complex bio-electric energies. We can encase these energies into physical bodies or into spheres and these spheres allow us to travel the universe in eternity. Whereas the solids exist, grow old then die. Like all species do except for a select few that we have come across. Placing our energy into sheaths for movement is as common to our existence as breathing is to you. It's a natural sympathetic ability."

"Let me guess, the solids asked you nicely at first to give them this natural ability."

"They wanted it. They wanted the same immortality and the same freedoms we have?"

"It would have been an amazing gift," Naomi realized.

"And we had no intention of keeping it just for ourselves."

"But what of the three of you?" Naomi asked.

"The three of us are known among our species as the Blessed. The death of an entire civilization emits massive electrical energies that can push back through time. The three of us realized, long, long ago, that we could sense these energies. We could sense the future doom of other civilizations. We believe we were created for a special purpose, a duty to help those worlds in imminent peril. And if our help is successful, reward them with a life of eternity after death."

"Incredible!" Naomi said.

"And, when any being ceases to exist, they still retain and emit a very faint energy signature that we can detect, decode, and rebuild back into what they were, like your sister for example. It's a very complicated process with risks and very taxing, yet necessary to further the process of helping a civilization save themselves from their own destruction.

"Again, incredible. What a gift that is, I mean will be, I mean could be to us." She was finding it hard to convey the enormity of what the sheaths' powers were. She composed herself, then continued. "And the solids found out you were helping others and neglecting them."

"It wasn't that we were neglecting them, it was that other worlds were in more urgent need of our help. Other worlds that were on a course of self-annihilation, or about to be destroyed by some future natural event. We had to help them first."

If Naomi had a lip to bite, she would be doing so. She could not help but wonder if she was on one of those worlds that was in peril. That would be an urgent question for later.

"I am guessing that didn't matter to the solids?"

"No, it didn't. As time went on, and with the finality of death for the solids continuing as usual, they pressed us constantly to help them. To show them how it was done."

"Give a man a fish," Naomi thought as a whisper.

"I don't understand?"

"It's just a saying we have. Please continue."

"How we do it on other worlds is not easy. Once the time is right, the three of us combine all our electrical energies into one burst that engulfs and penetrates every substance on a given world. These charged particles remain innocuously imbedded in every individual, dormant, but learning, then when death comes, these particles activate, which allow this continuation after death. And we tried and tried to do the same with the solids, but there was something interfering with the process."

"Did you ever find out what that was?"

"There was an unknown incompatibility between us and the solids. A devastating one that interfered with the process. Like they were made up of anti-energy."

"Like creating a short circuit?" she thought. "Or an incompatibility in blood types that can be dangerous."

"Not just dangerous but obliterating on a galactic scale! We tried. We really tried to help them! But to continue trying meant risking their existence. It was not meant to be for them."

Naomi was having trouble decoding all the information from Kia into a recognizable program. What she needed was a time out and it came just in time. They had just passed out of the illumination of the Milky Way and were now deep into interstellar space. There was a calming sense of weightlessness inside their sphere that was hard to explain. Her galaxy was becoming a distant spiral, so she turned her gaze to the next nearest galaxy, which was elliptical in shape. So fascinating, this was, like watching a drive-in movie from a moving car.

"You're thinking of... popcorn?" Kia noted.

"I know it's silly," Naomi admitted. Then a new sensation nudged at her. "What's happening?"

"For what is about to come, I would prefer not to hear your thoughts until you verbalize them to me."

Without asking for permission, Naomi was hit with a new sensation, which was the construction of two distinct energy zones within the bubble, each with its own membrane, like two embryos inside one egg. With that done, she felt liberated in knowing that her emotions were her own.

"Are we heading there?" Naomi asked, referring to the nearby elliptical.

"No, my home is a few more galaxies beyond, so we will detour around it." Then she continued with her story. "Before long, the solids' frustration with us grew to anger. They felt like we were not doing enough to find a solution, so they resorted to abducting a few of us. They must have found a way to capture and contain us in a way. Then began the torturous experimentation. This signaled the beginning of the war."

"War? How can you fight a war?"

"We couldn't. They were a hundred billion Solids spread over four planets, and we were but sixteen billion Sheaths spread over two. Their bodies were more experienced with movement. Their civilization was mechanical. We were spiritual and intellectual with bodies used only as a case for our energies. We were overwhelmed quickly, and we surrendered just as quickly."

"And then?"

"They gave us two choices. Angry annihilation, or to follow their demands… slavery."

"You chose slavery?" Naomi guessed.

"We didn't want to die. We are beings used to immortality. Perhaps it was a cowardly choice."

"It's not cowardly to want to live. It's instinctual."

There was a pause in the conversation as they over flew the elliptical galaxy and then sliced through an intense quasar that bobbed in the middle of an irregular. Kia then steered their sphere towards a beautiful blue dwarf galaxy, which was very distinct among the others that dotted the landscape. It was clear they were heading in that direction. She could then feel their momentum decrease. The fantastic scene unfolding was like being in the International Space Station on the dark side of its orbit and looking down at the lights of the various cities. She wondered what kind of life lived among those thousands of galactic lights they were buzzing past.

"What happened next?" Naomi asked, eager to get back to the story.

"We had only one thing left that we could give them… food. They would abandon the experimentation of us, and in return we would search the universe for food to feed their voracious appetites."

"What does that mean!?" Naomi didn't like the sound of that.

"The solids eat, well, other types of solids. Not cannibalism, but other animals raised and farmed on their worlds. They also knew that the resources they had would not be able to sustain their massive population. Remember that special ability of reanimation I mentioned before? They were now aware of that, and the three of us were ordered out into the universe in search of… food for them."

Naomi felt a holographic lump in her throat. Are humans going to be food for these solids one day? Could she have misunderstood Kia's intentions? That doesn't make sense. *Why would she show me this? Even more telling, why would she block my thoughts? Kia would want to know what I was thinking. No, I need to hear it all before judging the sheaths' purpose.*

"When we free a civilization, every being is embedded with certain of our electrical properties, mainly negative and positive properties. How they live their lives is imprinted on those properties. When they die, and they build up enough positive aspects like love, compassion and morality, then they are free to explore the universe. Those that build up negative charges like malevolence and hatred or commit violence are sent to the solids and reanimated. In essence, those that deserve a long afterlife are free to explore."

"And those that don't?" she could imagine the fate that awaited them.

"Sent to the solids and reanimated as food."

"Cattle!"

"What does that mean, Naomi?"

"Animals led to slaughter. Is that what I'm going to see?"

"Nothing will be left to the imagination," was Kia's direct response.

"Except this: why did you need to bond with me? Why do you need to bond with anyone? Why not just come to Earth, and give us an afterlife, then move on to the next?"

"As with any process, there was an extensive learning curve. In the beginning, long, long ago, we knew truly little of the process. One thing we wondered was how our special abilities would interact with aliens and their alien environments. We had catastrophes early on because we assumed that we were the only ones with an afterlife."

"And you weren't?"

"We found out the hard way that a few civilizations already had afterlives in some form. We did have success for the first sixty- two."

"Luck?"

"It would run out on the sixty-third. They already possessed an afterlife. When we discharged our energy to create their afterlife, we also created a contradiction."

"I'm afraid to ask what the result was."

"It was catastrophic. The result was the formation of a dead zone in space, where light can't escape and intense gravity swallows all."

"A black hole!"

"Yes, our energies cancelled each other out and created a massive black hole."

"So, these black holes we discovered back in the seventies, you created them!" Naomi wasn't asking a question but stating an incredible fact.

"Unfortunately, these event horizons took many, many years to enlarge to the point that we could detect them, which is why so many formed. We stopped immediately until we could find a safer way to proceed. Now, thankfully, we have a very standard system of contact, planning, and execution. It's worked well. We have yet to create any more of these black holes."

Another incredible discovery she would have to keep for herself because who would believe her? That realization still didn't diminish the impact of what she was hearing and seeing.

"And these black auroras? There must be a connection," Naomi wondered.

"They are very disconcerting. They are the beginnings of these black holes waiting for detonation. That's why we cannot spend too much time on your surface, and why we must be absolutely certain that death is your final existence."

"Unbelievable!" Naomi exclaimed.

What was also unbelievable was the speed that they were approaching Kia's galaxy. They plunged through the outer barrier like a bullet through a curtain on fire. Naomi's energy flinched, like hitting her funny bone, and she braced for a potential impact of sorts, yet there was no change inside their protective sphere. The transition from intergalactic space was uneventful. She wouldn't have minded if Kia could hear her thoughts and feel her emotions because they would relay awe. But for Kia to have excluded her, what is to come must be bad.

CHAPTER 26

"There! Ahead. Those two lone points of light in that region. That's my home." Their sphere of energy stayed at a constant speed, easily telling Naomi they would not be stopping in for a visit. "Do what you must to prepare yourself for when we arrive at the solid's home."

"I don't think there is anything more I can do," she admitted. "However, stopping in to see a bit of your world might help in the preparation. Could give me some insight."

It was worth a try. Naomi really wanted a sneak peek into Kia's life. It must surely be so alien and so incomprehensible, yet so amazing. She wanted to see what these sheaths could build with the bodies they had. How similar would it be to human civilization?

"As much as I would like to show you what we have accomplished, this is not the time."

"I understand." She didn't fully understand. She chalked it up as another mystery to pile onto her already fragile psyche. "How often do you return home?" Naomi didn't think it could hurt to ask that.

"Often enough to ensure that the treaty is holding. To ensure my people are safe and thriving. To ensure the solids have left them alone."

"It must be hard for your people to be under constant threat. That another race can decide whether you survive or not. That your future is not guaranteed. It must be difficult for the three of you to be the guardians of their survival."

"But at what cost? I am hoping, after you see what I am about to show you, that the ends will justify the means. It has appeased our guilt for a long time."

Naomi wanted to feel Kia's emotions as well as to show her emotions to Kia. She wanted the barrier between them to come down, but not yet. "Let's just get to it."

Naomi felt their sphere veer off toward the much larger of the two binary stars. The sun of the solids, she thought poetically. "Do the other two sheaths know what you are about to show me?"

"Not... completely."

The comfortable interior of their bubble felt none of the effects of this sun even as they travelled within a thousand kilometers of it. They experienced no scorching heat, no crushing gravity, and no tissue destroying radiation. Just awe-inspiring beauty. Brilliant solar flares were expelled outward, past them and around them. Orange and yellow fusions ebbed and oozed on the surface, as if they were hovering above the bubbling cauldron of lava inside a volcano.

Naomi wished they could stay a while longer, but they were soon zipping past the largest of the solids' four home worlds. It was a stunning yellowish in appearance, but they did not get close enough for her to see much detail. Could that mean the solids had a sulfur-based existence? Her imagination was running wild, as she knew little about chemistry other than from her classes in high school.

The next fly by was the second, which Naomi estimated had a similar orbit distance as Jupiter was from its sun. It had the same yellowish appearance as before, but she could see more detail: saffron colored clouds swirled in a pattern like her own earth's clouds, and she thought she could even see some surface detail. It was like looking at Google maps, but without the magnification. To her amazement, she thought she could detect the feature of a canyon though which some bright liquid was running through. It couldn't be water! What could it be?

They never stopped there and ignored the third, so it must be the furthest of the four planets that was their final destination. They began slowly braking, like a car coming to a traffic light. Taking in this entire star system as a panorama, she had a stunning three-hundred-and-sixty-degree view. Naomi took in the sights which included this planet and three other points of light along with the massive star as a backdrop.

They entered an orbit of sorts and Naomi noted the depressing dull grey atmosphere and the gloomy brown surface in stark contrast to the vibrancy of the other three. It was depressing for a reason, and Naomi was about to find out why. They passed through an upper level of clouds, then land masses appeared which were separated not by oceans, but by rivers of some slow-moving alien liquid. Hundreds of these rivers, like strips of bacon in a frying pan, were churning and bubbling, moving slowly like molasses.

Naomi could not detect any structures until they approached the equator, then from high above, she spotted a large land mass. They were descending quickly then suddenly hundreds, if not thousands of long rectangular buildings came into view. They were all massive in size, as large as distribution warehouses like Amazon or automotive plants on earth. Surrounding the exterior of all these structures were outdoor fields, all bordered by fencing, neatly separating themselves into thousands of corrals.

"Cattle!" Naomi thought once again.

And corrals full of somethings, or someones!

They swooped down to a height of a hundred meters, and it took Naomi a moment to be assured she wasn't going to plummet to the ground. She was becoming more comfortable in her bio-electric skin and enjoyed the sense of floating, like being inside a helium filled balloon.

"What are we seeing?" Naomi asked.

She could still feel her beating heart, or at least the concept of one. She couldn't see skin or chest, yet she could sense the vibration or the thumping, but it couldn't be pumping blood.

They continued to move across the land, hovering at times then moving on at a constant altitude. Kia remained silent, leaving Naomi to form an opinion as to what was happening below. There were fields upon fields, tens of thousands of sectioned off fields, each the size of a soccer pitch. Within each of these corrals were moving figures. They appeared like cockroaches, ants or wriggling maggots, moving without any co-ordination, at times crawling over each other. Crowded with no room to move freely.

"What are we seeing!" she asked with more conviction.

"Inside each of those containments, are the live bodies of thousands of varied species from civilizations all over the universe. Down there are only those that didn't warrant an eternal afterlife. They are the evil, the criminal, and the corrupt. Each of them died, were channeled here, and then reanimated."

"You mean each of those moving pieces is a person?"

"Not a person in appearance as you are accustomed to, but they are all sentient beings like yourself. All alive, with conscious thought. Memories of their lives all intact. Completely able to feel pain, sorrow, and agony... and some, even regret."

"Bring me closer!" Naomi demanded and, as if anticipating Kia's question, quickly added, "Yes, I'm sure."

Kia lowered their energy balloon gently downward as if venting some of the hot air. Naomi could hardly comprehend the scene below. She shuddered at what it might be, which sent a vibration though their internal barrier that Kia could pick up.

"Slow your thoughts," Kia advised. "Calm yourself, because it is not going to get any easier."

Naomi did her best to follow her adviser's advice as they were a mere thirty meters above the wriggling masses. She could easily make out each individual as living, moving bodies of all shapes and sizes. Totally alien in appearance.

Space was a vacuum, but not here, as she could hear muffled sounds, a perverse chorus of moaning and frightful cries of anguish.

"Lower," Naomi begged.

The groans grew louder and more intense, which gave them meaning. These... hostages appeared to be in a constant state of discomfort, make that agony. Yes, many of the cries were of searing pain.

"We call these places the corrals of the corrupt. This is what awaits all the evil in the universe."

Does calling it the corrals of the corrupt ease their guilt? Does that make this right, Naomi wondered, and only she could hear that thought.

"Concentration camps. Auschwitz. Belzec, Treblinka."

Naomi had studied this in depth, yet this was far worse. How could this ever be worse? Wet markets! That's what this is! Oh, my god! She remembered watching the cruelty of the caged animals, and the processing plants and the thousands of animals all in close quarters waiting to be slaughtered for food. Chickens so pumped up with steroids that their upper bodies grew too large for their legs to hold them up, toppling over then struggling to stand again. Any means to get them to slaughter faster.

She was seeing this below, as clear as could be.

Cattle herded one by one, single file to a metal hammer that would smash their skull, then send each carcass on a conveyor, only to disappear into a facility to be converted into steaks and burgers. She spied all those large buildings and connected the horrific dots.

"Is that what this is?" she wondered again to herself.

However, was it possible to feel any kind of sympathy as they looked so alien, and that they were the evil scourge of the universe? She didn't like hiding her feelings.

"Kia, I want you to know what I am feeling. It's important you know."

"Of course."

The barrier was down.

"Over there," Naomi ordered as something caught her eye.

She was beginning to notice the aliens that looked alike would huddle together in groups or packs. She saw six figures in the far-right corner and the sphere was now hovering over them. They were completely inhuman in appearance, yet sentient, Naomi realized. They were large enough for what the solids needed, about the size of a full-grown steer. They had thick abdomens and crawled on six legs. One of them stood up on two of its wobbly hind legs, searching for a way out. It easily measured twelve feet in height and weighed as much a full-grown grizzly.

"Are these animals?"

"Only in their actions. These came from deep inside a galaxy you call the Black Eye and from a star system in the constellation Coma Berenices. We gave them the gift a few centuries ago. Today, they still have a thriving civilization, family units like yours, industries, and education. They have transportation and communication, all adapted to suit their appearance. They are the last of their kind to come here, because they found the will to evolve into a peaceful world."

"Incredible. But they look like animals."

"It's unfair what you are thinking."

"I know, I'm sorry. I just assumed intelligence must look like us. How could they overcome violence, and we can't?"

"Is that regret?"

"How about ignorance. Yet if we only knew of this place?" Naomi wondered.

"Let your eyes decide," Kia suggested. "As far as that pack, their society succeeded in preventing the doom that awaited them which led to the complete unification of their species. Unification is always necessary for true peaceful longevity. Unification and peace are a universal association."

Is that our destiny? she wondered? *Unification and peace. Or is our destiny what I am seeing below? A more likely future?*

She cringed at the thought. Naomi wanted to see more so they floated over to the next corral. Inside this enclosure she saw a group of about fifty creatures. By creatures, she gave them that term respectfully. She also feared that by saying he or she, their suffering would add more emotions than Naomi could handle. It was enough to know that these were sentient beings. Each of these aliens had three spindly legs, a long corkscrew-like neck and a head shaped like a watermelon. On the head was one single large and terrified forward-looking eye.

"Are they aware of what's happening to them?"

"Fully aware. To them, they died just seconds before being reanimated here, and with all their lifetime memories and all their senses intact."

"Is this the fate that awaits us?" Naomi decided to ask. There was uncertainty in her tone.

"That's a question about your future I cannot answer, but be assured, for now, that only those who do not deserve an eternal afterlife will come here." Naomi's trust in Kia's words was growing strong and she had no reason not to believe her. She failed to pick up on Kia's last two words.

Another alien caught her eye at the far-right end of the corral. It, Naomi continued not to give the alien a pronoun to lessen the heartbreak, had two large wings atop a small body which was supported by four thin, trembling legs. It tried to stand tall enough to spread its wings to get airborne and escape, but Naomi could tell it was too weak. There didn't look like much meat on this alien for the solids to harvest, if that was their plan, and it was beginning to look like that would be the gruesome end to that creature's life.

The sphere's further drop in altitude brought in all the sounds from the environment into play. Naomi was startled by an alarm as a drone came from the direction of a nearby building then hovered in place over the crowded corral. Below the drone, a white flashing light was turned on and the thousand or so aliens all froze in place as if being unplugged.

"Pavlov's dogs." Was the first thought that came to Naomi.

Thousands of eyes of all shapes, sizes and colors stared up at the floating aircraft. Naomi was struck by the universal constant expression that eyes give off. Fear, panic desperation and the feverish need to survive no matter how bleak was easy to discern among the masses.

The wide-bodied drone began to spin as a compartment opened in its belly and pieces, or chunks, flew out like fertilizer from a spreader.

"Food?" Naomi asked rhetorically.

Every alien in the confinement went into a feeding frenzy. The strong stepped over the weak to grab what they could. Those with more efficient appendages did better than those not suited for this type of dinner service. A minute went by as those with food prepared to fight off those that didn't. Naomi estimated about five percent didn't get anything to eat at all.

This was one of the saddest scenes she had ever witnessed. The heart crushing wails and cries were hard to listen to, even if they were the scourge of the universe, as Kia inferred. Does that still mean they deserve this? If this were to be the final destination of the human scourge, and if humanity knew what was here, would that end the violence back home? An interesting question that she asked herself again.

The somber gravity of the scene below did not mean she was oblivious to the fact that she was witnessing alien life. Alien sentient beings. Completely inhuman, yet still historic proof that life did exist among the universe. Another mystery solved, and another mystery she could tell know one.

This stunning revelation had to be pushed to the back burner as another sight caught her attention. Kia gently glided their bubble over to the northeast corner of the corral. This was the closest area to one of the many buildings and two shapes emerged from a doorway of the factory. She watched in awe as they walked, in their own unique way, into the corral.

"They are...solids!"

"Yes, they are the solids."

Naomi again struggled to control her biorhythms. If she were connected to an EKG, it would show an obvious tachycardia.

These solids were grotesque in appearance, which was a personal opinion, with few human similarities. They had two legs which made up half of their height, which Naomi guessed was close to fourteen feet. Four articulating arms sprang out from their midsection, like those of a crab. The two upper ones, she assumed, could be used to bring food up to their mouth, and the two long lower ones could be for mechanical use. Their heads looked like a hatchet fish: three bulbous forward-looking eyes and a mouth with no lips made its face evil in appearance.

"What are they doing?"

"Keep watching."

How could she not take her eyes off the poor alien that the two solids were approaching? It was lying prone, barely moving its body. It had two large antennae with two baseball shaped eyes wavering in the alien atmosphere. Sad, lonely eyes, pleading for help and compassion. Naomi could swear it was her that this alien was pleading to as its eyes searched skyward. One solid kicked at the helpless being to see what kind of fight it had left. All the kick did was initiate a desperate shrill that tugged at Naomi's heart.

She had to keep thinking that this alien had the history of a Hitler to not feel sympathy. It worked, but only barely.

Both solids turned to reveal stunning tails that wrapped themselves around the desperate alien, dragging it slowly out of the corral. Nearby, a group of about sixty aliens formed a line, like spectators watching a celebrity walk the red carpet. Similarly, they all kept quiet, not wanting to attract any more attention to themselves than necessary.

"What is going to happen with that body?"

"It will be shredded into feed for the others in the corrals."

The part of her bioelectric essence that was her stomach acid churned as if she just swallowed rancid meat. She was feeling loathsome and contempt toward these solids, however wondered if she had all the information.

"Are they suffering?" Naomi asked.

"Does it matter?"

A good question, she thought. Her obvious answer was yes, however, was it truly obvious? Was it easier to ignore their suffering because they did not look like her? She wanted to see more.

"Just because they don't look human, doesn't mean I can't feel something for them," she said defensively.

"It does please me that you feel the way you do. However, do you feel the same when your chickens and cattle are slaughtered?"

Another great question. Kia said the solids numbered in the hundreds of billions. With so many to feed, don't the solids deserve to survive if this food meant survival? If the solids' resources are growing thin, are they not allowed to look elsewhere to feed their population? The similarities between the solids and humans were thought provoking.

"Let's take a look inside one of their processing plants," Kia suggested.

Naomi didn't know how much more she could take, emotionally and philosophically.

"Do they know we are here?"

"They know I'm here. They don't know you are inside with me."

"They don't mind you poking around?"

"I am no threat to them."

Deep inside Naomi's brain, she was running a sub-routine, casually formulating a strategy on how the sheaths could be free from their obligations to the solids. None had come to mind so far. Naomi was still curious as to why Kia was showing her all this. Perhaps she should have left the barrier up.

Kia proceeded into the building by passing though the wall while at the same time, Naomi braced for impact as if she were in a pick-up truck with no seat belt and about to crash head on. Instead, they passed though the wall of the factory as easily as any cell phone signal could.

Naomi was immediately hit with the sound of machinery. Conveyors and processing equipment spread throughout the interior of the sprawling factory. But what drew her attention the most were the audible screams and wails. Torturous cries of agony.

"What's going on!" Naomi demanded.

"This is where each body is processed into food for the solids. They are dismembered, separated into parts, then either cooked or processed raw. In another building, the food is packaged then shipped out."

"Why the screams?"

"They are transferred here from the corals alive and processed alive. No anesthetic. Nothing to quiet the pain. However, some species can regenerate limbs or other body parts, so after dismemberment, they are sent to a special holding area where they are kept alive until they regenerate enough to be harvested again and so on, until their defeated will to survive ends their suffering."

Kia sensed a surge in impulses from Naomi that were strong enough to cause a dangerous instability within the bubble that Kia had to quell. She immediately put up the barrier between them.

"Please, Naomi, once again calm yourself."

Easier said than done, and that was a huge understatement.

"I'll try. I am trying," she shot back.

Naomi felt dizzy and nauseous. She had to relax before she lost control. In her thoughts only, she was taking in deep, controlled breaths and mentally felt a little serenity. Since the death of her sister on that tragic day, meditation was still one of her best friends.

"This is all so brutal and unnecessary!" she blurted out. The calm from within did not last long.

"Does it matter?" Kia reiterated.

"It shouldn't. Or should it? I don't know. This is too much to take in."

"Perhaps if you saw the bigger picture here?" Kia suggested.

There was silence from Naomi. "Do you understand that you have what no one in the universe has?"

"I do understand that once you give us an afterlife, those undeserving will be brought here, reanimated, then tortured for food."

"Once again, does it matter? Look at the bigger picture."

Naomi had not seen it yet.

"What I see in our future will be butchered humans. Experimented on to see what recipes produce the most palatable meals. Nothing wasted. Bones, organs, tissues. All to feed an oppressive species. You should be the first to object, or are you simply numb after eons of acquiescence?" Naomi asked.

"Do you see it yet? It's in what you said."

"I... need time to think. I want to leave, now!"

"There is still more to see."

"I've seen enough."

"As you wish."

Naomi felt their energy sphere begin to ascend, then off in the distance, a huge structure caught her eye. It was impressive, about eighty stories tall and came to a sharp point at the top.

"What's in there?" Naomi asked. "It's massive."

"I don't know. No one knows. We can't penetrate it."

"Isn't that a concern?"

"If there was a way to look inside, we could find out."

"It could be important," Naomi continued.

"We have been trying for centuries, but there is just no way to look inside."

"Fine. Then there is nothing else to say about it." It wasn't fine, because Naomi was damn curious. Since she wasn't doing the steering, that unknown structure quickly became a spec in the distance as Kia guided their sphere upwards through the alien atmosphere. If only she could take some samples back to earth. Totally alien and completely undiscovered samples, or even reveal the knowledge of this, yet it would be useless as no one would believe her. Plus, any samples could be...

And suddenly an incredible thought hit her and all else was forgotten.

"That's it!" She suddenly realized.

What Kia was hinting at. Totally alien.

The chemicals that made up these solids' environment and their existence and their bodies, could be deadly to humans. And... vice versa! Kia felt a special surge from Naomi's side of the border that was not dangerous at all but comforting as Naomi was beginning to reason it out. In no time they were back in the quiet of space. The silence was soothing like aloe on a burn.

"You take the helm, Naomi."

"Me? I don't think I can. I've just got too much on my mind."

"Take the helm," Kia urged. "It will be important."

Naomi knew why it would be important. She did her best to darken the disturbing images from before and replace it with the brightness of her beautiful home. She imagined Earth in its wonderful splendor. A stunning blue orb with its white cloud tops floating on a black canvas background. Feeling confident she had her destination locked into the sphere, away they went and in seconds they were outside of Kia's galaxy and seconds after that, they were piercing the Orion Spur, one of the long arm spirals of the Milky Way.

No rest stops on the way. No reason to stop for a pee or a lunch break. No flat tires or frustrating traffic jams to slow her down. Just an overwhelming sense of euphoria as their energy bubble slowed to a stop in orbit above Naomi's home.

So beautiful, this home. So peaceful, yet so restless on the surface. Why? One beautiful home with so many borders that kept us from really seeing the beauty. Naomi wished for a giant pencil with an even bigger eraser to rub out the lines on a map that kept humanity from achieving everlasting peace and longevity.

"Well done, Naomi. Well done."

Kia took over the rest of the journey, and once again they were standing in Naomi's living room. Kia felt like a heavy burden had been lifted from her. She had told her story for the first time. Now it was up to Naomi, Victor, and Joel.

Naomi said good-bye to Kia as the room flashed a blue light and she was back in human form, alone. She felt the floor with her toes and stretched out her body. This second out of body experience was far more impactful than the first, meaning it would be more of a mental recovery than a physical one. Yet the full body stretching sure felt great.

What time is it? she wondered. The answer was seventy-five minutes later than they had left. Just over an hour to travel the universe... and back.! That thought further overwhelmed her. She felt like she had just written a seventy-five-minute exam and didn't know if she aced it or failed. Sleep was what she needed. It would be a struggle at first to pass into slumber. There was one major decision that she still needed to make: to seek out the other two or proceed on her own. Her yearning need to know left her with the answer. An easy one. It was time to meet the other two.

Who is first? Flip a coin? Heads it was.

CHAPTER 27

Tuesday, October 28
10:26 pm local time

Kia was gone, leaving Naomi alone on this dirty dusty road, no doubt setting off more social media posts about black auroras. She stared up at the thousands of stars twinkling in the sky which she saw as newly opened destinations, should the sheaths allow. The temperature was comfortable for the clothing she had picked out, a simple black dress and worn sneakers. She had awakened after a few hours of needed sleep and had asked Kia to take her here.

Naomi approached the front door and made a fist, but stopped short of knocking as she took a few seconds to gather her thoughts. One more deep breath, then she rapped on the wooden door. The outside light came on, yet no one answered. She was a lone woman at night on a lonely Arizona road knocking on a stranger's door, but she felt safe even though the violence of this country was well known. She knocked again, timidly, barely loud enough for even her to hear. She saw the knob turn and then the door cracked open.

"Yes, what can I do for you?"

"I know this may sound strange but..."

"You're one of the others, aren't you?" Joel figured as he kept the door ajar just enough to show his face. He had never seen this woman before, but now that he was sober, he was not as stupid as before.

"Yes, my name is Naomi. And you are?"

"Joel."

He ran his eyes up and down Naomi's body, then studied her face. "You aren't the one waging war against the corrupt leaders of the world, that's obvious."

"Why, because I'm a woman?"

"Yes, because you are a woman." Joel opened the door a little more. "You seem irritated. I meant it as a compliment."

"I'm not offended." The truth was that she was too curious to be offended. "So, then what am I capable of?"

"Hmmm, how about MH370? Amelia Earhart. Stuff like that."

"You seem to know me more than I know you."

"It's not hard when we are playing this game from the inside. It's not a tough deduction. Then I should ask you, what do you deduce I am up to?"

Naomi looked around to see if there were any prying eyes. Ever since her chat with Colonel Weiss, every bush or rock could be hiding someone. "Can I come in? We have a lot to talk about."

Joel signaled with his eyes toward the interior and then opened the door fully, welcoming her in.

"Have a seat, over there." Joel pointed. "Can I get you something to drink? Unfortunately, maybe for you, I don't have any alcohol?" he added slyly.

"I get it," Naomi said, understanding right off what he meant. "Water is fine."

With his head buried in the fridge, he shouted out, "So, who did you know that was able to travel the universe with you?"

"My sister. She was killed when our town was attacked."

Joel reappeared with the bottle of water. "I'm sorry to hear that. Your town, somewhere in the middle east?"

"Very astute. Just outside of Jerusalem."

"That attack. The one on the news. And I can also surmise that you did not need an airplane ticket to get here."

Naomi rolled her eyes.

"So. What did your friend gift to you, exactly?"

"Nothing much, just all the answers to any question I ask her."

"From past events, I assume."

"Yep."

"Too bad. It would really help if you knew the future."

"In this case it would, but in general, I'm not so sure."

"I don't know. It would have sure helped me to make some better choices." Joel felt himself getting sad again, so he used a technique he learned and quickly altered the path of the conversation. "The planet is still buzzing about your amazing discoveries. I'm still buzzing. I can't wait to see what you discover next. Can I borrow your friend if I happen to lose my house keys again."

Naomi almost choked on her water. She knew he was kidding but got the message.

"How much has your friend told you?" Naomi asked.

"Not a lot. However, I think you know quite a bit more than me, if not all of it." He noticed the angst expression on Naomi's face. "And I have a feeling it's not all good."

"Then you don't know why they are doing this."

"I've wondered but then again, I'm not sure I want to know."

"You weren't curious?'

"I wasn't until you showed up," Joel added. "Of course, I would be stupid or naïve or surprised to think that they are doing this out of the kindness of their hearts." Joel would also be stupid not to notice the growing anxiety on this visitor's face. "You know something that's going to make me want to start drinking again, don't you?"

Naomi nodded along with a shrug, then spent the next few minutes telling Joel of the solids and the sheaths and her trip to the solids' home system. The entire time Joel was staring wide-eyed at Naomi, but not really at her but through her as his imagination was attempting to put into pictures her incredible story. Once she was done, he felt like he had just finished skydiving.

"If I had heard this tall tale in one of my meetings a week ago, I would have thought you were crazy. Now I understand when my wife and I were with L.J., he specifically mentioned not to visit their star system."

"Then you lost your wife. I'm so sorry."

"Thanks. But seeing her once more was..."

"It was, wasn't it." Naomi smiled.

Joel nodded.

"Weren't you the least bit curious as to why they wanted you to stay away?" Naomi asked.

"Not really, Naomi. I was just so caught up with spending time with my wife, seeing her free. Being able to talk to her and to hold her one last time..."

"I understand. Again, I'm so sorry."

Joel nodded then took a sip of his soda. "The whole process was amazing." He took a moment to reflect, then had to focus on the present. "But if I get what you're saying, you believe the sheaths' freedom depends on our existence?"

"Wouldn't you? It all seems to point in that direction. They seem to be taking risks with us that they normally wouldn't take with any others."

"Well. Mine hasn't said anything to me?"

"Kia hasn't come right out and said it either. In fact, she speaks in riddles at times, which is quite frustrating. I think she wants me to figure it out on my own."

"Why don't you ask her."

"Because I kind of want to figure it out on my own."

"I get it. Well, what you saw must have been traumatic."

"It was just so depressing, but it was also necessary. They are providing me with a reason. An explanation for what they are doing."

"Or a justification?"

"As much as Kia and her people justify it, they want the hold the solids have over them to end. They want to be free of having to be the suppliers to the solids. Yet, curiously, they have struck a very complicated agreement with these solids that has lasted an awfully long time."

"When is freedom ever simple," Joel added.

"It appears that a few things are universal. Slavery and violence, as well as the desire to end both and be free." Naomi spent a few more minutes filling in the rest of the story, which left Joel in stunned silence. The good news was he didn't need alcohol to deal with it.

"I can see why they want to take some risks. They want to be free. I, more than most, should understand. L.J. did allow me to alter my plan despite the potential danger, so they must think it is especially important that humanity survives."

"Unbelievable, isn't it?" Naomi said.

"I can't even believe what we are talking about. Black holes. Solids and sheaths. Travelling the universe. Eternal afterlife. Our future doom."

"The good news is we are all still here, the planet's still here. For now, anyway."

"Which leads us to what you told me. That you believe one of us, one of us three, have been given the chance to change our destiny," Joel realized.

"Then you do grasp what's at stake. Our survival could coincide with the death of the solids. I think Kia and the others are worried that every planet they save is one more planet that finds peace and one less planet that can fill their quota. And if the quota dries up significantly, the solids could start using the innocent for food. That thought is scary. Should they run out of evil, the solids will demand what's left. The innocent energy and the good energy. Kia could be forced to randomly pluck..."

"My god!" Joel spurted out. "My wife."

"...yes, reanimated to endure the torture and the pain as they are sent to slaughter. My sister and all those that follow." Naomi raised her brow, then added, "Even us, one day, might be plucked out of our eternal shells and sent to that horrific place, to be diced into food for those disgusting solids."

That deserved a moment of silence. Not a long one but enough for Joel to feel some frustration. "Once again, I say that if all this had happened a few months ago, I would have thought your story was loco, and I would be down at the local pub."

"And now?" Naomi asked, concern obvious in her voice.

"Now I feel... rejuvenated, for lack of a better word. I don't know how, but L.J. has rejuvenated me. I feel like I've been given a tool to further our cause. A very substantial tool. And now, I might be the one to change everything."

Tool or weapon, Naomi thought which confirmed to her that she was right to come here. She was more curious than ever to find out what Joel was planning, and Joel could see that in her face.

"I can tell you want to know what I am up to, that's obvious."

Joel got up to go to the bathroom without any notice. Naomi could hear his urine stream and had to chuckle. He was not what she imagined. He was the same age as her father, she guessed. But his face was more worn. No doubt from a life, or maybe just a few months, filled with stressors, and judging from a slight nervous twitch in his left hand and his numerous comments, he was a recovering alcoholic.

This made her wonder how the three of us were chosen. We all lost a loved one, which was a common thread, yet everyone has lost someone so it must be more. This man was not well off, living in a simple place, alone and near a dirt road and out in nowhere'sville. That can't be why they selected us. She shook her head and laughed. She did feel at home here, though. Perhaps it was their common vision for the future of humanity. Both her and Joel seemed to have the same belief that there were billions of people with unlocked potential that, due to their economic or political situations, couldn't open that potential. They both believed in unity and equality.

"You know, Naomi..." Joel called out from the bathroom. She could hear the toilet flush and was thankful to hear him washing his hands. Then Joel stepped back into the living room, shaking the water from his hands. "...you're not at all what I was expecting."

"Please tell me what you were expecting."

"Oh, someone older, in her forties, hippie type clothing, a few piercings, folky jewelry. Like a fortune teller."

"If I told you I left my crystal ball at home, what would you say?"

"I would say her name was Kia. But I do like your hair. That part does suit you."

Naomi ran her fingers through her hair in case it was out of place.

Joel sat down, then added, "You do remind me of my youngest daughter when she was your age. Free spirit. Smart. Wanting to know everything. And she too was a little adventurist with her hair color."

"I will take that as a compliment." Naomi could feel the skin of her face redden. "Now..."

"Yes, what have I been up to?" Joel was back sitting on the couch. He put his feet up on the coffee table. "It started quite innocently. My friend," Joel said, putting the word friend in air quotes, "kind of caught me at a bad time in my life. The night before I met L.J., I..." he decided against telling her about his unfortunate happenings at the saloon. "had this weird dream that I was this successful gambler who could never lose. Winning millions that I could donate to my foundation."

Naomi's eyes lit up.

"Something I said?" Joel asked.

"It's just that the night before I met Kia, I had a dream that people all over the world were coming to me with questions, so many questions about everything, and I had all the answers to..." she stopped and nodded. "Odd that I would just make the connections now. I guess having someone else with the same experience was the trigger."

"Which all means?"

"Well, dreams are mostly random electrical patterns, and the sheaths are mostly beings of electrical energy."

"Do you think?" Joel wondered aloud. "That they can see our dreams?"

"It's possible and fascinating!"

"Well, however it came about, I never did take what I was given seriously at first. I'm sure no one ever does. But as time went on, I became a believer, and it will be the answer to accomplishing a lifelong dream."

"I can tell you're getting excited; I can see it in your eyes, hear it in your voice," Naomi said.

"To make all of humanity, all eight billion people around the globe wherever they live, all... equal!"

"To... unify humanity!" Naomi whispered.

"Yes. Of course. That has always been our goal."

"That's what Kia stressed. It's the key to the longevity of all civilizations."

"Do you think that is the reason I was chosen?" Joel asked.

Naomi was in thought mode. It could be how the sheaths, as they travel the universe, try to help save one doomed planet after the other. Giving them, giving us, the tools to save ourselves. Yet what of my ability? It appeared to Naomi more and more that it was the other two that held the key.

"It's possible. Very possible, Joel. I need to know as much as you can tell me."

"I can start by telling you that Kelly and I met at a homeless shelter, likely before you were even born, and we spent our lives together in this battle for equality. Charity events, fundraising. Travelling when we could to the poorest nations. During our long flights, we would joke and fantasize about what we would do if we were ever to have supreme power over everything. You know, just passing time." Joel leaned his head back and laughed. "I never would have thought, ever in my wildest dreams, that I would be in the position to take all the wealth in the world and spread it among the poor."

"That is very ambitious, and I love it! And your new friend, L.J, says he can do this?"

"I would never have believed it possible either if he hadn't proven himself," Joel stated.

"Proven himself?"

"Yeah, one morning I was waking up after... an unfortunate incident, and there was this guy in my living room. He, well it's hard to describe, but he gave me the means to make a lot of money. I thought the whole thing was a prank, but once I realized that he was able to manipulate certain, uh could alter… well I still don't understand how, but I sent the majority of what I won to the foundation that is in honor of my wife Kelly."

"How much was it?"

"Millions!"

"L.J. took a chance on you, on humanity. You could have kept it all. You could have had corrupt intentions. Maybe it was just a test. A test or your morality?" Naomi said with a warm smile. "And Kia did say your L.J was a bit of a free spirit, but I had the sense Kia was more worried about his actions than she let on."

"Should I be worried?" Joel asked.

"I'm not sure," was all Naomi would reveal.

She did have a theory about what could be happening, yet now was not the time to go over it in her mind. She wanted to hear more of Joel's story.

"Not sure? Let me elaborate and maybe you'll know for sure," Joel said. "Once I realized what L.J. could do, I thought solving world poverty one bet at a time would take forever, so I proposed to him to take the worlds wealth and distribute it among the poor in one fell swoop."

"That seems impossible. Yet you believe he could do that?"

"He says he can, and I wasn't going to ask him how." Joel noticed Naomi drumming her fingers on the arm rest of his chair and her gaze focused on nothing in particular. "You have something?"

"Perhaps it is possible. I mean money and bank accounts are nothing but electronic transactions today. And they are beings mostly of electrical impulses."

"Well, however it's done..." Joel looked at his watch. "...in about eight hours, Jeff Bezos and Elon Musk will have the same net worth as, well, everyone else."

"Even you and I?"

"Yes, even you and I."

"Hold on, Joel. Have you thought this through?"

"I realize it might be extreme; however, if you have seen what I have seen, the hopelessness and the despair of the poor, most through no fault of their own, it's just... unfair."

"I know first-hand the struggle of so many. I agree. It's very unfair, and unnecessary."

"Then you see it too, my vision," Joel said, pleading his case.

"Don't confuse my worry for disapproval. There's no doubt that your plan will affect the entire world, but couldn't it also be overwhelming? Plus, you're going to piss off a lot of people."

"Those who I'm going to piss off are the one percent that have all the wealth? The way it is now, it isn't working for the vast majority. Delivery drivers, teachers, cooks, servers; they work just as hard as entertainers, athletes, and CEO's. Some even more so, and their jobs are just as important."

"You don't have to convince me, Joel. All I'm saying is there will be a lot of chaos in the short term until we adjust to the new conditions."

"I don't profess to have an economics degree from Dartmouth, but more than two decades of being in the trenches, well, that makes me qualified to at least try this. A lot of people will just have to learn to sacrifice and adapt to a world of equality."

Naomi's sigh was a hefty one; Joel could feel her breath. Even so, he was not about to back down from this once in a lifetime opportunity.

"If you are right that one of us will set in motion the events that will save humanity, how can this not be the start." He could tell she wasn't convinced. "Perhaps our future destruction is man-made, like a war. You can't fight a war without money, and you can't find men to fight that war if they have real hope. Then without war, think of all the off shoots of global equality. What if our future demise was another global pandemic? With access to clean water, food, and medicine like everyone else, we can lesson, if not eliminate, the chance of a global pandemic."

"I get it. I see your point; however, how do we know that your plan doesn't quicken the end of humanity?" Naomi was doing her best to get Joel to delay his plan until she could talk to the third.

This also was a great segue as breaking news appeared on the television. The banner across the bottom read, *Syrian war ends.* Above were scenes of citizens dancing in the Syrian streets as well as many other cities across the globe. The internet was alive and well everywhere.

"You see, change is already happening. As a result of the third, no doubt," Joel pointed out.

"But it's still not enough," Naomi worried.

Joel noted the same thing. "You would think the Syrian president lying in a puddle of goo would be enough. That image alone should be enough for our sheaths to come to us and say we did it. It must be something else."

"That is worrisome. I wonder if you could delay your plan until I can talk with the third? We need to know more about him."

"Perhaps this is our destiny. All three of us, unified, to stop the madness." Joel was fixated on the flat screen and all the joy and celebrations going on. "See that girl there." Joel paused the television. She was about fifteen. Her face was dirty, and her clothes were well worn. The long war there had taken its toll on her, but she was happy now. "Her ability to do great things has been retarded by a decade of war and poverty. Soon, billions of minds will be free to invent and to build and to design a better way to live. New medicines, new technology. And at the same time, live better themselves."

"The possibilities could be staggering!"

Joel resumed the telecast then Naomi asked him to pause the show. On the screen Naomi looked at a man, tears running down his face as he held his emaciated child is his arms. Those were tears of hope. Not false hope, but real hope that change was coming in time. Naomi was suddenly on board with Joel's plan as she envisioned a future of prosperity for all, and especially for that little girl. However, a lot could go wrong as the transition began. It could be too much too soon.

Again, Joel was fixated on the television. "Look what happens when we start to rid the world of violent old men who need to hang onto power at all costs."

"We?"

"Don't you believe the three of us are connected in some way? This third has the right idea. Aren't you curious as to who he goes after next?"

"I will find out soon enough," Naomi hinted.

"Along with the rest of the world. Take a look," Joel said, pointing at the screen with his thumb. There was a bulletin that four more world leaders had been reported missing. One from Eswatini, one from Burundi, and two from the middle east. "Are they in hiding, or does the third have them? That's four more countries that will have people dancing in the streets."

Naomi was shaking her head, not in disgust, but in awe and disbelief. More news was blanketing the screen. The Chinese leader had mobilized five thousand troops to protect his residence. 9-11, the last pandemic, the Iraqi war, Russia's successful invasion of Ukraine. All that past coverage combined couldn't compare to what was occurring around the globe.

"How about you bring me with you?" Joel asked.

"To see the third?"

"Of course. My mind is going crazy trying to guess who it is. A man or a woman. I think a man."

"Why a man? Because of the violence?"

"Yes, because of the violence. Isn't most of the violence in the world committed by men? So, the odds would seem to suggest that. And an older man. He's obviously suffered a loss like us. Possibly a poor man."

"I think he's wealthy, but the rest of your guesses are pretty good."

"You could be right, but if he is wealthy," Joel noted. "That could cause some problems for him." And a lot of conflict, Joel figured.

"And wealthy means I need to find out what his motive is for what he is doing. Is it for greed, or is his plan virtuous?" Naomi wondered. Finding out this mystery person's motive was at the top of her list. Hell, she still wasn't convinced of Joel's motive, which led the conversation in this next direction.

"You know, Joel, each of us have been given an enormously powerful weapon, I mean tool." Naomi made the mistake in words on purpose. "We need to make sure of our motives. We need to tread slowly."

"But what of the hundreds of thousands of people dying every day with no afterlife while we tread slowly?"

"I know, I know." Naomi sighed. Damn, another angle to consider. Still, that did not stop her from proceeding with extreme caution.

"I can tell that you're not going to take me with you," Joel surmised.

"I don't even know if it's possible to fit you in our bubble. Kia said she and I were in a symbiotic state. And I highly doubt L.J will risk any unnecessary transports. Hell, the next could be the last for us all, if you know what I mean." Naomi looked skyward to remind Joel.

"Man, I sure hope you're wrong. The last thing I want to do is cause a black hole." That was a phrase he thought he would never say in his lifetime. "How much time do you need?"

Once again, Naomi was lost in the breaking news as a video surfaced of three more countries joined in a military blockade around their respective leaders. A correspondent in the Belarusian capital reported seeing tanks and anti-aircraft guns being placed around the Palace, as well as hundreds of heavily armed militias in convoys heading into Zaslawye. Yet, there were also stories of mass deserters from generals down the ranks to privates. People were getting the message. They were just as fed up with the leaders they were once fighting for.

"They are only admitting their guilt," Naomi said softly.

Quickly, the telecast switched to Istana as a helicopter fled from the residence of the Brunei leader. There was no doubt who was on board.

"Soon there will be dancing on the streets in downtown Brunei," Naomi said in wonder.

"Yet, still not enough to prevent our own annihilation?" Joel theorized. "L.J and the others would certainly have let us know."

Yes, they most certainly would have, and without delay, Naomi thought through a furrowed brow. In fact, whatever alien celebration the sheaths had would be going on right after that event. What was going on in the world now, how could it not have altered, if not stopped, humanity's annihilation. This thought was setting off alarm bells in her mind.

"What's it going to take, I wonder," Joel said, loud enough for Naomi to hear. He was hoping for some affirmation, but she was engrossed with the breaking news. He doubted she even heard him. "Those oppressive leaders will soon discover that they will have no more followers."

"I can't believe what's happening. It's incredible. It's historic."

They both looked about the room because they were wondering the same thing.

"I know, Joel. Why haven't they come? Why haven't they come to tell us?"

"Has to be something else. Something greater," Joel wondered nervously. It preoccupied both their thoughts. It also made him want to begin right away. Then again, better to wait until she was gone. "Naomi?"

"Yes, Joel?"

Joel muted the sound on the television.

"When you found out that there was no afterlife, how did you feel? I mean; you are Jewish, right?"

"Is it that obvious?" Naomi wasn't offended. "I am more of a skeptic when it comes to the Bible and even religion in general, you might even say I might be one of many atheist Jews. But my sister was more of a modern Jew so to speak. She was more orthodox than me. She believed in resurrection and reincarnation. She believed that after death, we are judged by the actions we take while we were alive. Then God will give the good people a better place to exist once they die."

"Like these sheaths?" That connection made them both reflect for a good thirty seconds. Then Joel continued. "I can see how that belief can help one live a good life. Unfortunately, religion has as many extreme fanatics as it has righteous followers, if not more. So, how did your sister react when she found out that there was no afterlife? That death is final?"

Naomi took a drink of water, which was warm by now, then wiped some sweat off her forehead. She rubbed some of that sweat between her fingers and glared at it. Then she brought up the glass of water and stared at it as if it were a gold watch being dangled by a hypnotist. Or was it having one of the universe's rarest substances being dangled in front of her that was making her hypnotic?

"Naomi? Hello, are you still with me?" Joel asked, confused.

She then followed a fly as it darted about the living room. It eventually collided with the living room window, just missing the tiny opening that would have granted its freedom.

"She knows the afterlife she has now..." Naomi continued. "... and I don't think it matters to her anymore as to what it should have been. I do know, for certain, that she was incredibly happy."

"So, you were right all along."

"It's not often easy to be right and have everyone happy at the same time. All I know is that she now has an eternity to debate it, and that makes me very, very happy," Naomi said with a smile.

"My wife was Catholic, and she believed she would meet God in Heaven after she passed." Joel wondered if Naomi was thinking the same thing. She was.

"Do you believe these three are..."

"Don't ask me. I am a devout atheist, apparently like yourself." Joel winked at her. "Aside from all that, if you break it down, my wife and your sister will be the pioneers of a new science. Of a new religion." Joel's expression was one of contentment until he saw a frown grow on Naomi's face. "What's wrong?" he asked.

"We may be the only ones who will ever know the truth because who can we tell that will believe us?"

"Hmmm, you're right. Tell our tale, and we would come off as whackos," he said quietly. "You know, one time I was golfing by myself and got a hole in one, and until now, I never told anyone about it."

Naomi nodded as she understood the metaphor.

"Imagine us walking into NASA and telling them we know how black holes are formed, then you tell them about the sheaths."

"Imagine us walking into my class and explaining how we have travelled the universe with our deceased loved ones and how after we die, we... well, you get the picture."

"Then how are we going to spread the news when it's time? How are we going to convince anyone?" Joel wondered. "How are we going to convince all of the people who believe in God and all the hundreds of different religious beliefs to abandon it all for just one reality?"

"How to properly spread the word, I agree is the dilemma. The ghastly things I saw on the solids' planet won't be a deterrent if no one knows what awaits them there in the afterlife."

"Your Kia. My L.J.; they must have a way. I think there are many things about them we still do not know."

"She knows all I have to do is ask her. Perhaps the other two have stuff we don't know about. One thing I want to ask her, if humanity survives, is if she will allow me to retain my ability. You know, having all the answers can help a lot of people."

"Have you thought that knowing the answer to everything can make a lot of people nervous. You might want to get an unlisted number," he pointed out.

"The risk will be worth it, because it will help a lot of people."

"Pretty bold for a..." he peered into her eyes and really studied her face for the first time. "...for a twenty-two-year-old?"

Naomi blushed. "I will take that as a compliment. However, it's all moot unless Kia is willing and has a way."

"I have a feeling they have more power than they are letting on," Joel said with a suspicious undertone.

Naomi shook her head. "I don't think they are as scary as you imagine. As I said, I think Kia has been honest and straightforward."

"But they are beings mostly of electrical energy and our brains are made of electrical energy. Do you see where I'm going with this?"

"Is that a new category of racism, Joel?" she asked facetiously. "It's the way they are. They just want to save our world and free theirs. They want us to explore the universe after we die and see worlds that are in a state of peace, and farther from war. They want us to see a Disneyland, not The Gulag."

"Have you seen some of the lines at Disney on a hot humid day? Some might prefer the Gulag." His attempt at humor was a flop, so he quickly moved on. "That would be great if that's their true motive. Knowing that my wife will see nothing but wonderful places of natural beauty for all of time gives them a sense of legitimacy. That I will, one day, be able to see them with her?"

"I guess it's human nature to question anyone that's different, and they are different."

"Well, we are on our way to changing that." Once again, Naomi motioned with her head toward the television.

Joel raised his drink as a toast. "Then to equality and unification. The cornerstone to a lasting civilization."

Naomi was quick to acknowledge that sentiment. Then he changed to another subject while watching the content on the screen.

"How long do you think our third can maintain his anonymity? He hasn't exactly been shy about his intentions."

"He's been resourceful so far. And I'm sure governments all over the world have been flexing their tech muscles trying to find him."

Joel chuckled. "And you and Kia have bested them all. When you show up, I'm sure the third will be very surprised to see you."

"Surprised? Maybe angry as well." Naomi added.

"Angry?'

"What he's been doing shows a lot of pent-up anger about something from his past, that's obvious."

"Then he could take this too far"

"These sheaths have given us a lot of power, the power to change the course of a planet's future. That can be overwhelming to someone unstable."

"Thank god we aren't," Joel said with a wink. Naomi winked back.

The fly was long gone, and the only sound was the low hum of a bulb that was nearing the end of its life. Naomi gathered up the courage to mentally summon Kia and leave to face the third. Meanwhile, Joel was pondering hard what his blue-haired friend just said. He was sure he wasn't being affected by the power that Naomi had warned of. Then again, there was no way he was going to mention a possible alteration to his plan.

Joel fidgeted in his chair and leaned down to pull up both his socks. He needed a new pair. His new plan would afford him the luxury of socks with good sturdy elastics. Instead of L.J. spreading the wealth with whatever freaky power he had, Joel thought it might be easier for L.J to let him have all the money, and that way Joel could dole it out as warranted. That much control has sent many, make that every, man down the wrong path. Was Naomi's speech about universal peace and unification a strong enough influence to keep Joel to his true self?

When he sat back up, he glared at Naomi, wondering if she could sense what he was thinking. No, she wasn't like the sheaths, and this was just a plain old living room. He then shifted his gaze to a different news bulletin; this one was about another shift of three degrees in the earth's magnetic field and a large black aurora spotted in the skies over Zambia.

"Looks like our third is back at it," Joel pointed out.

He chewed on his lower lip as they interviewed the CEO of Quantas Airlines. He was talking about the potential suspension of flights should the shifts become lengthier and more severe.

"I better get going," Naomi said, as if she was about to call an Uber.

A quick flash of blue penetrated the blinds of a window facing Joel's backyard.

"My ride's here. Promise me you'll wait until you hear from me."

Joel was still fascinated with the happenings on the television.

"Joel!" she exclaimed.

"Yes, I promise." He then acknowledged her face to face. "Yes, I promise. Enjoy your trip," he finished.

Joel watched Naomi go into the kitchen then heard the back door close. He quickly went back to CNN as new drone footage showed the Palace of the leader of Saudi Arabia being surrounded by tanks. Joel didn't want to wait, yet he promised. A tug of war raged in his conscience. Impatience was strong and was gently pulling his obligation to Naomi into the mud. His lifelong dream was just a thought away.

Meanwhile, Naomi was joined by Kia out back of Joel's spread. Only a dim back porch light lit the area and Naomi began sniffing the air like a bloodhound.

"Do you feel it?" she asked.

"I do." Kia answered. "Something is watching us."

"Something? You mean someone."

"I'm not sure. I've never felt anything like it."

The fact that Kia had experienced all the universe had to offer for as long as time is old, and she had never felt anything like it before? That thought unsettled Naomi.

"It's hard to explain, but I have felt this before," Kia then realized with a hint of fear in her voice. "It is a someone to me." There was no fencing behind them, and she could easily say it was just a wild animal encroaching on them. If only it were that.

"Let's get going, Kia. I don't like it here anymore."

"I agree. Are you ready?"

"You know the destination?"

Kia nodded, then absorbed Naomi's energy into her sphere and they were off to visit the third.

From the kitchen window, Joel's curiosity could not help him from witnessing this amazing process. His eyes sparkled from the reflection as Naomi was swept away. Then another sphere of twinkling light caught his attention as it followed Naomi's sphere, then both vanished, leaving Joel shaking his head, wondering if it was just an illusion or if he saw what he thought was something else.

"Could there be a fourth?" he wondered.

That thought did not sit well with him. He felt a tad nauseous, and he needed to tell Naomi about what he saw, but how to contact her?

Because he was stupid enough not to get her number, there was only one way. How long would it take for L.J. to hear him?

CHAPTER 28

Wednesday, October 29
5:45am local time
One-hundred and fifty-thousand
kilometers from Earth

"I don't understand," Echo thought to L.J.'s sphere which was hovering next to his.

Kia had just arrived after dropping Naomi off in the vicinity of Victor. Echo's energy bubble was losing its roundness, much like a soap bubble wafting in the air, but not bursting. It was his way of showing agitation.

"I feel it also. It's disconcerting. I sense both your presences, but is there something else nearby?" L.J asked.

"Or someone," Echo said. "Similar properties to our electrical thoughts, yet not exact," he added. "Could there be a fourth? Could we have sent a fourth?"

"That was never an option. We decided, long ago, never to send a fourth," Kia stated forcefully. She could then feel a shift in negative emotion directed at her sphere. "What's wrong?"

"Why did you bring Naomi to our system? Why did you bring your human to see it all?" Echo asked. "Perhaps they sent someone to ask you just that. Perhaps something bad has come of it. Since the beginning, we've told all the others to stay away, yet you decided to allow her to know it all. You might have upset a few of our directors."

"I wanted someone to know the truth. I wanted to find a way to end the solids' tyranny over us for the last time. We've discovered a way, finally, and we need her help and her trust. The more she believes in our cause for freedom from the solids, the more she will trust us and help us," Kia explained. "When she speaks, the others will listen to her, which makes it even more imperative to gain her trust."

The other two were deep in thought. They didn't want to respond without fully hearing Kia. Not just hearing her but learning from her emotions as well.

"I understand, Kia, why you did what you did," Echo lamented.

L.J. agreed by sending that same feeling. "There is another..." he stopped as they both felt nothing coming from Kia.

There was another reason Kia revealed it all to Naomi and she didn't want the others to know. A reason that brought on a powerful emotion that made her put up her barrier, effectively shutting the others out completely. An emotion she had been feeling for a long time until it had welled up inside her and was ready to burst.

It wasn't time to reveal to them that she wanted this to be her last mission. That it was her time to end her existence like many others had before. Much like someone in the final stages of a painless cancer, she was losing the will to continue. It would take all she had to keep this from them. In their eternal friendship amongst each other, shutting one off from the others had occurred only during the early times of their exploration, at a time when they were just starting out and learning the nuances of their abilities.

Echo and L.J. felt the exclusion but didn't want to push the topic further at this crucial time. Kia would let them know when she was ready. A few moments later, Kia had calmed down and was communicating again.

"Let's move closer and wait. And just be ready. If that energy is a fourth sent to us, then they will seek us out eventually."

"Agreed," Echo said.

"And if it isn't?" asked L.J. There was no response.

The trio began the slow trek to Earth to either wait to be summoned or, hopefully, wait for the spectacle that told them that this planet was safe from future destruction. In the meantime, all three were wondering the same thing. Why hasn't that spectacle already happened? Based on what Echo's companion had done, that should have been more than sufficient to alter these humans' future. Something was wrong, and they all could not help but think it had to do with that fourth energy.

CHAPTER 29

Wednesday, October 29
5:50 am Local Time
Nkotakhota Wildlife Reserve.
Malawi

It was a gorgeous sunrise as Victor leaned one hand on a rough railing, which ran the length of this wooden deck. The other hand held a hot cup of black Ceylon tea. There was little visible steam rising from the drink because it was already a balmy seventy-three degrees out.

Victor visited here often for two reasons. One was for the area's sheer beauty. The other was because this was his reserve, bought and developed solely as a refuge for the animals, and a place of education for the many poor children that lived in the nearby shanty towns.

As proud as he was of this, he had more urgent concerns, one of which was the black auroras being tracked on social media, and he couldn't help but notice a correlation between these events and his meetings with Echo. The other auroras positively confirmed his suspicion that there were others like him, each with their own new friend. And necessity being the mother of invention, there was now an app to track these auroras, which coincidentally, his company had developed in rapid speed. He would check this app shortly; however, all his electronic devices were inside, which allowed him a little peace and quiet among the early morning songbirds.

This calming moment was interrupted by a slight vibration nearby. He looked from side to side but saw nothing; he wasn't a stupid man. Victor was certain he would eventually get a visit from one of the other two. Who would it be?

There was only one small lane that led to the front of this bunkhouse, and he did not see the need to walk around to greet this visitor. Nor would he walk down to the water's edge to see this person arrive by boat. His spider senses were spot on as the visitor was here, arriving the same way he had been travelling of late.

"Would you like some tea?" Victor asked without moving his gaze from the sunrise.

There was still a mystery to solve. Would the visitor be a man or a woman? Based on his deductions, he guessed female, older like himself. While he didn't know why he or the others were chosen, it was his opinion they used a formula known only to them.

"No thank you," came a woman's voice. Footsteps approached him. "Beautiful view!"

"Can't beat it." He turned to greet his guest. "Nice to finally meet you. I'm Victor, and you are?" He tried to remain cool.

"Naomi." She studied him for a brief period in a way to not make it obvious. "You're what I expected. Sort of."

"Sort of?" Victor smiled.

Naomi noticed that his teeth were white and straighter than normal for a man his age, which she guessed around fifty-five. He appeared wealthy, as dental work like that doesn't come cheap. Yet the rest of his appearance screamed poor. Tattered shirt, ragged shorts, worn flip-flops, no jewelry or expensive watch on his wrist. His house was charming, rustic, and simple. Still, he was wealthy. He just had to be, because if he was the one responsible for these high-profile kidnappings and tortures, he would need the means to remain anonymous. That meant sophisticated technology, and that meant money.

Victor could tell she was eyeing his appearance. No doubt forming a judgement. Well, she wasn't alone. He saw a youthful woman, a free spirit based on her hair color and seventies style dress. Highly intelligent, he decided based on nothing but his intuition.

"L.J., my mentor for lack of a better word, had been tight lipped about answering my questions. Information is very hard to come by."

"No doubt you've asked as many questions as I have."

"I think all of them," he joked. "But I am not privy to all the answers you are, am I right."

Naomi raised her brow and smiled slyly.

"You helped to find MH370." It was a statement more than a question.

"You are very clever, sir."

"Sir?" He said that with the voice of an incredibly old man. She got the gist. "Please, call me Victor."

"I'm sorry, Victor it is."

"Have you met our third?" He asked, narrowing his eyes. Naomi also narrowed hers. "Hmmm, let's do this right, Naomi. No secrets. Mutual co-operation. Trust."

"It's hard for me to trust people, especially strangers," she admitted.

"Because I am a man? An older man?"

Naomi was quiet and avoided eye contact.

"It's all right. I don't trust old men in general either as you can see by who I've... uh, well let's get to that later. And there is no doubt you have a legitimate reason not to trust me; however, we were chosen for a reason, you, me, and our third. We have a common goal. So, how about it?"

Victor extended a hand. Naomi moved a step closer then reached out and shook it, cautiously at first, then with more acceptance. There was an air of relaxation that was desperately needed.

"You have made quite a stir," Naomi stated. "More than a stir. A tidal wave."

"Your tone says you approve."

"The world is changing because of what you are doing, and it's long, long overdue. Yes, I approve."

"You know, the only approval I could hope for would be from my little girl, but yours, that's important also."

Naomi sensed a pinch of vulnerability when he mentioned his little girl. He was as close to her as Naomi was to her sister, she was certain.

"Your little girl, is that who you lost? Were you able to visit with her?"

"I lost my only daughter. And the visit with her... it was incredible. It was... exhilarating, but even more so, it was inspiring. This amazing gift Echo gave me could give us all inspiration after losing a loved one. Grief, sadness, and pain would be so much less. When my Charlie died, a part of me died with her. My wife was devastated. We should have turned towards each other, but at times we grew apart."

Victor could tell by Naomi's somber expression that she was truly listening and was very understanding. It felt good.

"And your first broadcast, that had a lot to do with her death?"

Victor nodded. "It was necessary and therapeutic. Beyond being selfish, if this can deter even one future person from causing others that same pain, it will be worth it. You know, Naomi, it's easier dealing with her loss knowing that she has a peaceful and eternal afterlife. Loss can be debilitating. Grief can be debilitating.

His mood turned bright, and he stood up tall and straight. "I was doing some daydreaming before you came. In fact, I've been doing a lot of that since they came."

"You're not alone," Naomi stated.

"Their arrival made me do a lot of fantasizing. I was just imagining when I die, being able to view my own funeral if I want."

"Would you want to?"

"I've been a good boy for the most part." Victor laughed. "Funerals from now on could be a celebration of something new and exciting. And the saying 'they are looking down on us' can be real and comforting. When I pass, I could see the love and support I've brought to others throughout my life, but some may prefer to just head out and explore the universe!"

"It could be an incredible choice to have. A life altering gift, an afterlife altering gift. It would change the entire way we approach and deal with life and death," Naomi added, emphasizing the word could.

"I know, and we seem to be on the path to screwing up the whole thing. What a chance we could be blowing."

"It appears it's up to us to unscrew the screwing up."

"Let's hope we aren't too late. I've always thought, strangely enough, that the only chance humanity had to clean up the mess we made was alien intervention."

"You aren't alone."

"Well, we are well on our way. If we are successful, humanity's attitude and optimism regarding life and death could make the days approaching our own death much easier to contemplate. I am sure in the days before I pass away, I will be comforted in knowing I can continue, not in a physical way, but a real, tangible, and spiritual way. Which makes it even more urgent that we move forward as quickly..."

"...and as prudently," Naomi reminded him.

"Yes of course, as prudently as possible. We can't waste this incredible opportunity they are giving us."

"You emphasized the word opportunity," Naomi said, fishing for more.

"I know that one of us can stop humanity's impending destruction." Victor's voice struggled to complete a statement that could be considered inconceivable. He then saw that Naomi was just as troubled with the notion that humanity was on the precipice of annihilating itself. "What's wrong?"

There was sweat slowly rolling down her face. Was it the stress of the situation or the rising heat?

"You could use a drink, Naomi. Have a seat over there and I'll get you some juice?"

Naomi agreed.

"I'm certain we have time for that," he joked.

A few minutes later, they were both sitting in deck chairs. Naomi lapped down her juice like an antelope at a watering hole. Victor noticed her nervousness as he rocked back and forth. The next few minutes were difficult as Naomi spent them telling Victor of her journey to Kia's star system and what the solids were doing. Now he knew another of the many reasons for the sweat. This time it was Victor's mouth that went dry as his swallows came up empty.

"This juice is quite good," Naomi said. "Quite fresh too."

"Never mind the juice, Naomi. If I had heard this implausible story..."

"I know from anyone other than me."

"Just give me a minute. I need to digest this."

Naomi would have been surprised if he didn't need time. She watched him squirm and could imagine the hamster in his head, turning the wheel and trying to make sense of all this. Would his reaction be acceptance of the solids' right to survive any way they could, or repulsion? Permission or rejection of the methods they used to survive?

"Is it wrong to think that what the solids are doing is okay?" he finally asked. "We spend a lot of our resources to feed and clothe and house the millions of violent criminals and murderers, whereas these solids use them as resources. Outsourcing all our criminals to the solids would..."

"I know what you're getting at, but do you not feel sympathy for Kia, L.J., Echo? They are the ones being forced to do the outsourcing and with the threat of their own destruction hanging over them."

"Do you really think the solids would destroy the ones who are supplying them with food?"

"I think there is fear on both sides. However, the solids and the sheaths have formed an arrangement that works for them. The result is peace between them and the solids that has lasted throughout time."

"Yes, but a forced peace, and the result is the torture of others. If you could have seen that processing factory and the feeling of despair and horror. Being skinned and dismembered alive."

"Despair? Interesting choice. Do you feel sympathy for them? As you said, since they look like animals, perhaps imagining them as cattle would make it more... palatable."

"Is that what you're doing? Making it palatable?"

Victor scratched his right knee, then did up one of the buttons on his shirt that had come undone. This Naomi was making him question whether the solids were justified or a monstrous race. Both on opposite sides of the moral spectrum. Then Naomi added more food for thought.

"Unfortunately, I know what was in those corrals. They were sentient beings. I know now that intelligence does not just walk on two legs, have forward looking eyes, or even a human face. Intelligence has universally unique and alien features."

"As does hatred."

"We don't truly know what crimes these beings committed. Minor or heinous? What is the measuring stick that sentences them to this horror?" How she could feel sympathy for who the solids were killing, yet contempt for the humans Victor was killing? It was confusing at first but was becoming clearer as time went on. "What it boils down to is do I, do we, accept the story we've been told? They want a peaceful universe and one that is accessible to all. I believe Kia," Naomi wasn't finished. "Do you believe me?" she asked with eyes that met his straight on.

"Sharing thoughts with them makes for an incredibly powerful experience and, well, that bond is hard to explain. I do believe you," he said with confidence.

"They have made a lot of sacrifices, the sheaths. They isolated their private little war to save so many civilizations. She had a reason for revealing her story, and I have no doubt it was necessary."

"I guess the proof is in front of our eyes. I sent most of the barbaric leaders running. Some will flee, some will commit suicide, and some I am not done with. Many lives will be saved, and who knows, we could be getting a visit any moment now telling us that humanity is no longer an endangered species."

He waited for a debate, but there was none coming. She sighed and Victor knew what was on her mind.

"I know. Why haven't they come to tell us?" He slapped his thigh, then added, "We can't second guess ourselves. We continue our paths until that event occurs. We can do it. You, me, the sheaths, our third. United, we all stand."

"I know we must. I agree," she said with a lot of enthusiasm. "I don't want anyone else to have to go through what I did. And I want as much as anyone to prevent whoever or whatever is threatening our future."

Victor was relieved to get Naomi's thumbs up, however, there was a noticeable concern lingering about Naomi that needed to be addressed.

"What is it?" he asked in a caring manner.

"I just don't know how much help I can be. If Kia could provide me the answers to our future, what a difference that would make, but she can't. It doesn't seem to me that I'm really needed as far as preventing some future catastrophe. I guess all I can do is try to help you?"

And help Joel.

That part she kept to herself. Joel's obvious contempt for the wealthy and his plan for economic equality could cause friction with Victor that they didn't need at this critical moment.

"Don't minimize your importance. Yes, Naomi, I believe you hold the key to everything."

"Me?" That statement sent shivers through her, even in this heat. "I... I don't know what to say."

"I see leadership in you. I see in you what our future needs, and that is youth and a vision of how humans need to unify to endure. You believe in that, and the alien that bonded with you sees that in you as well. You may not know the future, but I see you leading a new generation of leaders. Kia sees it as well."

That statement packed a wallop, and she guzzled down the remainder of her juice then put the empty bottle on the table beside her. She got up and went to the railing and looked at the rising sun. Could what he was saying be true? She felt a shiver which did not stand a chance in the humid morning air. If this was all true, she felt ready. Ready for whatever Kia had in store for her. She turned around and faced Victor.

"But what about your bond...?"

"With Echo? It's more like a business arrangement. Yours is different."

"How do you know that."

"It was one of the few things that my friend mentioned. Plus, in the brief time you and I have known each other..."

"Very brief," Naomi interrupted.

"Still, I see and feel something special. Your Kia sees it too. I see her leaving you with an incredible gift. If humanity has a future, I see a future where you can answer the question of who is guilty and who is innocent. Punishing the right people is an enormous responsibility but think beyond just helping me: truly think of the potential. Retaining that gift from Kia could mean you can free all the innocent people in jails all over the world. Imagine hundreds of mothers and brothers lining up to ask you if their loved ones in jail are innocent or guilty. No more trials will be needed. No more juries, just you with all the right answers. And imagine, of the hundreds of thousands of missing people all around the globe, you will know precisely where they are and what happened to them. That is closure for mothers and fathers and brothers and sisters. The possibilities are endless."

It was like Naomi was wearing VR goggles as she stared outward at nothing, seeing all those possibilities.

"Not to mention the mysteries you can solve. Who killed JFK? I ask you and you tell me. Was there water on Mars, and you tell me. What happened to the dinosaurs, and the answer comes to you like two plus two. You, my child, will be in high demand!"

That demand meant tremendous responsibility. Every utopia had at least one snake in it, she thought. There are a lot of people who want their secrets to remain buried. But snakes can be tamed. Naomi brought up her forearm and did her best to wipe away the sweat that had returned on her forehead and face.

"You're hoping the same thing, I can see it," Victor said. It's the same look Charlie would give me when she wanted something badly. "You want your gift to stay with you when they leave."

"Is it that obvious?"

Victor nodded.

"Have you gotten any hints from Kia?"

"None. It's another thing I haven't asked."

"Is that because you are afraid the answer might be, yes?"

"In a way."

There was another pause for thought. Then Victor spoke.

"Are we ready for that much responsibility? And power?"

"You most of all should know what it can do to a person, having too much power. Maybe some things are best left unknown for now," Naomi realized.

Victor had stopped rocking his chair. She was right. "The sheaths may not have the ability to transfer their abilities permanently, as much as they might want to in this case. Or even if they can, it could be a sheath rule not to. Their version of the prime directive. Of course, it would all be moot if we fail to stop our imminent destruction."

"Have you ever wondered to ask how they do it all?" Victor asked.

"Not really. Well, not yet. I probably wouldn't understand even if it was explained to me. Kia and the others have abilities that are just best left to mystery and imagination. Sure, it's fun to speculate, but right now speculation is good enough for me."

"So, what is your speculation?"

"A layman's opinion?"

"Is there any other? We're in uncharted territory."

She tossed him an impish grin. "I think it has to do with electrical energy, which seems to be the most common property in the universe."

"Electrical energy?"

"They are beings made up of electrical energy. Apparently, electricity, electromagnetism, and all their forms are the most abundant properties in the universe."

"Next to water."

Naomi cleared her throat. "That is another fascinating theory I'm working on, but in this case, I think they can convert or manipulate electrical energy and impulses in a way that is far more advanced than anything we can conceive of. Every cell in our body conducts electrical impulses. Electricity is the key to survival. Without it, our species would have died out long ago. Kia and others like her are pure electricity. They understand it on a level that is absolute. Since our cells and our brains and our thoughts and our dreams are electrical impulses... put that all together and I can see how it's possible to do what they can."

"I think I understand. So why, then, don't they manipulate our thoughts?"

"Simply, they don't want to. Maybe it is some sort of prime directive as you said, but anyway, they wouldn't know what to manipulate our thoughts toward."

"I get it." Victor imagined it all. "This is all so fantastical. To know that when we die, we continue to hold onto a tiny amount of electrical energy, just one atom of that energy, that these sheaths can then adapt to or transform in the ways we've seen! They just need a tiny sample to remain. It's like our electrical DNA. Blueprints of who we are. Like photos."

"And can we speculate as to how they can perceive the event that ends humanity?" Victor suggested.

"All right, I think it's like an explosion."

"An explosion?"

"Any future explosion or release of billions of deaths would create a massive singular blast of electricity. So powerful that I believe time itself would be no match for the sheaths' ability to perceive it. But only perceive it as a catastrophic event without the specific details."

"Fascinatingly sci-fi. Multiple timelines? So many possibilities, which still brings us back to the million- dollar question. Why hasn't that end sensing event happened here yet?" Victor asked. "It's unfathomable to think I haven't done enough to change our future. I always believed it would be a crazy unstable leader unleashing a nuclear holocaust."

"It must not be that, then."

"Then this mystery person, which I have yet to meet, and you undoubtedly have, must be the one to change our future."

The cat was almost out of the bag. Naomi tried to cinch the bag up by changing the subject.

"When do you think this event will occur. Weeks from now? A year. Decades?" Naomi asked.

Victor resumed rocking his chair. It was obvious she didn't want to discuss the other for some important reason. He decided to let it go for now.

"I believe it will be sooner rather than later. We just went through a near catastrophic war in Ukraine. With Russia victorious, that leaves a lot of other nations emboldened. After the attack near your town, the entire middle east is close to war. Violence in the United States is at a historic high. People around the globe are living in fear. The sheaths couldn't have come at a better time. The end could be just around the corner."

"If it is war that destroys us, then I guess you haven't grabbed the right person yet," Naomi pointed out.

"I guess I have to go through every single brutal leader until I get to the right one. Still, I shouldn't have to."

"How so?"

"The ripple effect."

"You mean all the leaders who are running scared? I get it. Then again, you might not have scared the right one. Or the right one might not care about what you're doing."

"He will. He will," Victor repeated.

"Just keep doing what we think is right, that's all we can do. These sheaths have put a lot of trust in us. We will make that difference."

"The enormous number of thoughts and events and knowledge released in the penultimate death of a civilization would fill up a trillion computers. And they do it naturally and all inside that tiny bubble!"

Naomi had never considered that fact. Naomi didn't see Kia as a massive supercomputer, but a being with a vulnerability. One with emotions and feelings.

"I see what you're saying, Victor, and as complex as they might be, they need our help. We need each other. They could be more like us then they are different."

"You have more insight into who they are than I do. Visiting their star system and listening to their story helped. It gave them a human vulnerability that you could relate to," Victor said.

"I sure would have liked to have seen them in their natural environment."

"I bet you asked, and I bet she said no."

"She didn't think it was the right time."

Naomi bowed her head.

"What's wrong?"

There was silence except for the creaking of Victor's rocking chair.

"Naomi?"

"Kia's been a little vague, but I am sensing a common human emotion coming from her that is strong, yet she's trying to hide it at the same time. I've been trying to process it just like everything else, but it's there and it could be serious."

"Whoa! How can anything be more serious than what's already happening?"

A small iguana had crawled up the side of the bunkhouse and was staring at the duo from close range, yet neither noticed it. A colorful finfoot had waddled onto the deck, hoping for a regular handout, but left as he got no attention.

"What emotion?"

"Depression."

"Depression? It's hard enough to tell if a human is depressed, but then again, I can imagine the constant exposure to the war and dealing with the planetary scenarios they come across time after time can be..."

"Depressing?" Naomi finished Victor's thought. "I have the impression that she's tired. An eternity of slavery has taken a toll. If we can succeed here, save ourselves, free the sheaths, then Kia's fantastic journey will be a success. It might help to rid her of that depression."

"And the other two... wait! Did you just say free the sheaths? What does that mean?"

"Uh, if you don't mind, I've given you enough absurd theories for one morning. I would rather sit on this one for a while longer."

Victor stared at Naomi, hoping his pleading gaze would change her mind, but he could see that she wouldn't budge. "Fine, but not much longer."

Victor nervously rocked back and forth in his chair to a point where he almost lost control. He slowed to a stop, then paused to gather his thoughts.

"I still keep circling back to why we haven't succeeded all ready." Victor was showing his frustration and his impatience. It was time to switch topics. Victor felt comfortable with his new friend. It was time to show her what hackers had been trying to find out. It was time to trust her.

CHAPTER 30

Wednesday, October 29
6:30am Local Time
Nkotakhota Wildlife Reserve.
Malawi

Victor finished what was left of his tea and unexpectedly excused himself, went inside then came back holding a photo. Victor pulled his chair up next to Naomi and handed it to her. It was a picture of his daughter, before the accident, before the wheelchair. Naomi studied the girl that Victor had his arm around. She looked at the picture, then Victor, then back to the picture. He was younger by about six years. They appeared to be celebrating a moment, yet she didn't know what that was. She handed the photo back.

"That is my daughter, Charlie. That photo was taken at a particularly important time in my life for a reason that will become evident. First, I have to say that I have read thousands of resumes but there is nothing like looking directly into someone's eyes to truly tell a person's character and strength. You have that strength, just like my daughter."

Naomi saw Victor holding that photo with delicate care. It was not crinkled or creased. It was pristine for its age which emphasized its importance in Victor's life.

"That picture, with you and Charlie, you said it was an important moment." She could tell it was a topic Victor was eager to discuss.

"My path in life changed drastically from that moment on. All my decisions came from that moment."

Naomi had lost track of time as their dialogue was captivating.

She leaned in anxiously.

"Charlie was twelve in that picture. Born with a silver spoon in her mouth. I was very wealthy back then, but you knew that, didn't you?"

"I had a feeling, but you said wealthy in the past tense. That wasn't a mistake, was it?"

Victor shook his head and continued. "One morning, I was about to leave on a business trip, and Charlie came to me, tears in her eyes, and said, *Daddy, I'm afraid.* I couldn't understand what could make her so fearful. We had an enormous, gated house. Private school. The best medical care. She wanted for nothing. Then she clarified. She said, *I am afraid about my future. The way the world is, I'm afraid.* I must have stared into her eyes for must have been an eternity and realized she truly was afraid. And it hit me. Hit me hard."

Naomi could sense Victor was reverting to that moment by his wavering tone and sad expression. He was reliving that moment, which lent to even more of an emotional impact to his story.

"Charlie made me realize that I was the source of her fear. Not I, as in her father, but I, as in myself and others like me, living lavish lifestyles while so many suffer. She saw me flying the world in my private jet, my empty jet spewing enough pollution for a hundred people. She asked why her one tuition for her private school was so much when that money could send a hundred kids in the poorest nation to school with books and lunch. Then guess what?"

"She asked you to put her in a regular school."

"The next week she was being bused to a public school." Victor wasn't sick, but he seemed to have developed the sniffles. "She also showed me these correspondences between her and a friend she was writing to who lived very far away. Her name was Tamanda. They had become friends, but her friend died three days before I knew anything about their friendship. She had kept it a secret from me. She thought I would be angry. Imagine what I thought when my little girl thought I would get angry at her for making a friend who was poor."

Naomi thought this was so sad and decided just to listen.

"She said her friend died of malaria and she was malnourished. The kicker was that I noticed a charge on my credit card that wasn't mine. I didn't understand it at the time, but it turned out that Charlie had used my card to buy the medication and some food, but the medication never arrived in time."

"I'm so sorry, Victor."

"Imagine how I felt. My own daughter couldn't ask her own dad for help. Her own rich, privileged, elitist father. Since then, I have been using all the resources at my disposal to develop places like this." Victor spread out his arms. "This is a refuge for endangered species of all kinds."

He winked and Naomi knew what he meant by endangered species.

"This is one of eighteen such places scattered about the globe. I manage this reserve and the others from this single bunkhouse. So many can benefit from this gorgeous piece of land overlooking Lake Malawi. This house is one of thirty-six similar bunkhouses spread about this seven hundred square mile sanctuary. And we just finished construction of a fourth schoolhouse, which is just three miles north of here. More than eight hundred school children receive nourishing food and valuable education, and hundreds of jobs have been created as well."

"You blame yourself for the loss of Charlie's friend, I can tell, but it did change you. You learned, you understood, and you changed. Perhaps that's why we were chosen by the sheaths," Naomi said softly.

Perhaps it is why, he thought to himself.

"And all what you have here comes from a promise to your daughter?"

"All of it. My greed, for lack of a better word, was more destructive than I could have ever imagined. My greed was destroying humanity and sucking the hope out of millions. Not just mine, but greed all over the world. How can humanity survive and thrive long term when one man can have a billion while a billion have nothing? Charlie opened my eyes. Who I was, was the example of a way of life that is unsustainable for humanity to endure. This fragile human pyramid that is our civilization must be strong from the ground up for it to endure. Pandemics, diseases, and many wars are born from poverty, and along with it comes the exploitation by those who have wealth and power. That needs to end." Victor shifted in his seat, emotions tempting to get the better of him. "Do you know the last words my daughter said to me before she passed away six years after that picture?"

Naomi could feel tears form and she was not concerned with holding them back.

"'Daddy, I'm so proud of you. Don't ever stop. I... love you.'" Victor's eyes welled up. He shook his head in an overt attempt to stem the flow. It worked for him, yet Naomi had a stream down each cheek. She then heaved a heavy sigh and let out a huge breath of air, which helped for more than one reason, which Victor was about to find out.

"It felt great to tell someone about that," Victor admitted. "I haven't told many. I would never have thought to tell all of this to a stranger."

"The word stranger should mean the joy and excitement of meeting someone new, but in today's atmosphere, it usually brings out fear and mistrust. I am honored that you feel the former. You know, I think our youth can teach us a lot if we give them the chance. We need more youth in places of power. They have an insight that these old men can never see."

"That will happen. There are a lot of voids that will need to be filled in a lot of countries, and they will be filled with more young scholars and scientists and no more politicians."

She raised her glass as a toast. "To Charlie."

He was quick to join her.

"You seem relieved after my story. Is there something else on your mind?" Victor asked.

"Might be everything. Your story might make all the difference." She leaned back, looked around then made direct eye contact with Victor. "I have met our third," she finally admitted.

"I already knew that." But it got his attention anyway. "And you just learned something about me that made you decide that now is the time to tell me?"

"You saw that in my eyes?"

"I see a lot of things face to face, remember," he responded with a slight grin.

"What I need to tell you about Joel is what he's doing with his helper, L.J. I was afraid to tell you earlier because I thought his goals would be in direct opposition to your way of life. I thought this may interfere with what you are doing. But now I see, pleasantly see, that there will be no conflict. It's fascinating how that worked out."

"Or lucky?"

"I don't believe that. Not with these sheaths. They have such abilities beyond our comprehension that we can rule out luck."

Victor agreed. "So, what is Joel planning to do?"

"All right, here goes." She squirmed in her chair then began. "He wants to distribute all the wealth and spread it out evenly among the poor. Everyone equal across the globe."

Naomi winced as if she were facing a small balloon with a sharp pin ready to pop it. If she had told Victor about Joel when she first got here, it could have been a large balloon. In fact, had she not learned of Victor's story, she doubts she would have told him at all. She saw Victor lean back, then rock back and forth a few times, visualizing the ramifications. He slowed to a stop then leaned forward.

"How can that even be possible?" he responded calmly. Victor then realized that was a silly question. "Of course, it's possible. If Joel wants it to be."

"We've been witness to incredible things," Naomi reminded him. "He can make it happen. They will make it happen."

"When?"

"I asked him to wait until I spoke with you." Naomi was relieved to see Victor be so casual about this. "You can see why I asked him to wait. You and Joel could have been very adversarial and that could have been a disaster!"

"Makes you wonder, doesn't it, whether these Sheaths knew exactly who to choose."

"One in a million, the three of us?"

"Or more," Victor surmised.

"Have we brought the concept of luck back on the table?"

"Not yet, Naomi. But as the sheaths said, unification is the key to success. You, me, and Joel will make an effective team. We want the same thing: just to live in peace and have real hope. And not to let a few destroy that for so many. Take the power away from the few."

"Most leaders are just cowards with cash," Naomi agreed. "They brainwash and browbeat the poor and the people with no hope, then script them into a cause that only they believe in. Most of those who fight don't believe in the cause they are fighting for. Instead, they believe they have no other alternative."

"I wholeheartedly agree."

"My one concern: is this all too much too soon?"

"The first time, when I was punishing Charlie's killer, I was too angry to wonder about the ramifications of what I was doing. Since then, the stakes have risen exponentially, but Echo is kind of a guardian. I feel safe with him. I have seen the successes. I have seen the joy in the people when these leaders are no longer around. Are we moving too fast? That's yet to be determined."

He could see Naomi's hands trembling slightly, so he tried his best to reassure her. "We humans have such amazing potential. We just needed a little help and a lot of hope. Not false hope but hope that has teeth. Hope that is real."

"Well, we are on our way. And the lives of eight billion people are hanging in the balance."

"And the three of us will be the only ones to know why the changes were necessary. When Joel's work is complete, the world will adapt, and we will be successful. Real hope is a powerful tool."

"Humans' motives for success will change," Naomi realized. "Borders will eventually fall as the news of equality spreads and we see the benefits of cooperation. We will be able to make honey again!" Naomi finished.

"Honey?" Victor asked.

"I will tell you later." Naomi smiled. "It's all coming together. The people are coming together. Once I go back to see Joel and tell him to go ahead, that should leave no doubt. That and what you are doing must be what the sheaths are waiting for."

"I'm confident that peace will win out. Imagine if we could only know or be aware of the fate that awaits some of us, being sent as food to the solids, then peace should become the norm."

Naomi closed her eyes and treated her mind to a wonderful vision. "Victor, when I was in space with Kia, and I was looking down at this incredible planet, what I admired the most was the beautiful, rare creation that we have taken for granted. When I was so far out and saw the earth as a tiny pinprick of light, I realized how alone we are, and that we need each other to survive. Instead, we have developed a system that has all but given the middle finger to the beautiful place we live in."

"That is the unfortunate reality that lines and borders create. They act like zip-ties, virtual handcuffs. I too was moved when I was up with Echo. I have confidence the borders will fall once we feel that global equality." Victor slapped his thighs, and Naomi saw he was about to get up.

"What's next for you?" Naomi asked.

"Our conversation has given me a lot of confidence going forward. I have two more people to pay a visit to and a long day ahead. I can tell you there is certainly no shortage of contestants. Since what I have done so far hasn't made the difference, I can only keep trying."

"Now I'm intrigued and impatient," Naomi said eagerly. "Can you give me a hint? Maybe it's the Russian leader?"

"I should have included him in with the Syrian leader, but I was just beginning. What punishment does he deserve?"

Naomi enjoyed the challenge Victor had given her. She reflected on the atrocities and the genocide but what horrified the world the most was... "No! Are you?"

"I already have a place picked out, which wasn't easy. Echo will get me into the military facility near Millerovo. The Russian leader wiped out Ukraine with these horrific weapons as the world stood by, afraid. I have the resources not to be afraid. I can't stand by and let him go unpunished. Besides, it could give the sheaths a challenge. Can they reanimate the body of someone so vaporized?"

Naomi's jaw had dropped. She wondered if she needed to reign him in. She wondered if she even wanted to, and that brought on an even larger question: how do the sheaths determine who goes to the slaughterhouse? Does a man who killed thousands go to slaughter as well as someone killing a man who had killed thousands? Will Victor become a candidate for the slaughterhouse? Does Naomi's acceptance of Victor's cause make her a potential meal for the solids? Another question she did not want to know the answer to... yet.

"I have two others to get to first before the Russian leader. It won't take long. I just need to go to North Korea, and then stop in at Mar-a-Lago."

Naomi's heart was pumping as she knew exactly who he was going to snatch.

"What are you planning to do to, I mean with, them?" *To* them she thought was right in the first place. She formed an idea, and she was very curious to see how close her prediction would be.

"Would you like to see what I have planned?"

"I think I need to."

"Walk with me?" Victor asked.

They both got up and she followed him to the far side of the bunkhouse. He then pointed to the north.

"I have a couple of underground safe houses near the north-west boundary of the reserve. You know, just in case."

"I get it."

"Of course, I never thought I would use one of them for this. It's all wired up now ready for my next broadcast. Recently, I went to..."

"You mean snuck into."

"Recently Echo and I snuck into the Wuhan Institute of Virology, and we took a vial of RaTg13. It's locked in a cooler in the bunker.

"Maybe you should just prop him up in front of a TV and let him watch all his money get distributed to all the people he loathes. That alone should kill him." She noticed Victor slow his pace as if her suggestion might be a better choice.

They continued along the narrow dirt path that wound its way through short bushes and small areas of grass. Naomi watched a small monkey on a nearby tree hanging by its tail and wondered if he was hoping humanity's reign would come to an end so he and all the other animals could begin to co-exist with the humans in the right way.

"You know, that's not a bad idea," Victor realized. "However, I did lose two close friends who listened to his lies and died needlessly. Them and another half million people who should still be alive from that virus.

"You don't think events are unfolding minute by minute that require us to make changes to our plans," Naomi urged.

Victor slowed his pace as he reflected on Naomi's thought. "Hmm. You may be right." Victor resumed his pace as Naomi was matching his stride. "He is doing precisely the opposite of unifying humanity. He's dividing us. He is pitting us against each other for his own selfish ego. His lies and corrupt behavior could mean civil war is a high possibility if he wins again. When he's gone, the threat will be gone, and so should a lot of our fear and hatred towards each other."

"I get it. Your country and ours are great friends, but we know, the world knows, the terrible path your nation is on and how other subversive countries are ready to take advantage of your instability. Removing him could stop a tragic chain of events. Once he's gone, Kia will let us know."

"I can go crazy trying to guess who or what will lead us down the path of annihilation." Victor was looking up to the sky, the haze slowly revealing a bright blue sky. Confidence grew inside him. "I am going to put him in one of the rooms and the North Korean leader in the other."

"Oh, how I would love to see the look on their faces when you show up. Tell me, how did the others react?" Naomi really wished she could go with him, but the risk would not be worth it. "Any remorse? Any pleading for life? Any apologies?"

"None of that. They are stunned at first. I give them a quick explanation, but they don't care what I have to say. Defiance to the end. It's the personality of megalomaniacs and psychotics."

"These two upcoming will be a quick and easy extraction. One may have thousands of troops protecting him, but I only need one Echo. The Korean leader's reign of seclusion and terror will end. Echo will bring him here. The world has proof of his people's starvation so I will let him feel the same pain his people are enduring. Hopefully, there are some in his country who can view this. It will be therapeutic for millions."

"That could take a few weeks." Naomi added.

"It could."

"Let's hope, once he's gone, that help comes quickly for the Korean people and the children. For everyone."

That led to a moment of silence to reflect on the changes that were coming fast and furious. They reached the garage sized bunker, then Victor completed detailing his plan.

"If you can see it, there is a small opening between the two rooms. The two of them will be able to talk to each other. I'm confident I can keep the broadcast location secret long enough. I'm exceptionally good at that," he boasted with a wink.

"Are you going to broadcast their conversation as well as the visuals?" Naomi asked.

"I usually don't, but I might in this case."

"That might not be a good idea."

Victor was going over in his mind what they would say to each other. One in English, the other in Korean, rationalizing, recruiting, defiant. Just like the three bombers before.

"You're right. I have the feeling you are right about a lot of things. About everything."

They returned to Victor's house in silence, save for the sounds of geckos, exotic birds, and that same monkey who was chewing on a mango he had manage to snatch. Both looked out over the railing as the sunlight cast a reflection off the slow-moving water.

"It's time I go," Victor said.

She felt the familiar tingle of electrical energy and she turned to see Echo for the first time. She lapped up his appearance like a fan seeing a movie star. He was dressed in a long black coat with scraggly hair and a leathery face. No doubt dressed to play the game of espionage. Or was it his normal attire?

Victor greeted Echo with a nod and said, "I'm ready to go."

Usually, Victor would spend a moment visualizing his desire, then feel the warmth of Echo's virtual grasp. Instead, he was interrupted by a request from Echo.

"Can you summon Kia?" Echo asked Naomi.

Naomi had never met Echo and was taken aback by his somewhat artificial, robotic, electronic sounding voice and stoic expression, which was in stark contrast to Kia's comforting and sensitive tone, something she noticed had become more human with each interaction.

Echo was, in his own way, trying to sound and look more human with each of these interactions but it was coming slowly for him. The three sheaths always tried to learn how to mimic the characteristics, personalities, and expressions of whatever species they were interacting with to help them bond better with their students. Even with thousands of species in their database and eons of practice, it still wasn't an easy task. However, Echo seemed to have mastered the expression of concern that both Naomi and Victor noticed in Echo's voice and face.

"I can. I just need a moment," Naimi promised. "Why don't you go do your thing, Victor, and when you get back, I'll have Kia here."

"All right, but we may not have a lot of time. Something isn't right," Echo replied, which did not sit well with Victor and Naomi.

They both disappeared leaving a shaken Naomi alone on the deck. It would take her more than a moment to compose herself as she was certain a profoundly serious event was about to happen. Could it be that when Victor returned, Kia will be able to reveal that humanity was safe from its own demise? Would Kia return and be able to reveal the event that would have destroyed the human race? Unfortunately, she couldn't be further from the truth.

CHAPTER 31

Wednesday October 29

Sebastien placed the coffee tray from the Central Café on his workstation, wiggled one cup free, then handed the rest to Julia. She inhaled the intoxicating aroma of her latte and Danish, which really helped to open her eyes. Sebastien managed only one sip before the alarm rang out, a sound they were getting accustomed to.

"Look, Julia! A magnetic shift of five degrees!"

Julia wiped the sticky glaze off her finger then punched a few buttons on her keyboard. "The pull is towards the African continent."

"Localize it."

"I can generalize it. All right, I have it. Fifty-eight thousand kilometers altitude above the African continent."

"Come on, you can do better than that," Sebastien urged.

"Give me a sec. Over Zambia, near the border with Malawi." She scanned more of the data, than put the visuals up onto the main screen. "There are reports of black auroras over the Kaningina reserve." They both looked in awe at the images being relayed from one of their satellites. "Send out..."

"I'm way ahead of you." Sebastien rolled his chair over to another console and sent out an urgent bulletin to all government agencies, with special priority to the FAA. He leaned back and both stared at each other with the same expression: fear.

"Talk to me, Julia. What are you thinking?"

"I've seen these figures before and I can hardly believe it. My undergraduate studies were in astrophysics, mainly studying the properties of stellar phenomena. One area of focus was in..." she put a trembling hand over her mouth.

"In? In?"

"The formation of black holes!"

"Black holes? Come on, what are you saying?"

"I'm saying we could be witnessing the formation of a black hole, right above us! Maybe more than one!"

"Come on!" That was his favorite go to expression when he was nervous. "Something must have brought these anomalies on. They don't just appear, do they?"

Julia shoved her chair away forcefully. That was not like her at all, so Sebastien went over to her.

"It's quite the bummer to start out the day, isn't it?" He put a gentle hand on her shoulder.

"There is another possibility," Julia stated.

"A good possibility or a bad one?"

"This could be a reversal of the magnetic field."

"So, a bad one." Sebastien flipped through his mental notes from a course he took three years ago. "That would be catastrophic also. Didn't the last one happen about eight-hundred thousand years ago? And didn't the effects last about a thousand years?"

"We might barely survive the radiation but how could we deal with the end of good cell phone coverage?" It was a stupid thought, but it lightened the mood. She glanced at the large room monitor and heaved a sigh of relief. "There, readings are normal again. This is crazy!"

"Can we predict the next one?"

"I'll start working on some models, but in my opinion, three, maybe four more of these incidents, and the elastic band that is the magnetic field is going to break."

"That's assuming the black hole doesn't swallow us up first." Sebastien stared at his coffee in a whole different way, as if it could be his last.

Julia savored her Danish in the same way. All they could do was to send the data and their findings to the required departments and hope this phenomenon would simply end on its own.

Then they both froze, just their bodies, as their eyes followed the most frightening data, they had ever seen. They were speechless as they read the numbers. One of them had to speak. It was Julia.

"My God. See the aurora near Arizona? It's... opposing the earlier auroras. Like this new one is positive energy, and all the earlier ones are negative. Or something like that. I don't get it.?

They're in a tug of war. Sebastien wasn't able to pass air over his vocal cords, so that was said in silence. No matter how you slice it, they knew what that meant. The loss of the entire magnetic field and the planet's atmosphere slowly being sucked out into space. Then the black auroras expand into the properties of a black hole which could cause the planet to compress into the size of a walnut by the gravitational forces. They both shook off their rigor enough to prepare texts and final messages to their loved ones, just in case.

CHAPTER 32

Wednesday October 29
4:15 pm Local Time

The North Korean leader had just settled down for a lavish dinner, yet he was very unsettled. Each servant was body searched as they laid out his plates of food, all seven of them. Now he was alone in his cavernous dining room. He cut his Kobe beef, then sniffed it for any odor that might be poison. He put the knife and fork down, the clanking echoing throughout the empty room. He chewed slowly and loudly enough for the eight skinny guards out in the hall to hear, all of them wishing for even ten percent of his meal.

Spread among the sprawling hillsides surrounding this estate in the northwest sector of North Korea, were nineteen ancient anti-aircraft guns and, blocking the only road in, four rusty Panzer-4 tanks, each spray painted to hide the fact that they were built in the seventies. The supreme leader spared no expense to protect himself from this internet madman. His palace was on full alert.

And roaming the grounds were two-hundred and thirty elite, malnourished guardsmen, their spirit all but pummeled out of them. They marched slowly and without much zest as they were disgruntled and weak and wondering how the hell they could get out of this country.

If Victor was a sadist, with Echo's help, he could pick them off one by one like playing the video game Hitman on easy. But he knew they were not to blame. So, instead, he bypassed all the outdoor armaments and boringly appeared one foot back and three feet to the left of the North Korean leader. At first, the president, saw a lot of bluish glittering light reflecting off the room's polished surfaces. Then he scratched an itch while at the same time, Victor cleared his throat, then put a finger to his lips, instructing the leader to keep quiet.

The language barrier would not present a problem, as they would not be here long enough to chit chat. Victor also knew that the North Korean leader probably had a World War Two era gun within reach, so he quickly grabbed a plate and flung it at the door. As soon as it crashed, the door sprung open, and eight men ran in but could only watch as their boss was whisked away in a method none of them could grasp.

They were somewhat privy to what was happening around the world, so they looked to each other, and they all had but two thoughts on their mind. One, they dashed to the table and scarfed down every piece of food in sight. and their second thought... good riddance to their supreme commander.

CHAPTER 33

Tuesday October 28
11:20 pm local time.

Victor used his network of worldwide web resources to locate the people he was going to snatch. He had a source of information that would make the CIA envious. This made his search and extraction a breeze, and now he was inside the sprawling grounds of the former U.S. president.

From a few nearby estates, and from maybe a few passing cars or two, a quick twinkling of lights might have been a distraction or an alert, but it was nothing that would have interrupted Victor's extraction.

"Wake up!" Victor shouted, loud enough to alert anyone outside this room.

The man in bed jerked upright, saw the two strangers, then rolled into the fetal position. Since his wife wanted nothing to do with him, he had been sleeping alone tonight and most every night. Four of his personal guards burst into the room, only to see three figures disappear. They were aware of the goings on around the globe and had but two thoughts. One, how much stuff they could loot, and two... good riddance.

CHAPTER 34

Wednesday October 29
6:20 am local time

Victor closed the door to the safehouse and locked it tight. Even through the concrete, he could still hear the wailings from the two men inside. They were speaking different languages yet saying the same thing. He brought up the livestream on his phone, and already the viewership was in the hundreds of thousands. He was very satisfied, which showed in his stride back to the bunkhouse. Along the way, two more alerts popped up on his phone. The President of Sudan was found on the front lawn of his estate, with a bullet in his head from a self-inflicted gunshot.

Interestingly, Victor had two thoughts. Was he the one and one less task to perform. The Belarusian leader was in front of the press, admitting his crimes and misdemeanors and begging for mercy. Victor cursed at the former and chuckled at the latter, as these pleas for leniency were aimed directly at him.

Victor arrived at his bunkhouse and climbed up onto the deck, then made his way around back. He was greeted by Echo, Naomi, and Kia, whom he was seeing for the first time. He didn't believe this was a standoff, us against them. No, the mood seemed graver. For them to risk a double incursion? This must be serious.

It was Victor who began.

"This extra visit doesn't look like a celebration. I take it you aren't here to tell us we're saved." The silence was the answer to his question.

"I just don't get it. I must have done enough. There must be something else that is fouling things up. Something you have never come across before?" Victor asked.

Kia responded after a moment of thought. "There is another presence or another energy here that is interfering. Something or someone else is interfering. We must find out what it is."

"Kia, you should be telling us all about the event. The world is changing as we speak. Victor seemed certain the last two would be it. I'm certain." Naomi was animated with her arms while she spoke, then she turned to Kia. "You aren't sensing anything?"

"Nothing. No spectacle," Kia informed them. "L.J.?"

He sniffed the air. "Nothing."

"Maybe I should have let Joel do his thing. That should really have been enough." She then noticed Kia was moving her head as if she were an owl watching for predators. "What is it?"

"Naomi, are you sensing anything on a human level of perception?" Now she stood tall, like a mole looking out over the tall grass.

"We don't have the perceptions you do, but on a human level, no, nothing out of the ordinary. How about you, Victor?"

He shook his head.

"We are being watched, but it's nothing out of the ordinary. It's not unusual to have energy spheres from past lives reveal themselves to us. They are free to travel the universe, look in on places and people like we did with the solids, Naomi. We've seen a few of these alien energies since arriving, but they don't have the power to interfere. Occasionally, and in extremely rare cases, one of the aliens in their bio-electric sphere suffers a short circuit and becomes briefly visible, but as you said, they are simply labelled as apparitions. Nothing of concern. It mostly happens with the spheres that are incredibly old. They aren't responsible."

"Ghosts! Spirits! Apparitions! Paranormal experiences!" Victor spoke these words softly. "I was always skeptical. Turns out they are real!"

"Another mystery solved," Naomi gasped. "But not the one we need solved the most."

"It's just one amazing discovery after another!" Victor exclaimed.

"Something is different about this discovery, isn't it?" Naomi asked.

"We are being watched and it's by an energy I've never experienced before."

"I'm feeling it now," Echo revealed.

Kia didn't look well. Naomi was worried for a good reason.

"Remember when I took you to visit the solids, Naomi? That strange feeling that was making me uneasy?"

"Of course. You said it was like an attack. When we were close to that strange building, it became worse."

"That's what I'm feeling now!"

Naomi's eyes darted about as she collated all that had occurred since meeting Kia. Then it hit her. She covered her mouth and let out a gasp.

"That building, the one we couldn't penetrate. Could that have been a testing facility? You said the solids have been trying to recreate your abilities from the very beginning. Is it possible they have succeeded?"

"That... that has to be it!" Kia shrieked. "They must have done it. That's what I'm sensing."

"What are you all talking about?" Victor asked, his voice cracking.

Naomi explained, as succinctly as possible, her perception of what was going on. "You couldn't give the solids what they wanted, so they went about trying to reproduce your abilities on their own. They've had eons to work on the process. It was just a matter of time before they succeeded."

"The solids had come to a realization that one day we would want our freedom," Kia elaborated. "They have sent one of them here to stop us!"

"If they sent a solid and that solid had been watching for a while, then they might know about our plan," Echo said sullenly.

"What plan?" Victor asked. Then he addressed Naomi. "That theory you wouldn't discuss before. This is what it's all about?"

"Water!" Naomi exclaimed.

"You have the means to give us our freedom, Naomi. You've figured it out. You have the rarest substance in the universe. The one thing that can stop the solids."

"There is nothing rare about water," Victor scoffed.

"Victor, they have been all over the universe. You know how massive it is. You travelled just a portion of it with Charlie. We know nothing in comparison to what theses sheaths have seen."

"Are you telling me that water does not exist anywhere in the universe beyond our star system!"

"Star system, or a little beyond that, but yes, Victor. That is exactly what they are saying," Naomi answered. She wasn't sure he heard her based on the stunned expression on his face.

"Unbelievable!" he managed to say.

"When we realized what you had, we knew we had a chance to be free. This beautiful system of yours holds the only means to end the solids' hold over us. Your water, once introduced into their environment, would be like a poison to them. We must succeed here. Your longevity, your survival means our freedom!" Kia exclaimed.

"We must receive that spectacle. We must make sure you survive. Then you will have that afterlife, and as the first humans are introduced into their food chain, the poison should spread," Echo added.

"So, you hope," Victor said.

"Yes, but it is real hope. The most important hope of all," Kia responded.

"And you will be free at last." Naomi was happy for her friend and for all the sheaths. "We must succeed."

"I hate to be a buzz kill, but there are still a lot of variables. And one major unknown variable is that energy. Are we in danger?" Victor asked.

"What would happen if one of the solids were to interfere? What exactly could one of them do?" Naomi asked, fearing the answer would be grave.

It was confirmed by the slight disassembling of Kia's shape. She was struggling to keep it together. Fear caused this brief instability.

"Incompatibility. Two opposing forces. Two opposite energies. It was why we couldn't help them. Now that they have succeeded in becoming incorporeal, like us, if this solid is here and does attack one of us, then it means the end of life, not just here on earth, but beyond."

"How far beyond?" Naomi asked.

"This entire star system would be destroyed. And most likely the eradication of this entire galaxy! And the destruction of the one thing that could end them and free us."

"These solids want to destroy one tree by burning down the entire forest," Victor surmised. Eliminate the one substance that could hurt them by making it extinct.

"Perhaps we should separate," Kia suggested.

"Or get everyone together," Naomi countered. "We need to discuss what to do. We need to be ready for anything."

"We need Joel here," Echo pointed out.

"Unfortunately, that is out of our hands."

CHAPTER 35

Tuesday October 28
8:20pm local time

Joel's mind was spinning like a merry-go-round on acid. Why?

Because he was waiting for the go ahead from Naomi. If that wasn't enough to cause him to trip out, he was absorbing more breaking news. No doubt another kidnapping by one of the others. This time it was the population of North Korea that was dancing in the streets. Seconds after the leader's disappearance, communication with the outside world slowly began to open up. The release of anxiety and oppression was like the opening of a valve on high pressure. There was jubilation and parading in the streets as the joyous news spread quickly to a hermit nation that were hermits no more.

Would that be the event that the sheaths needed? Joel quickly changed to a live stream of the event. The world was still in the dark as to who this mystery blogger was. The most brilliant hackers in the world were stumped, but Joel had an insider who could quickly set up a meeting.

He saw the viewership had surpassed eight-hundred million, the massive interest brought on by the two men being held. It was a split screen and on the left was the ex-president in distress. There was no sound, but the action spoke volumes. He was shouting something through a hacking cough and sweating profusely. His orange combover had dropped down to cover his eyes. The man on the left of the screen was doing nothing but sitting on a chair in the empty room. In the top left corner of his broadcast was a HUD. It displayed the North Korean President's vital signs. They were perky and excitable but, in a few weeks or sooner, they were sure to redline. Once depression, anxiety and the effects of isolation take hold, his condition should deteriorate rapidly.

More breaking news as images of a dead Sudanese president spread on television. A massive cloud of carbon dioxide hung over the country brought on by the exhalation of relief of millions of embittered civilians.

Joel wondered if these livestreams would soon become mundane, like views of cute cats on TikTok or glaciers melting at the poles. Now he really wanted to meet the third. It wouldn't be a contest as to who could save the planet, it would be a collaboration as to how to save the planet. He did a recap in his mind of a new world of hope, peace and equality happening before his very eyes. But why hasn't this been enough? Why hasn't he been told by L.J. that....

Then Joel's heart took a beating as he was startled by a knock at the door. He rocketed out of his seat and speed walked to the door then skidded to a stop on the tile floor.

Why would L.J. knock to tell him the exciting news? Old- fashioned and unnecessary. That bar fight was long an afterthought, but some might have longer memories. He peaked through the window and saw a man in uniform.

Good grief.

It wasn't the police. It was a military uniform. Joel knew squat about the military other than from the show M.A.S.H. He had a similar look to that of Henry Blake, so he must be a colonel. Opening doors seemed to offer adventure as of late so why not. He cracked it an inch and could see the man in full view.

"Good evening, sir," said the stranger.

Joel examined the street and did not see any vehicles. There was a nervous excitement from within as this could be a fourth that Naomi spoke of.

"I'm Colonel Weiss," he revealed as if he wasn't sure of his own name.

Then the stranger's form began to blur and sharpen then blur and sharpen, followed by that familiar tuning fork sensation, only this time, it was affecting Joel's stomach. Not a full fledge want to vomit, but enough to feel uncomfortable. That feeling also came and went just like the stranger's body, which had settled into a clear image.

"The others sent me here to bring you to them. It's..." His voice cut out, yet his lips kept moving. "...wanted... you... wanted. It's important... all get together to discuss the situation."

Joel was watching his lips and trying to follow his words, but they were out of sync. It was almost comedic.

"I am more than ready," Joel answered naively.

The colonel smiled but it was a grin that reminded him of Chucky the clown. This made him no longer naïve.

"Why didn't my bio-friend, Griselda, come and get me?" Joel asked.

"Well, she's having difficulties."

Before Joel could slam the door shut, he felt a pull, much like the first time he was pulled into L.J.'s sphere, only this was without his consent. In seconds, he found himself high above his house and accelerating. With L.J., it was invigorating and inspiring. This felt like a kidnapping. He was on a bus with no doors and no bell to ring and no idea where his destination would be.

CHAPTER 36

Wednesday October 29
7:38am local time

"Something is on the way!" Kia shrieked.

"This is it. What's coming is the new reason our future annihilation hasn't been revealed yet!" Naomi said. She had reasoned it out. "This is the event we need to stop."

"But how?" Victor shouted.

"Naomi's right. What is to come is what's blocking our spectacle."

"I'm so confused, but you tell me what to do and I'll help any way I can," Victor offered. He stood by, awaiting orders.

It was closing in fast. They all could feel a surge of electrical energy which passed through them, making the ground tremble. High above them, they saw with astonishment, a massive black aurora had converged like a black oil slick in the sky. It must have been as high as the altitude most jetliners fly, Naomi guessed, and it was dropping in on their position fast.

"What should we do, Kia?" Naomi wanted to help, but she felt this was way beyond her pay grade.

The slick was at twenty thousand feet, then ten thousand. Back in Copenhagen, Julia sent out alarms, and Sebastien was having a coronary as the formation of a black hole had begun its process.

"I have an idea," Kia informed everyone.

Noami had been her friend for long enough to feel her resolve, which did help to nullify a small part of her fear. They just had to win this as the stakes were high: the survival of humanity, and the galaxy.

"I know what you are going to do," Echo realized. "You're going to confront the solid. You are going to sacrifice your life to save these people."

"And to set us free," Kia added.

"Is that the only way?" Naomi asked.

She didn't want to lose someone she felt was a friend. She didn't want to lose someone she'd come to respect and who was her teacher in many ways. Naomi had formed a bond with Kia that went beyond the physical.

"When we decide to end our own existence, we will have power and strength far beyond anything we've had before," Echo explained. "Kia will add to her the energy from all those we have helped before as they lend their support in her fight against this enemy. Their way of saying thanks. It's the quintessential belief of how unity will and must always prevail."

"Or is this the exception to the rule?" Victor wondered softly.

"Will it be enough?" Naomi asked even more softly.

They would soon find out as the black slick was close enough to cast a shadow like a solar eclipse at totality. It covered a thousand acres, and they felt the temperature drop thirty degrees. The wind picked up, giving Victor and Naomi the same sense that a nuclear bomb was being dropped on them.

"But Kia, I still need you. There must be another way," Noami begged.

"We don't have time for a debate, Naomi." Kia used her hand to usher her away from her side.

Echo had shut off his feelings to the other sheaths as he had a better way. He shut off his feelings especially toward Kia.

The black slick was descending at a rate like that of a rookie chopper pilot coming in for his first landing. The dark shadow shrunk to cover just Victor's refuge, then just his bunk house. Then it vanished all together in the snap of a finger. That snap was also literal, as the resulting jolt knocked Victor and Naomi off their feet. But the same effect seemed to repel off the sheaths, like water beading off a freshly oiled surface.

Naomi helped a staggered Victor to his feet. Two figures appeared from around the left side of the house. Naomi recognized them both. Her body tensed and she gritted her teeth so hard her jaw ached.

"Colonel Weiss. Of course!" she exclaimed. "It all makes sense!

"Not to me," Victor said.

"You bastard! Have you always been one of them? Back on the ship?" Naomi had an epiphany. "Was that when this all started?"

Meanwhile, Joel was using the deck railing to inch himself toward Naomi. He required a pound of Gravol after that harrowing ride.

"Is this Joel?" Victor asked.

"Nice to... finally meet you," Joel managed through his heavy breathing. He was practiced in the art of staggering; therefore, it wasn't long before he recovered his land legs.

Kia moved in front of the human trio then addressed the enemy as if speaking for all the sheaths and all the lifeforms everywhere. This would be a standoff of historic proportions, and the stakes would be more than a few horses or a mission in Texas.

"Why are you here?" Kia began sternly.

It was not in the sheaths nature to be forceful at all. Yet being amongst humans was giving her that much-needed trait. She was finding a way to be believable.

"I know what you want to do." The solid addressed the entire group, then turned all his attention to the slave. "I have a duty to stop this genocide of my people. We have the right to survive."

"Is he right?" Victor asked.

"I have seen how they survive, Victor! It's barbaric! But I also understand how they view their survival, which is why we must find a way to co-exist. Colonel, we must find a way to peacefully co-exist for the sake of the universe."

"No." The solid was adamant. "We have spent a thousand millennia trying to achieve your abilities, and my presence is proof of our success. We do not need the sheaths anymore, and we can't risk leaving this galaxy intact. This substance you have is too dangerous for us. This substance that gives you life can end ours."

"How many aliens lives did you experiment on to achieve this?" Naomi asked, stepping out from Kia's shadow.

"That is none of your concern. We did what we did to survive, nothing else. In fact, it took another few thousand of your years to finally track the three of you together. And I see why you kept your abilities to yourselves. The universe is a wonderous place. Full of fresh food, which will ensure our survival for eons more."

"Is he saying what I think he is saying?" Noami exclaimed.

"I am saying exactly that. Once the three of you are gone, we will take your place among the stars. We will go out into the universe; we will convince as many as we can find to visit our beautiful world. The corporal and the incorporeal."

"And turn them into food!" Naomi was seething with anger. "Leave these people alone! They are innocent. They want nothing but to explore and to be with family. And don't you dare go near my sister!"

"Or my wife!"

"Or my daughter!"

"It's a big universe," Colonel Weiss offered, which made no one feel better.

"I can't allow that to happen." Kia stood strong. "Once we are gone, you plan to destroy our world, am I right?"

"You won't be needed anymore. And your existence is too much of a threat. You might as well admit that you cannot stop me. This is a one-way mission for me. I will spare no energy to win this fight. Are you ready to die for these people. But I have an offer. Sacrifice one of you, without resistance, by letting me merge my energy with yours outside of these protective spheres. Let me destroy this galaxy, and I will spare the sheaths planet. If you agree, before we begin, I will return home and let the solids know there is an agreement. You, Naomi, asked for co-existence. Those are my terms."

"No deal." Kia snapped back. "For these people, for all the species in the universe, and for freedom? No deal. To quote a human phrase, all for one…!"

The trio of humans grew empowered by Kia and the other two sheaths. They felt like they were fighting a war they believed in.

"You won't win, colonel," Echo added his defiance. "We have been doing this a lot longer."

"You are old and obsolete, like muskets and slingshots. I am modernized and powerful, and the Colonel has left me with valuable insights."

"Is he still in there?" Naomi asked. She tried to prolong this conversation as she was sure the delay would help Kia prepare.

"Very little. His memories, knowledge, and electrical energy has been absorbed and overtaken and whoever was inside this head has been obliterated." He clenched his fists and shook out the tension in his legs. "I can see why you sheaths needed to create solid bodies. You can lead a lot more of a productive life with movement."

"There must be another way, Colonel," Victor tried.

While Victor engaged the solid, Naomi inched closer to Kia and whispered in her ear. "What are you going to do?"

"I'm almost ready." Kia was preparing herself for a massive burst of energy. Like a nuclear reactor ready to power a million homes. Or a nuclear bomb ready to destroy.

"For what?"

"I'm going to bring the solid into my sphere of energy like I did with you. I need to form a barrier between his energy and mine and hold it in long enough until I get to a safe distance. If I can make it outside of your galaxy in time, I can lower the barrier. The convergence of our opposing energies should ignite with the power of a million exploding suns. He will be stopped."

"You can speak freely and openly." The colonel was obviously eavesdropping. "I know what you want to do. It is my idea, also; however, the detonation of our opposing energies will occur here."

Noami moved around to stand in between Kia and the Colonel. Victor and Joel were too paralyzed with confusion and fear to offer any assistance. They were content to be mere movie-goers with a front row seat.

"Colonel, I'm pleading with you one last time. Don't do this."

The Colonel shook his head, his meaning clear. The time for action was near.

"Kia! I need you." Naomi didn't want to let her friend go.

"You will do fine. You are a leader. More than you'll ever know."

Kia put a caring hand on Naomi's shoulder, and she felt a surge like nothing before. She felt protected, like a mother would protect her child. Yet, there was another purpose for her touch that she couldn't explain. Kia took her hand and guided Naomi over to Victor, who helped her as she was about to pass out. Naomi was overwhelmed, they thought, but there was more to it than that.

Victor and Joel sensed a finality in Kia's touch as they backed Naomi away from the confrontation. The Colonel's physical body began to lose cohesion. Kia matched his change and both bodies turned to energy.

Kia's charged particles slammed into Colonel Weiss like they were propelled by a Supercollider. Their properties merged like two massive spiral galaxies colliding at the speed of light. Kia immediately created a super strong barrier to contain their enormous energy from seeping out of this battle sphere. She then created a wall, like an electrified fence, between Colonel Weiss and herself. This barrier was vital to protect their energies from combining. If she couldn't hold it before they reached a safe distance, it would mean the destruction of this entire galaxy.

Their white-hot sphere hovered briefly, filling the bunkhouse with the smell of charred wood.

"Let's move away from here," L.J. ordered as the glowing sphere accelerated upward, like a hypersonic ballistic missile.

Naomi had regained her senses by then enough to see the vapor trail and hear the sonic boom. Could this be the end of everything? That was a thought affecting all involved.

"Let's get to the shore," Victor suggested as he felt the heat on his skin. They all moved in one small group, except for Echo who remained behind.

"Are you coming?" L.J. asked verbally so that everyone could hear.

"I have something to do."

L.J let the group continue to the shore. He would rejoin them shortly.

"Something to do?" L.J. asked.

"I have to do this," Echo said adamantly.

"I know you do," L.J responded, kindly and with immense respect. He walked slowly away to take care of Victor and Joel and to reassure Naomi.

"When will we know?" Naomi asked when L.J. rejoined them.

She felt helpless and scared.

"Soon. Very soon," was all L.J. could offer as comfort.

CHAPTER 37

Wednesday October 29
7:55am

This was a heroic battle, not just between good and evil, but to prove that unification was stronger than singularity. Save for three lone humans on planet Earth, not one other *living* being in the entire galaxy was aware of the consequences of the struggle taking place.

The Colonel began his barrage on Kia's barrier, which was as thin as a layer of molecules but as strong as a mile of concrete. He used a thousand jackhammers in an attempt to break through before they reached a safe distance. Kia was so focused on this wall that she had to sacrifice speed. She willed their bright orb toward the most direct route she could imagine that would bring them out into interstellar space, but they had yet to leave the confines of this star system.

The solid was leaving nothing behind as he used a full power bombardment. He was confident he would be able to bust through in plenty of time. The resulting joining of these two contrary energies would be the largest detonation since the big bang. Space itself would be torn apart, forming a suction of all nearby matter, like opening a drain in the bottom of the ocean. Asteroids and moons would be fodder and planets like nearby Mars and even faraway Jupiter would be no match; they would all be pulled into this gravitational chasm. The Earth and lastly the Sun would join along with all the matter in the milky way, eventually everything would occupy the same area of space.

The last known vestiges of the rarest substance in the universe would evaporate, along with the threat to the solids. The extinction of humanity and the water that brought it life, gone forever.

"I'm not going to let you destroy what we have created," Kia thought boisterously.

The solid had a confident response. "Your technology is old and antiquated. Ours is and will be advanced and relevant. This is the first battlefield for the both of us. And the last for both of us. My fellow solids will learn from my victory as we proceed forward to secure our future and control the universe."

Kia's defense was being pummeled by a much younger and more powerful foe. She didn't want to win here, just hold on long enough to escape this galaxy.

The entire world's planetary observatories were trained on the light that had grown in brightness. Kia's sphere had reached out past the orbital plane of Pluto yet was as bright as the sun. Worshippers of all kinds were kneeling in prayer to the mysterious bright light as wild fantasies were being tossed about the internet. The main thread: was this light an alien responsible for all the changes happening around the globe?

"I can feel you fighting, but you lack aggression. Passivity has always been your weakness. It's why we have been able to enslave you for such a long time."

Kia tried her best to stall as she attempted to gather the energies from every being she had freed, but that energy was having difficulty reaching and penetrating the sphere. Every assault from the colonel was a distraction. Focus on the barrier or gathering strength from the outside. It was hard to do both. If she could hold the colonel inside until...

"Our strength comes from hope. Not false hope, but giving others real, tangible hope. It's authentic and it's legitimate," Kia reminded the solid.

"We asked, no, we begged you for that hope. All we got in return were promises and eons of false hope."

"We did the best we could. Our attempts to help were genuine. As you see from our place in this battle, we were two incompatible beings. Proof our gift to you could never have happened."

Kia felt a sudden and overwhelming sense of realization from her enemy. The body blows from the colonel eased off. Their sphere was shrinking and dimming. There could be a truce, she thought. She relaxed her barrier a little, then a little more. There was hope, but as always been the philosophy of the sheaths, false hope can be debilitating.

The solid, a pioneer, the first of its kind to escape its prison and to try to conquer the universe, went in for the kill. He tore through Kia's barbed wire defense with the cutting force of a thousand acetylene torches. She felt regret for trusting and failure for letting down the universe. For letting down humanity and her fellow sheaths. She clung to a ledge, dangling from a cliff a thousand feet up with the colonel stomping on her fingers with steel cleats. Her wires were exposed, and short circuits were weakening her resolve.

Suddenly, when she felt all was lost, that real hope returned in the form of a familiar energy. Echo was there to lend a saving hand.

"Kia, I sent out a distress call throughout the universe, and they answered. I have the support of the energies of every being we have helped since the beginning. I have the right kind of hope. Let me do this, my friend. The Universe needs you. The sheaths need you. The humans and a young woman need you."

"But..."

There were no buts as Echo expertly and forcefully pushed Kia's energy out and took her place in the battle. She was on the outside looking in. She sensed the loss of a friend she'd known since the beginning of time. She was able to connect one last time before Echo would place all his concentration on defeating the solid.

"Thank you, my friend. I will never forget this. I will never forget you."

Kia hovered in space, wounded but alive. She watched the battle sphere grow in size and brightness again. Echo fortified his position, riveting a steel wall between him and the solid. Easy to do with the backing of an entire universe. Then he knitted an impervious outer energy shell that the colonel was unable to escape from. He was a thousand-pound gorilla with a full nelson on a waif of a rat.

"Lonely, isn't it," Echo chided. "Welcome to the strength that unity provides."

"I..."

"Lost for words?"

Kia reluctantly left her friend and returned to the group on earth and was there in seconds. She stood next to Naomi, whose smile was both grateful and reserved. Astonishingly, they could all still see with their naked eyes the light that was the war between the solid and the sheath, with freedom hanging in the balance.

It was the light of hope for, and as long as it kept shining, that hope was alive. Victor and Joel knew what they were staring at. It was as bright as ten Venus's in the morning sky, and Echo had managed to drag the sphere out to a distance of eighteen thousand light years. It was speeding away at a pace that gave Kia the confidence to put her arm around Naomi.

"Can he do it?" Naomi asked.

"We will find out soon," Kia answered to the group, although only L.J. could feel her concern.

The rat that was the solid inside the sphere would not give up. Biting and clawing, causing bloody scrapes on the furry gorilla. They were nearing the galactic barrier, and the barrier energy gave an unexpected boost to the rat bastard colonel. He knew they were only seconds from escaping this galaxy and failure. Once outside, Echo would drop the barrier, thus joining their conflicting energies.

Echo would feel the strafe of desperation as the solid geared up for one final assault. First it was bee-bees, then as they entered the galactic barrier, the colonel turned the fire power into shotgun blasts, but Echo had a bullet-proof vest sturdied by hope and reinforced by the support from all those the sheaths had helped before.

The solid never had a chance.

The brilliant sphere emerged from the galactic barrier and reached interstellar space. Without wasting another nanosecond, Echo tossed away his vest. Energy and anti-energy converged for the first time in recorded history. It was a cataclysmic event that caused a spacial laceration. The tear tried to draw in matter, but there was nothing to draw in. This allowed the energies from one sheath and one solid to mix and mix and mix until the pressure cooker exploded in one of the most violent events since the big bang. An explosion with the power of a million stars lit up the black void, taking up almost a tenth of the entire gap between the Milky Way and its neighboring Andromeda. The galactic void would need a new designation.

From a very distant Earth, the resulting light could be easily seen with the naked eye. However, there were only three humans that would ever know the meaning and the origins of the new light.

Victor felt his skin and shook his legs and arms. "We're still here!" There were smiles all around.

"He, did it?" Naomi asked. She had two fingers crossed on each hand.

"He did it!" Kia exclaimed. Then she separated herself from the group and stepped closer to the shore. L.J. joined her and they both were disturbed by something. Joel and Victor shrugged but as usual, Naomi knew.

"The spectacle. It's coming to you," Naomi stated. Then it dawned on Victor as well.

"Of course. The solid interfered with what would have occurred."

"With that threat gone, everything should be revealed," Naomi whispered to Joel and Victor.

They could all see L.J. was about to tell an incredible story. An incredible story that would have a special impact on the three mortals.

"Tell us, please."

"Yes, please," Joel added.

"Do you see it?" Kia asked L.J.

"It's unbelievable. Two spectacles. I am seeing two separate spectacles!"

"I understand! You are seeing what would have happened if the solid had won, and also what would have happened..." Naomi couldn't finish.

One of them had indeed done it. She was sure it wasn't her, but either Joel or Victor had already changed the future. Had Joel gone ahead with his plan, and he was the one? Had Victor already changed the course of Earth's history, but it was the solid's appearance that kept him from succeeding? Who was it! And what was it? She slyly looked at both men. Judging by their bulging eyes and nervous postures, they were also aware. The answer as to who was clear.

"The solid's interference has brought on a new experience. An unprecedented experience. Had the colonel succeeded, I see rubble, darkness, and extinction," L.J. foresaw. "I see an immense area, void of energy, void of life. It was a massive, immense, all-encompassing annihilation of an entire galaxy. What was once a bright spiral, filled with color and life, is dark. That is what I see, had we failed to stop the solid."

L.J recited the vision as if watching a movie in reverse. "Now I see the scattered remnants of death come together to form life. Echo's victory kept the status quo. A beautiful spiral galaxy of spectacular colors and systems and light. Incredible energies of all species scattered about billions of stars that make up this vast palette. All is as it is today."

There was no time for an intermission, as there was another reel being loaded into the projector.

"You see another spectacle?" Naomi asked L.J.

"Yes, the solid was an anomaly that interfered when it shouldn't have. I see the event that would have unfolded naturally here, had we not come."

"What do you see?" Victor asked impatiently.

"I see the inevitable end of human civilization. Had we not come, that was your future."

Joel, Victor, and Naomi heard no birds chirping or water lapping on shore. They only heard L.J, who would finish the story. Would he tell them of a nuclear Armageddon? Would he tell them of a global pandemic that wiped out humanity? It couldn't be a natural disaster. It had to be something they could have prevented.

"Give him a moment," Kia advised. "These spectacles can be traumatic to us as well."

"Of course. Whenever you're ready."

L.J turned and locked eyes with Naomi, then Joel who swallowed nothing but air. Then he stopped and did not leave the gaze of Victor's blue eyes. He felt drawn to him and took one step toward L.J. He realized it was his actions that had changed the future.

L.J. had seen the entire visual, thousands of years of earth's future after its demise and was able to condense and compose and assemble it into a frightful tale of what would have been.

"About five decades from now, I see remnants of structures and cities. Your structures and your cities. I see insects and animals in abundance. All lower forms of life in abundance. Now I see scattered humanoids, no life, just bones and broken skeletons. No industries or associations. Before that, the few that survived would feel misery and hopelessness. Despair, sadness, starvation. All life forms remaining are irradiated. I sense their bio-electric patterns overlayed with neutrons, gamma rays, and alpha particles."

"A nuclear war!" Naomi realized.

Joel looked around and imagined his surroundings should he have been one of the unlucky to still be alive in a world L.J is describing.

"Little of what he will describe will make sense to us," Kia explained. "But you will understand. He will describe the event in great detail. Some visuals will be from further in the future, then to most recent. It will be up to you to make sense of it. After he is done, there is no doubt you will understand," Kia added. "Are you ready to continue, L.J.?"

"Yes, I'm fine." He continued to gaze into Victor's eyes. "You started a chain of events that led to the capture a particular man. Had you not started what you did, this one man would have begun the events that would have led to the destruction of humanity."

"It was me!" Victor went back through his resume to see who it could have been. He was thinking by talking. "It couldn't have been any of the men that were in prison. They were minor players. Not capable of a global event."

"It must have been one of the world leaders," Naomi easily surmised.

"That's it. But which one?" Joel asked.

"I know." Victor was nodding confidently. "I know. It's not a leader that is in power, it's a leader that will be in power!" He let his claims sink in then said. "L.J., please continue." he urged.

"Had we not come, a former president would get re-elected. He reviles unity and craves the success and power of other world leaders, mainly Russia, China, and North Korea. He is emboldened by the triumph of Russia over Ukraine as the world watched and did nothing."

The three humans were listening as if L.J was swinging a gold pocket watch in front of them. Back and forth. Back and forth.

"Using executive orders, this president begins to slowly take away the voting freedoms of the people that would be a threat to his presidency, easy to do as he had strategically put these measures in place prior to his election victory. Those on his side, he would give special powers and money. This division breeds protests in every city. Months of civil unrest breaks out as the president uses the military under his command to quell all opposition. News organizations are censured and face prison if they report anything negative against the supreme leader."

"Right out of the Russian play book," Naomi gasped.

"And many other autocratic men throughout history. Barbaric and ruthless. Divisive," Joel added.

"Civil war breaks out between the affiliations you call Republican and Democrat."

Victor was frozen in fear. They were so close to having to live through what was being described. He was American. Had the sheaths not arrived, he would have had to take up arms and fight and murder those who were backing his own elected president. Many of those could have been his friends trying to kill him.

"Once again proving your belief that division is deadly," Kia added.

"And proving that old angry men should never be in power... ever again," Joel said.

"This president uses his military might to overwhelm the other party. I see fighter jets firing and bombing the people opposing his absolute power. The anger against one another in America, built up over the last decade, is unleashed as an all-out war. The republican side is now mostly Caucasian and wealthy, but they are massively outnumbered. It's a war between the rich and the poor as much as it is between ideologies. The poor have them massively outnumbered, but the rich have the military might and the monetary might. There are tens of thousands of corpses in the streets, in fields and hidden in mass graves. Livelihoods are halted. Businessmen are fighting their employees, teachers their students, celebrities, athletes fending off and murdering teammates who had opposing views, and fathers take up arms on their respective sides even if it meant the killing of their own children. I see power outages, explosions, and fires in every city."

There were three overwhelmed humans listening to a future that was inevitable, had the sheaths not come. Victor was stupefied that the annihilation of humanity was not a century away, but a single election away. Stupefied at first, but that turned to an acceptance of what would have been inevitable. The Divided States of America? The signs were strong before the sheaths came. A second civil war, but in an advanced twenty-first century? We learned nothing.

L.J continued in horrific detail.

"With more than seven million dead, America in chaos and near collapse, Russia and China collaborate to take advantage. I see an eight-month American civil war that allowed the other powers to amass a force of millions of soldiers and thousands of war ships, fighters and bombers all locked and loaded. Like I'm looking from above, I see this army up and down each coast. They demand the surrender of the United States of America. The president realizes the futility of a war against two nations so unified that he believes the only defense that can keep him in power is to unleash a massive assault of every available nuclear weapon. I see the skies full of smoke trails as six hundred and fifty long range ballistic nuclear weapons streak across the planet. But with little time to prepare, only half will reach their target. Countless others will go off course, striking areas around the globe."

"China and Russia thought they were well prepared to intercept the American death machines, yet almost four hundred of the warheads strike all their major cities, including Moscow and Beijing. China and Russia's attack was more successful. With precision, they target every large city in the United States with over nine hundred warheads, only a few going astray."

"How... how many died overseas?" Naomi asked.

"Eight hundred million are incinerated in the initial bombardment. Eighty percent of the American population is also gone. Many more will suffer in excruciating horror as your planet is irradiated. Fresh water is scarce, and ninety percent of the world's crops are unusable. Humanity descends into anarchy. The last human perishes forty-seven years later. Your extinction is complete."

Kia and the others were near exhaustion. Victor had to sit down and guessed the others could use a seat as well. He guided the small group over to a familiar area by the shoreline. Several chairs arranged around a fire pit made for many a relaxing time and this was one of those times they needed to relax.

"I don't know what to say to all that," Victor said, his mind racing like a car with bad brakes. Anxiety, then relief. Unease, then relief. Uncertainty, then...

"What happens now?" Joel asked.

He looked around at the others then couldn't help but look up with astonishment at that new light in the sky. It was having a calming effect. The others were staring up at it also. What would it symbolize? A beacon of hope that only Naomi, Joel and Victor would understand. And a remembrance of what needs to be done to prevent the events Kia just recounted from ever happening again.

"L.J. and I will leave here and prepare. This is a unique situation."

"Because of the solid's interference?"

"Your star system is safe. The only source of water in the universe has been preserved. And you have earned the gift of an afterlife. In time, the solids will no longer be a threat to us or anyone, and this should set us free."

"Are you sure there is no other way to ask for a truce with the solids?" Naomi was always trying to be the diplomat.

One of her motives for a truce rather than the solids' death, and it was tugging on Naomi's conscious, was that keeping the solids alive was a strong deterrent if humanity knew what awaited them in their afterlife should violence continue. Another question added to that tug: *will Kia make all of humanity aware of what awaits us after we die? Will we all become aware of a real heaven and a real hell?*

"It will not be long before the solids realize the first one failed. They could send others. Perhaps the next will be stronger and more advanced. They will keep searching for us, and they will spare no effort to eradicate this galaxy."

"I guess there is no choice to be made," Victor surmised.

"When we leave here, your afterlife will commence. It might not be wise to interfere with the natural progression of that afterlife. Those of you that are undeserved will be reanimated, as is natural, on the solids' home world and will be simply thought of as a new food source like the others."

"Will it act as a poison?"

"It could create another cataclysmic event. "This is all new and unpredictable," L.J. added. "Water had never been found before. What effect it will have will be unpredictable, however it most assuredly will be deadly in some form or another. It could happen in hours, years, or centuries. We have no way to know."

"Will you go back and watch the end of the solids, if it does come?" Naomi asked cautiously.

"I will return." Was the correct answer to Naomi's question.

Nothing else was added. Then there came a human smile that spread across the two sheaths' faces. It was contagious, as Naomi knew why. It had not spread to Joel or Victor.

"What? What is it?" Joel asked.

"Come on guys," Naomi chided. "The death of an entire race is what draws them to help. They have or are receiving that sense of doom from the solids home world now, aren't you?"

The sheaths' silence said it all.

Joel threw back his head, laughed, then said, "You are receiving the energies of the future death of all the solids. And you are the only ones who can save them. The irony of all ironies. It's incredible. To be a part of all this is incredible! It looks like a new beginning for everyone."

"And you can save them if you want," Naomi said. "You can demand they dismantle their experiments in exchange for freedom and the promise not to unleash what you have found here."

That required a moment of reflection from Kia and L.J.. Meanwhile, Victor had slipped off his sandals and he was scrunching his toes in the soft sand. Naomi was wondering what that pit next to the shore would look like at night with a roaring fire in it. Joel was wondering if he should go ahead with his plan or if it was even possible to go ahead. The silence was broken by Victor.

"Is it possible for us to spread the word of this new and incredible afterlife?" Victor asked. "The people need to know but we will not be believed."

"Don't worry. We will take care of that. Because you see us now in this human case, you forget what we are made of. The thoughts of every being in the universe are made up of similar electrical energy of some degree or another. Once the power of the afterlife is given, that knowledge about the new afterlife and all that it entails will follow and it will become a normal thought for every human," L.J. revealed.

"It will be a new belief," Victor realized.

"And a new religion?" Naomi wondered in awe. "One religion for all of humankind?"

"When we leave here, we will go in orbit and prepare for the modification."

"You say that like you are about to rearrange the furniture in my living room," Joel said.

"That wouldn't take much." Naomi laughed. It felt good to just laugh at something ridiculous again.

Joel got it, but Victor was left in the dark.

"Don't worry, Victor. Joel will invite us all over for a victory drink... of Pepsi," Naomi said.

"Consider it done," Joel said.

"I'll be there for sure." Victor nodded. "It's incredible what you are about to do, Kia, L.J. The power it must take to continue life after death on a planetary scale must be immense."

"It is what we do."

"It is time we leave," L.J. informed them.

That sent a sadness through the group. For Naomi, she felt something more.

"I'm... scared." Naomi admitted. She stood and took Kia's hand. It wasn't warm, but Naomi felt the warmth of a bond that was like no other.

"In time, that fear will subside. You have a power that will require calm and patience."

"But it will be gone when you leave."

"No, it won't. I left that in you for as long as you want it. For as long as you live, you will have the answers. You will finally know it all!"

Naomi's eyes lit up. She was hoping that fear would subside soon because it hadn't yet.

"That touch. Before when you left to fight the solid."

"I wasn't sure what condition I would be in if I was successful. I've never ever left a gift behind, but you and your world have given us the gift of freedom. You are the first to be left with your abilities. It's my, it's our way, of saying... thank you."

Joel stood up slowly as he absorbed the magnitude of what Kia revealed to Naomi. L.J. rose and put a hand on his shoulder.

"Finish what you started, Joel. It will fulfil your life's dream. I will leave you with that."

"I... will. Thank you. Kelly will be so proud. And knowing that she will be able to witness it all makes it even more special."

"Victor, your work is done. Echo would be proud as well, I know it. You had a cause you believed would make a difference and it did. You have set a lot of people free all over this world."

They all looked up at Echo's Light.

"His sacrifice will not be forgotten. The enormous number of souls that lent a hand to Echo's victory will help spread the news to the entire universe about what happened here."

"Will our loved ones find out?" Noami asked.

"The universe has become a much smaller place to me," Joel thought. The others agreed.

"This planet will become a beacon of hope that will be available for all visitors to see."

"The best tourist destination in the universe!" Joel said.

"Absolutely, Joel," Naomi agreed. Then she addressed Kia. "Will you visit, now and then?" she asked sadly.

"We will return to see the progress, now and then."

Kia and L.J. began to fade. Naomi's tears flowed, made up mostly of happiness. Joel and Victor were doing the manly thing, keeping the water on the surface of their eyes. L.J. had left but before Kia vanished in her usual way, she leaned over and whispered something in Naomi's ear. An expression of absolute wonder spread across her face as Kia vanished.

"What!" Victor asked.

Based on what he'd been a part of over the last two weeks, what Kia said must have been amazing. Joel was equally curious.

"Yeah, what did she say?"

"I'll tell you later. We have a lot to do and a lot to consider. We have a new world and for the first time, humans everywhere have real hope. And you, Joel, have one more thing to do. One more very important thing, if you want."

Joel knew what he would do. Kia had described a world where the rich overpowered and nearly destroyed the poor. He would not let that happen again.

EPILOGUE

Kia and L.J. hovered in their sphere twelve-hundred kilometers above the Earth's surface and prepared. This was always the most satisfying ending to their visits. Like a massive orgasm after weeks of roller coaster foreplay. And this victory was doubly triumphant.

"Are you ready?" Kia thought.

"More than ever."

Carefully and precisely, they began a controlled build-up of energy. Building and growing to the power of an unmeasurable number of gigawatts. The resulting brilliant glow, like that of a glass forge, caused billions of human souls to witness another light in the sky. Kia and L.J. reached maximum potential, then released a massive burst of thought and desire that washed over planet earth. Like gamma rays, these particles penetrated the human psyche. Like a computer code, and with technical precision, a new directive was entered.

The realization of a continued life after death is now common knowledge. The exploration of the universe, and the bonding with loved ones beyond the physical, is now common knowledge. Along with it, the realization of the fate of those who commit violence is implanted. This fate will last as long as the solids exist.

"It's happened, I can feel it!" Naomi shouted.

"It's like I've always known," Victor added.

"It was euphoric, like it has always been." Joel was equally pleased and equally accepting.

"How is it possible, that in two short weeks, we were on a path of total annihilation and now on a new paved path of hope and equality?"

"If aliens and humans can work together, can unify in a common purpose, then anything is possible."

"I wonder if there will be a buzz on the internet," Joel wondered. "It will be epic! I keep thinking everything is epic and it truly is. And Joel, you have one more thing to do but before you begin, let me get something." He ran to his bunkhouse and returned with two glasses of champagne and one glass of juice which he handed to Joel.

"How did you know?" Joel asked.

"I've seen a lot of resumes in my life." He handed Naomi her glass and they toasted skyward to the three people that meant the most to them.

"Victor, you said I have one more thing to do?"

Victor nodded. Naomi knew what was coming next.

"I have two more things to do. I made a promise to myself. I have some long overdue healing and mending to do," Joel said." Can I borrow your phone?"

"I understand." Victor handed him his phone, put an understanding hand on his shoulder, and nodded. "Take as much time as you need. We'll hang out here."

Joel's hand was shaking as he did his best to dial the number on the first try, which was a bust. The second try he connected, and Naomi and Victor could only hear the first few words as Joel walked away.

"Honey, it's dad. How..."

Kia's tears were still flowing as there were smiles all around.

"Isn't this all wonderful?" Victor added.

"Just perfect and it's only the beginning."

They both sat down and really reveled in the peace, quiet and calm, like they had just run a two-week intergalactic triathlon. They needed to wind down and these ten minutes were therapeutic. Joel returned and it was obvious he was very emotional but had the widest grin on his face. They knew it had gone well.

Joel joined them around the fire pit for one last conference.

"I could ask Naomi if it went well," Victor laughed.

"That's right, you could. It's going to take me a while to get use to this. I don't feel any different."

"Do you want me to test you?" Victor asked jokingly. "Who really shot JFK? Wait don't tell me, yet."

"You look different. You look confident and happy," Joel noticed.

"I agree," Victor said. "What do you think will be written in the history books a hundred years from now?"

"I'm just glad we will have those hundred years."

"Well said," Naomi replied.

"Okay, let's do this," Joel blurted out.

"Are you sure?"

"More than ever."

"Are you ready, Victor? This will change your life as much as anyone," Naomi prodded. "What did you estimate, Joel. Eight billion people all with the same worth?"

"All with the same worth."

"Those Harvard economists will be wearing out their pencils in a hurry." Victor laughed.

"We'll figure it out. We are on track to become one race, the human race."

"What do you have to do?" Noami asked.

"L.J. said I just need to want it to happen, really concentrate and be very committed, and it will happen."

"I'm not ever going to try to explain how, so are you ready to turn Buckingham Palace into a bed and breakfast for everyone?" Noami asked.

Joel leaned back in his Adirondack chair, with one last crucial decision to make before he began. One thought and all the wealth spread evenly, or one thought and all the wealth would come to Joel for him to spread out.

He had made his decision.

"All right. Here goes nothing."

THE END

Printed in the USA
CPSIA information can be obtained
at www.ICGtesting.com
JSHW020452011024
70766JS00001B/23